OLD BAGGAGE

Merry Christmas Amy
2019

To our suffragette,
Step out of line and
be You.
    love Mon
        XOXOXO

OLD BAGGAGE

A NOVEL

Lissa Evans

HARPER  PERENNIAL

NEW YORK • LONDON • TORONTO • SYDNEY • NEW DELHI • AUCKLAND

HARPER PERENNIAL

Originally published in Great Britain in 2018 by Doubleday, an imprint of Transworld Publishers.

OLD BAGGAGE. Copyright © 2018 by Lissa Evans. All rights reserved. Printed in the United States of America. No part of this book may be used or reproduced in any manner whatsoever without written permission except in the case of brief quotations embodied in critical articles and reviews. For information, address HarperCollins Publishers, 195 Broadway, New York, NY 10007.

HarperCollins books may be purchased for educational, business, or sales promotional use. For information, please email the Special Markets Department at SPsales@harpercollins.com.

FIRST U.S. EDITION PUBLISHED 2019.

Library of Congress Cataloging-in-Publication Data

Names: Evans, Lissa, author.
Title: Old baggage : a novel / Lissa Evans.
Description: First U.S. edition. | New York, NY : Harper, 2019.
Identifiers: LCCN 2018043844 (print) | LCCN 2018046189 (ebook) | ISBN
        9780062895455 (E-book) | ISBN 9780062895448 (paperback)
Subjects: | BISAC: FICTION / Literary. | FICTION / Historical.
Classification: LCC PR6105.V35 (ebook) | LCC PR6105.V35 O43 2019 (print) |
        DDC 823/.92--dc23
LC record available at https://lccn.loc.gov/2018043844

19 20 21 22 23 LSC   10 9 8 7 6 5 4 3 2 1

For my sisters:

Mary and Judy

PART I

1928

M attie always carried a club in her handbag – just a small one, of polished ash. That was the most infuriating aspect of the whole episode: she'd actually been *armed* when it happened.

The New Year's Day fair had been audible from the moment she'd left the house – a formless roar that receded as soon as she turned off the track and took the path through the woods. The quickest route to the Underground station was along the narrow lane to Hampstead, but there was (as she'd pointed out to The Flea only this morning, apropos of their neighbour's new motor-car) very little point in living with the Heath absolutely on one's doorstep if one didn't take every opportunity to tramp across it. Besides the exercise, it was a rare walk that didn't provide one with at least a nugget or two of brain-food, as evinced by Mattie's December column in the *Hampstead & Highgate Express* in which she'd compared a dead duck, frozen into the pond, with the Prime Minister's current position. She'd been bucked by the news that the paper had already received thirteen letters in reply, several of them furious.

Last year's beech-mast crunched pleasingly underfoot. It was a day of splendour, the air still, the sky cloudless between bare branches, every vista possessing the hard-edged brilliance of cut glass: all was ruled lines, crisp sounds, sunbeams like polished stair-rods – a marvellously true, sharp world.

Lately, Mattie's view of it had been becoming increasingly impressionistic. 'I find I am living in a perpetual Pissarro,' she had remarked to the optician. 'Aesthetically pleasing, perhaps, but I miss the *detail*.'

'I'm afraid that a deterioration in eyesight is inevitable as we get older, Mrs Simpkin.'

'*Miss* Simpkin. And I am not yet sixty; I'd really rather you didn't speak as if I were creaking along in a bath-chair.'

Her new eye-glasses had restored clarity; she might now be walking through one of the landscapes of that tiresome moralist Holman Hunt.

In a tree above her there was a vicious chuckle, and she looked up to see a magpie sidling along a branch, the crown of its head marked with an anomalous white patch, like a tonsure.

'Afternoon, Abbot, not seen you in the garden for a day or two. Busy dismembering blue tits, no doubt.'

It cocked its head, its wicked gaze fixed upon her. Had she been responsible for naming the species, she would have chosen *vigilans* rather than *pica* as its suffix; thieves, they might be, but their watchfulness was paramount. The Abbot glanced over Mattie's shoulder and she turned, automatically, to check behind her.

She had not lost her own habit of vigilance; in the past, it had been imperative; in the past, she had written articles on the subject.

OLD BAGGAGE

For those of us in constant danger of re-arrest, there is no other option. Are you certain that the fellow coming up the path is the usual postman, or might he be a plain-clothed police officer? That ordinary cove standing eyeing the goods in a shop window – is it possible that he's eyeing your reflection instead? Be like Janus – look before and behind; be like Argos, possessor of a hundred eyes.

For now, though, there was only the empty path, barred with shadow. Leaving the shelter of the trees, squinting in the sudden sunlight, she crossed the sandy heath towards Hampstead ponds. The fair was immediately louder, the chaos of noise separating as she drew nearer to wild screaming and the yelp of barkers, the crash and clack of flung missiles, the laboured jollity of a steam organ playing pre-war melodies, 'Daisy, Daisy' succeeding 'That Daring Young Man on the Flying Trapeze'. A helter-skelter was visible, and a spinning ride, chairs on long chains whirling around a central spindle, the occupants twisting like marionettes.

Just ahead of her, a rabbit shot across the path. Ten yards behind it, a spherical Jack Russell laboured in pursuit, slowly followed by a gasping Labrador. Their owner was stationary a short distance away, paused in the act of lighting his pipe.

'Did you receive the canine diet sheet I passed to your housekeeper?' asked Mattie.

'And a Happy New Year to you, too, Miss Simpkin,' said Major Lumb, his voice carrying well in the still air. 'Fine weather. Shall we avoid snow this year, do you think?'

'They would live far longer and be much happier were they to lose several pounds.'

'And I would live far longer and be much happier were my next-door neighbour to stop issuing unasked-for advice. Please pass on my greetings to Miss Lee and wish her a thoroughly sanitary 1928.' He tipped his hat and turned to follow the pair of animate barrels through the grass.

'One meal a day and no tidbits,' called Mattie at his retreating back. The only reply was a puff of yellowish smoke.

She snapped open her handbag and took out a small notebook and pencil, thumbing through to a section entitled 'COLUMN IDEAS'.

Speaking out, she wrote. *Public silence breeds private misery. Dare to be a Daniel.*

She was closing the notebook again when the steam organ changed its tune: 'Daisy, Daisy' gave way to a jaunty march and the melody looped out of the past and caught her like a snare, so that she stood with the book in her hand, her bag open, her feet nailed to the path.

> *As I walk along the Bois de Boulogne*
> *With an independent air*
> *You can hear the girls declare*
> *He must be a millionaire.*

And instead of the tapering tower of the helter-skelter, she was seeing her younger brother, Angus, his dear, handsome face lop-sided, his indented forehead like a battered tin mug, his lips struggling to supply the words. 'Just try the nouns this time,' she'd suggested, rewinding the gramophone, and he'd managed a ghostly vowel for each, while she'd sung the rest with desperate vigour.

> *As I walk along the Bois de Boulogne*
> *With an independent __*
> *You can hear the __ declare*
> *He must be a __.*

The handbag was whisked from her grasp before she'd even registered the footsteps behind her, and she was left standing open-mouthed as a young man ran down the slope towards the fair, stuffing her bag under his plum-coloured jacket as he went, glancing back at her and then slowing – actually *slowing* – to a casual stroll as he neared the striped shooting-booth at the perimeter.

'Thief!' she shouted, starting forward. '*Thief!*' Her foot touched an object that rolled, and she looked down to see the miniature of whisky that had fallen from the bag as he'd tugged it away. She snatched it up – it was full, a decent weight, heavy enough to startle, too light to maim – and then she straightened, took aim and flung it side-arm, as if skimming a stone. The slope was in her favour; the missile maintained its height, kept its trajectory, and she was able to feel a split second of wondering pride in an unlost skill before a red-headed girl ran, laughing, from behind the booth, dodged round the thief and received the bottle full in the mouth.

'I am really most dreadfully, dreadfully sorry,' called Mattie, hurrying down the path. The redhead had been joined by a boy and the pair of them were kneeling, staring up at her in round-eyed disbelief, the boy pressing a handkerchief to his companion's mouth.

'You're a bloody lunatic,' said the boy.

'Ooh fooh a *oll* a ee,' said the girl.

'That was accidental. I was aiming at a man who had stolen my bag and I would awfully like to—' She stepped to one side and looked round the booth at the shifting crowd. 'I really must try and catch him. As I say, I am enormously sorry. May I see?' She reached towards the handkerchief and the girl jerked away.

'Don't touch her,' ordered the boy.

'I have myself been the recipient of a large number of superficial injuries, many of them deliberately inflicted. In the case of a blow to the mouth, the only worry is whether the teeth are broken or the outline of the lips transected.'

Momentarily, the girl lifted the cloth and Mattie glimpsed an upper lip the size of a frankfurter and a row of undamaged teeth.

'Cold compress,' she said, exiting round the tent. 'No other treatment needed. Awfully sorry.'

For half an hour she hunted the fairground. It appeared that plum-coloured jackets were commonplace this season. She accosted four or five self-declared innocents before accepting that the thief was certainly long gone; there really was nothing further she could do.

༄

The Flea was in the drawing room, taking down the Christmas cards, re-reading each one to ensure that she'd not missed a change of address, or an item of news that might require a note in the diary.

'Come to the Grafton Gallery,' Mattie had suggested. 'I've had a sudden urge to look at the Monet *Haystacks*, first *with* lenses and then without, and we could take tea at Brown's afterwards.' But The Flea had wanted an afternoon to herself, a chance both to restore order after the seasonal anarchy of the past few days, and also to conduct a rather difficult interview with the daily; in any case, she always preferred the Tate, where every painting seemed to tell a satisfying story and a chair looked like a chair and not a collapsible music stand. In particular, she enjoyed the John Martins – vast, apocalyptic canvases showing the wicked sliding into the filthy abyss while the good sat placidly in spotless linen on the sunlit plains of heaven. Sunlight was, of course, not only the best bleaching agent but also the best disinfectant and, moreover, absolutely free! It was something that she always told her mothers.

> *To my dear Mattie and Florrie,*
> *Wishing you a splendid Yule-Tide and a peaceful New Year and also a splendid Yule-Tide.*
> *With kind regards from Aileen*

The handwriting on the card careered downhill amidst a shower of blots; poor Aileen, clearly back on the bottle. Last time they'd seen her she'd been bright-eyed and wearing a correctly buttoned coat – her people, she'd said, had paid for a spell in a strictly run convalescent home, 'very like Holloway, only with smaller rooms', and she'd emerged not only dry but full of plans: she was, she'd told them, going to write and illustrate a novel. She'd apparently forgotten that during her last spell of abstinence she'd claimed to be 'going in for' photography and in the one previous to that she'd been very close to opening a tea-room on the South Downs with accommodation for lady walkers.

The front of the card showed a view of the harbour at Polperro, with snow on the quayside and a sticky brownish stain obscuring most of the fishing fleet. Poor Aileen, unmoored and drifting.

> *Christmas greetings to dearest Mattie and Florrie*
> *Writing this from Northumberland, where I have been attending my daughter Kate during her confinement. I am delighted to say that I am now grandmamma to a bonny boy who looks the spitting image of his grandfather. Are you coming to my 'Forward Thinking' lecture in January? (The 14th, at Conway Hall.) I have chosen 'Wages for Mothers' as my theme.*
> *Your loving comrade*
> *Dorothy*

The picture on the front of Dorothy's card was of a serenely smiling Virgin and child, but Dorothy had drawn a speech balloon from the Virgin's mouth, so that she appeared to be saying 'I should be receiving an allowance for this!' Mattie had laughed out loud at the picture but the graffitoed image had made The Flea uncomfortable. She'd seen enough dismal rooms where a cheap illustration of the Holy Family was the sole non-utilitarian possession – the one pleasant view on which a weary woman could rest her gaze. 'Not everything should be shaped into a joke,' she'd said, a little sharply; she herself had grown up in a household where unchecked laughter had been seen as a bodily failing, rather like breaking wind.

She placed the more colourful cards in a pile ready for taking to New End Infants School and, after wrapping herself in a shawl, started to cut up the others for spills. The house was, as usual, freezing. Mattie never seemed to feel the cold, but then she was built along solid lines, whereas The Flea (as a friend had once remarked) looked rather as if she'd been constructed out of toothpicks. There was a fireplace in every room, of course, but the heat never permeated much beyond the grates and the corridors were a lattice of draughts.

It suited Mattie, though, who required space and air and who would undoubtedly have preferred to live in a tent. 'Doors should generally be open and the sky visible at all times,' was one of her maxims, usually uttered while flinging open a casement.

She had bought the house in 1922, after coming into a legacy. 'I was walking across Hampstead Heath,' she'd announced at the end of a Women's Freedom League fundraising concert, 'and I stumbled across our dear old Mousehole *festooned* with "For Sale" signs. Been empty since the war, apparently. Plenty of room for anyone who wants to hunker down there.'

Dorothy had nudged The Flea. 'Didn't you say you were hoping to move?'

And The Flea, whose bedsit in Tufnell Park had a dark

line of mould creeping across the ceiling and a shared kitchen lambent with silverfish, had negotiated a short stay. 'Thank you, but just while I'm searching for something else.'

Mattie had refused payment. 'I am not a landlord.'

'And I am not a charity case. I shall donate a sum to the WFL.'

After a week, it had become clear that Mattie lived on porridge, apples and baked potatoes. The Flea had made a steak-and-kidney pudding.

'If you stayed for longer,' said Mattie, scraping her plate like a schoolboy, 'you could cook in lieu of paying rent.'

'I'm fully capable of doing both,' replied The Flea, rather tartly.

That had been six years ago.

'We're good companions,' said Mattie. 'The arrangement works well.'

From the passage came the clank of a mop bucket being set down, and The Flea felt a flutter of unpleasant anticipation. She put down her scissors, walked over to the door, bracing herself for the interview, and opened it to find Mrs Bowling just inches away, hand poised to knock. Both women flinched.

'Did you want to speak to me?' asked The Flea, recovering first.

'I did, yes, Miss Lee. I'm sorry, but I've got some bad news for you.'

'Oh dear.'

'Yes, I'm afraid so.' Mrs Bowling paused, portentously. 'You see, Miss Lee, I have to hand in my notice.'

'Oh.' The Flea tried to rearrange her features into an expression of regret. 'I do hope there's nothing wrong.'

'I wouldn't say there's anything *wrong*, exactly, Miss Lee.'

'You've been offered another job, perhaps?'

'In a manner of speaking, yes I have.' Mrs Bowling paused again, her expression enigmatic. ('The Kentish Town Sphinx,' Mattie called her. 'You cannot ask that woman whether she's seen the bathroom plunger without her reacting as if she holds the Secret of the Ages.') 'You see, what happened is that my daughter-in-law Enid went into labour on Boxing Day.'

'And is the ba—'

'*Twins.*'

'Oh my goodness.'

'A little boy and a little girl. My son said he's going to name the girl after me. He said, "I hope she turns out just like you, Mum, because you're the best one there ever was."'

'And are they—'

'The midwife said she'd never seen a healthier pair, *never*. But Enid's just a scrap of a thing and my son's told me he wants me to come in every day and help with the babies. "Mum," he said, "you shouldn't be out slaving for strangers when there's work at home to do," and my husband agrees, he said to me, "I'm sure Miss Lee and Miss Simpkin will understand that *family* needs to come first." And, anyway, my youngest has just had a promotion at the Post Office so we can manage now without my little bit of pin money.'

The Flea actually had to bite the inside of her lip to keep her composure.

The tremendous cheek of the woman! Mrs Bowling's tenure as a more than adequately paid daily help had been marked by a gradual diminution of labour: all shipshape for the first month or two, and then a slow shrinkage of the areas subjected to scrubbing, a lowering of the height dusted, a neglect of less-frequented corners, all accompanied by a stream of chatter about the comforts of family life. No one, she implied, who had never had children or a husband could possibly understand true joy or sorrow – and it had begun to seem to The Flea that these two aspects were linked, and that a type of contempt for her spinster employers, living their barren lives, had led to a carelessness about how they were served. Mattie, of course, had noticed nothing – had swished past like a Daimler – but the idea had gnawed at The Flea until at last she'd determined to speak out, at least about the cleanliness part. And now this cup had been taken from her.

'I suppose I could stay another fortnight,' said Mrs Bowling.

'No, that's quite all right,' said The Flea. 'I'm sure we can manage without you.'

She had just sat down again – feeling more at ease than she had for days – when the doorbell jangled.

'The most infuriating thing has happened, Florrie,' called Mattie, opening the back door and racing up the scullery passage. 'I was crossing the Heath towards the—'

'Mattie, we have a visitor.' There was a warning note in

The Flea's voice. The kitchen door was ajar and through the gap Mattie could see a policeman's helmet on the table. Its owner, a sergeant, stared at her as she entered the room, and then rose with what felt like deliberate slowness. He had sharp features, and brown eyes that were slightly too close together; a terrier's face.

'Miss Simpkin?'

'Yes.' She remained standing, her chin up and her knees a little bent. *When questioned, imagine you are about to receive a tennis serve; with your senses on the alert, your stance easy and your muscles poised, you'll be ready to return all shots – with backspin!* Behind the policeman, The Flea hovered anxiously, hands clasped.

'My name is Sergeant Beal. I'm here about an incident at the Heath fairground earlier this afternoon.'

'Yes, my handbag was snatched from my grasp. Did someone report it?'

'The incident I'm talking about involved a missile being thrown at a young lady.'

'No, the missile in question was thrown at the thief. The young lady happened to interpose herself between us. I think you will find there is a considerable difference between these two statements.'

'Mattie,' said The Flea, levelly, 'you are not in the dock.'

'Nevertheless, I would prefer to keep the facts straight.'

Beal picked up his notepad and, with deliberation, thumbed through to a page of close writing. 'The young lady claims you threw a bottle at her.'

'A *miniature* bottle. Please don't make it sound as if I lobbed a jeroboam in her direction. A crime had been committed and I was attempting to delay the escape of the perpetrator. The injury to the girl was entirely accidental, not to mention minor, and I apologized profusely. I cannot see why this is a police matter.'

There was a pause. Mattie had the sudden feeling that she had hit a mis-shot.

'You said that a crime had been committed,' repeated the sergeant.

'Yes, my bag was stolen.'

'Which is most definitely a police matter. And yet you didn't, yourself, report it.'

'No.'

'Why's that?'

There was a pause. 'I chose not to. As is my legal right.'

Beal nodded, as if she'd just confirmed something. 'I gather we're not too fond of the police, are we, Miss Simpkin?'

'*I* – I presume you are using the first-person plural ironically – *I* infer from your remark that you know something of my history. The question therefore answers itself.'

'The tea's ready,' announced The Flea, brightly and hurriedly. 'Let's all sit down together, shall we? Would you like a cup of tea, Sergeant?'

'Thank you, Miss Lee, that would be most welcome.'

'Let me clear a space.' She moved the piles of cards to the window ledge, and took her time about setting out the tea cups, waiting until Mattie had reluctantly taken a seat before she began to pour.

'Given that I did not report the incident,' said Mattie, 'may I ask why and how you arrived on my doorstep?'

'One of my constables was patrolling the fair, and he

came across the injured young lady. She gave a description of the person who had thrown the missile and this description was recognized by the constable in question, who had attended an incident involving yourself last summer.'

'Which incident?'

'An argument between yourself and a carter.'

'Oh, that incident. The fellow was refusing to allow his poor animal to stop for water on the hottest day of the year. All I did was unbuckle the harness and attempt to lead the horse away until such time as—'

'Mattie.' The Flea's tone was like a nudge to the steering wheel; Mattie veered away from the side road and back to the main thoroughfare. 'As I say, the injury to the girl was quite accidental and not, I think, serious, and my apology was immediate.'

'The young lady,' said the sergeant, his voice suddenly hard, 'looks as if she's been in a prize fight. She works in the first-class ladies' cloakroom at St Pancras and says she's sure she won't be allowed back there until the injury to her lip has healed. She is thinking of pressing charges.' He leaned back, seeming to relish the silence that followed. 'In the meantime,' he added, 'could you give me a description of the thief, and also of the handbag?'

'He was wearing a purple jacket,' said Mattie, stiffly, 'and he had dark hair, but I barely saw his face. I can tell you nothing useful about his appearance.' Though as she spoke, she recollected that glance back; a broad face, sharply cheek-boned – almost Slavic; she had been reminded of her Serbian refugees.

'And the bag?'

'Black leather. Rather large.'

'Its contents?'

'A purse, a 1928 diary, a pair of nail scissors, a fountain pen, a third edition of Fuller's *Worthies of England*, volume two . . .'

'A large book,' supplied The Flea, as the sergeant's pencil hesitated.

'. . . an apple, a string bag, a handkerchief, a Jew's harp and a small wooden—'

Mattie stopped herself just in time.

'. . . shoe tree.'

'And how much is in the purse?'

'Just over two pounds, but there is also a betting slip which, should Casey's Bride win the 4.20 at Sedgefield, will yield a further three guineas.'

Beal tucked his notebook and pencil into his pocket and rose to leave.

'Thank you for the tea, Miss Lee. Miss Simpkin, we may need you to come to the station to give a signed statement. You shall be sent a letter in due course. In the meantime, I'd advise you not to take the law into your own hands. Again.' He checked his watch. 'Casey's Bride?'

'Three-year-old gelding out of Joe's Heaven and Penelope. On striking form this season.'

She stayed seated as The Flea showed the sergeant out, and when she heard the front door close she reached for her tea. Her hand was trembling. How ridiculous that a single fairground tune had led to this; for thirty seconds she'd visited Angus, dear Angus, in that dreadful hospital in Weymouth and for that she'd been robbed and

threatened with court. Her guard had slipped and the bar-
barians had come smashing through. *Vigilance*, she
thought, for the second time in as many hours. *Vigilance*.

'That poor girl,' said The Flea, returning.

'Yes, it was fearfully bad luck for her. For both of us.'

'Mattie, you could have taken her eye out!'

'No,' said Mattie, with certainty. 'No, I was aiming for
the spot between the fellow's shoulder blades. She would
have had to have been frightfully short to be struck any
higher.' She took a deep breath and set her cup down.
'However, I would rather not be the subject of an assault
charge. I wonder . . .'

'What?'

'If the girl might accept payment for days missed at
work. Compensation, so to speak. I could go to St Pancras
and ask for her address. She's a redhead, it won't be hard
to describe her.'

'I could do that,' said The Flea, quickly. 'I'll be working
in Somers Town tomorrow, right beside the station.'

'I don't mind going.'

'And neither do I.' The Flea's tone was bright but firm.
Mattie looked at her companion over the top of her spec-
tacles. 'You fear I may mishandle the situation.'

'It's more that you're very *memorable*, Mattie. After all,
what we are talking about is . . .'

'Bribery.'

'Yes. Any visitor would need to be unobtrusive. And
don't forget I often have to raise quite delicate matters
with my mothers, topics of discussion that I need to' – she
picked her words – 'sidle around.'

'I lack tact.'

'Yes.'

'Hmm.' Mattie gave her eyes a rub. 'You may be right. In which case, thank you. In the meantime, I urgently need to replace my diary, all my lecture dates were in there – do you have a record of them?'

'They're on the new kitchen calendar.'

'Ah. I wasn't sure, so directly after the incident I went across the road to the Drill Hall to look at the poster outside and . . .'

'A week on Wednesday,' said The Flea. 'Seven o'clock.'

'. . . and whoever pinned it on to the noticeboard has done so rather carelessly. There is a pleat right down the centre of the paper, eliminating an entire syllable of every line. My lecture is apparently entitled "Some Experiences of a *Mint* Suffragette", though I fared rather better than Mrs Gretel Neumann and her daughters, who this week will be giving a demonstration of Traditional Germ Folk Dancing. One for you, I thought, Florrie: you could bring your flit-gun and douse the front rows of the audience with prophylactic Jeyes Fluid.'

There was a moment of silence and then The Flea flushed pink and, almost against her will, began to laugh.

'Thought that might tickle you,' said Mattie with satisfaction. She drained her tea and then stood and stretched. 'A *thoroughly* irritating day,' she said. 'What I need is some violent exercise. I shall walk down to the bookmaker in Camden and see if he'll honour my mark.'

'Across the Heath again?'

'Yes.'

'Then please be careful. I still don't understand what happened – was there a struggle, were you injured in any way?'

'No. I was distracted by something and made myself an easy target.' Humiliating to think of how she'd been standing, daydreaming like some silly flapper.

'But distracted by what?'

Mattie shook her head. 'It really doesn't matter; it won't happen again.' She went to the hall to fetch her cape; it was crisping up for a frost outside.

Twenty minutes later, breasting Parliament Hill in the twilight, she saw a fox trot into the bushes, its mouth crammed with something that struggled. London lay sprawled below, yellow streetlights like a cheap glass necklace, the diamond pin of Venus hanging above. She could hear the jangle of the fair in the distance; the music was still playing, dangerously sentimental, and she took a deep breath and began to sing 'The Marseillaise', matching her footsteps to the rhythm of the lines. A spooning couple turned to stare; she nodded at them, pleasantly. People always stared. If one didn't creep around, if one said what one thought, if one shouted for joy or roared with anger, if one tried to *get things done*, then seemingly there was no choice but to be noticeable. She couldn't remember a time when her path hadn't been lined with startled faces; they were her reassurance that progress was being made. What tremendous luck, she'd often thought, that she'd been born into an era of change. She could not have stood to have been like Dorothea Brooke, deprived of grand gestures, incrementally adding to the growing good of the world.

∽

For work, The Flea wore a plain coat over a blouse and skirt, but her hat had 'Health Visitor' embroidered across the band. She exchanged it for a felt cloche in the public lavatory at St Pancras, pausing for a moment between hats to marvel at the shortness of her hair. It hung just below her ears – more of a bob than a shingle (she had rather lost her nerve in the barber's chair) – but, nonetheless, it was nearly eight inches shorter than before, and the novelty was still delightful. 'I should think I gain nearly twenty minutes of useful time a day,' she'd said to Mattie, 'what with all the washing and brushing and pinning.'

'It isn't time that I begrudge,' remarked Mattie, whose own hair, plaited, had the thickness of a steel hawser, and who harboured a secret suspicion that, like Samson, she might pay physically for its removal; she wore it pinned into a great silver wheel that framed her head.

The Flea's own hair was limp and fine, dark brown threaded with grey, and the shorter length made her pointed little face appear almost girlish. *I shall never grow it long again*, she thought, and the idea was quietly thrilling.

The red-headed girl's name was Ida Pearse. 'But I'm afraid she no longer works here,' said the supervisor at the first-class ladies' cloakroom, mouth pursed, as if balancing a marble on her tongue. 'She kept getting styes, and that's not at all nice for our ladies to see, is it? So last week I had to ask her to leave.'

'Could you tell me where she lives? She . . . she left her umbrella at our house.' Even to her own ears this sounded implausible – she had always been a poor liar – but the supervisor was scarcely listening; after one glance at The Flea, her gaze had slid past in search of someone more obviously first class.

'I couldn't tell you, I'm afraid. Excuse me.' She plunged forward with a sudden smile as a customer approached, and The Flea was left standing beside the counter. The waiting room behind it was beautiful: a leaf-patterned carpet, and leather sofas; frosted glass in the window, a central table with a sheaf of magazines and a bowl of potpourri.

In one corner, a girl in a maid's uniform stood beside a small table, ready to hand out pins, or hairgrips or hand cream. The Flea caught her eye and gave an encouraging smile, and after a moment of hesitation, and a glance across at her supervisor, the girl came over to the counter. She was about fifteen, plump-faced, her eyes like buttons on a pink cushion.

'Can I help you?'

'Do you know Miss Pearse's address?'

'Miss Pearse?'

'The red-headed girl who worked here.'

'Oh, *Ida*.' She bit cautiously on the name as though it were an over-seasoned pudding. 'She had to leave.'

'I know. Styes.'

'And cheek.' The girl glanced towards where the supervisor was pouring a glass of soda water for a customer and then lowered her voice. 'She corrected one of the ladies.'

'Corrected her on what?'

'Geography.'

'What aspect of geography?'

'I don't know. But we're not supposed to contradict the ladies. I don't ever,' she added, complacently.

'So do you know where I could find Ida?'

'Wilson Road. She lives with relations. Her auntie takes in ironing.' The tone was disparaging.

'A useful service,' said The Flea, rather crisply, forgetting for a second the need to be unobtrusive, remembering instead her own childhood: two steam-filled rooms, walls pearled with moisture, piles of folded linen which couldn't ever be touched or even brushed against, so that she and her brother had learned to walk crab-wise, arms pressed to their sides. 'Thank you,' she added, turning away from the counter.

She knew Wilson Road well. 'Black Alley', it was called by the locals, the bricks thick with railway soot, the thrum of trains audible in the rooms at the front of the buildings, the ceaseless clatter and hum of the Euston Road at the back. 'He can't sleep if he can't hear no traffic,' one of her mothers had said of her baby. A nice, clean, healthy baby he'd been, in well-scrubbed quarters, while directly outside rats had rustled in a row of lidless bins. On that occasion, The Flea had threatened the landlord with a summons, and new lids had been quickly supplied; you could use the law against the landlords – you could demand a visit to a workshop, request gutters to be mended, walls to be whitewashed, windows to be unscrewed – but to enter a home you needed an invitation. And you never knew until the door was open whether you'd smell carbolic or sour milk, whether the mother would be able and energetic or a weary slattern with a row of ailing offspring, and, if the latter, you could never criticize – only hint, nudge, suggest, interleave tact with sympathy, otherwise you'd never get in again. You were a *visitor*, and visitors should always be polite.

'Excuse me. I'm looking for a lady who takes in ironing. She might be called Mrs Pearse.'

The small boy sitting with his feet in the gutter and a kitten on his lap jerked his head towards a stairwell.

'Top floor, Miss.'

The Flea was halfway up the stairs when a young girl of fourteen or fifteen came clattering down, a knotted bundle in her hand, a puffed purple smudge on her upper lip, auburn hair visible beneath a cheap beige felt.

'Ida Pearse?'

The girl ducked her face towards the wall.

'Who's asking?'

'My name's Miss Lee. I heard about your nasty accident on the Heath and I called to see how you were.'

The girl flicked her a glance and then returned to her study of the brickwork. 'What do you mean, you heard about it? Are you something to do with the police?'

'No, I . . . my friend was inadvertently responsible for your injury.'

'What, *her*? The old bottle-chucker?' Ida turned. The bruise was like an inked-on moustache, vivid against the colourless bread-and-marge complexion, the sparse, pale eyelashes. 'Sent you to say sorry, has she? Too scared to come herself?'

25

The Flea managed not to smile. 'Quite the reverse, I had to persuade her to let me visit. I work in this area, you see.'

'How did you find me, anyhow?'

'A policeman called and told us you were worried you'd not be allowed to go in to work, so I went to the cloakroom at St Pancras and . . .'

Ida flushed. 'That cow of a supervisor,' she said. 'You'd think I got the styes on purpose, you'd think I'd chosen them out of a catalogue. She said it was from the dirt, and I'm as clean as Christmas, I bet I wash more than her. So you going to tell the police I was lying then, and I'd already been sacked?'

'Of course not.'

The girl gnawed at her lower lip, indignation fading. 'I don't even know why I said it.'

'You were upset and shocked, I'd imagine. Did you try bathing your eyes with borax?'

'Are you a nurse?'

'A sanitary inspector and health visitor.'

'Salt water, I tried. I boiled the water first.'

'Yes, that's sensible.'

'But I've got another one coming already – look.' She dragged down the skin of her cheek, and The Flea peered at the cream-tipped swelling on the lower lid.

'My aunt says it's the soot from the railway.'

'That could be a factor. Perhaps it's just as well you no longer work at the station.'

'I suppose she told you about the row, too?'

'What row? Oh – something to do with geography?'

'All I said was, "Where are you travelling to, Madam?"

because otherwise you're just standing there, aren't you, and you might as well be a hat rack or have your mouth glued shut, and the lady said, "Manchester," and I said, "Oh, I've never been to Lancashire," and she said, "It's Yorkshire," and I said – politely – I said, "It's not, Madam." Because I *know* it's not, my boyfriend's dad's from there, except he's not my boyfriend any more, he went off with someone else after the fair, he said I looked a fright and I had to go back to Auntie's on the bus with my scarf over my face. It's been a rotten, stinking, horrible week.' And she was crying, suddenly, blotting her eyes against her sleeve, all the starch rinsed out of her. 'I've got to take this over to Warren Street now,' she said, shifting the bundle of linen to the other hand.

'Are you working for your aunt?'

'Just for my keep. Why?'

'I'm wondering . . .' The girl's nails were neat and short, and as clean as Christmas. 'I'm wondering if you're look-ing for another job.'

Mattie wore her purple, green and white sash for lec-tures, and her Holloway brooch, but not her hunger-strike medals. 'I have no wish to look like the veteran of an historic war,' she said. 'The battle is not yet over; every day brings fresh skirmishes.'

With five minutes to go, the Drill Hall was three-quarters full. From her position in the wings, Mattie looked out at the audience with dissatisfaction; they were all so *old*. She hastily corrected the thought – most of them were a similar age to herself, and at fifty-eight she felt no different, bodily or mentally, than she had at thirty – no, it wasn't their age that was dismaying but their demeanour. Women were knitting; a man on the front row peered through a magnifying glass at a copy of *Punch*; there was chat, there was light laughter and the rattle of a tin of mints being opened. There was no anticipation, no rigour: they were clearly there for entertainment and not education or debate, and the swift sword of her rhetoric would be blunted on a row of bolsters.

Only The Flea was on the alert, standing in the aisle with boxes of slides to hand, the air around her swimming slightly from the heat of the lantern. Rather than her WSPU sash, she was wearing a discreet pin in the Union's colours ('If the audience are looking at me, Mattie, then they are looking in the wrong direction'). She caught her companion's eye and gave a little nod of readiness.

'Good evening,' said Mattie, stepping forward to the lectern. 'My name is Miss Matilda Simpkin. I hope, over the next hour and a half, to convey something of the history and methods of the militant suffragette movement, to slice through the integument of myth and slander that has so often overlaid the truth of its beliefs and actions, and to expose to clear view those of its aims that have yet to be achieved. For until women are represented as well as taxed – until the laws that govern one sex expand to cover both – we will not be free to work for our own salvation: be it political, social or industrial.

'Let us begin with the venerable argument against the female vote – an argument that centred around the character of that frail creature known as *woman*. Her horizons were narrow, her sphere domestic, her opinions as light and capricious as the flutterings of a moth; how could she possibly be trusted to choose wisely and independently? Let us see a collection of these Victorian flibbertigibbets.' She signalled to the caretaker and the hall dropped into darkness, apart from the long cone of yellow light from the magic lantern and the softer splash of the reading lamp that illuminated Mattie.

'Mary Somerville,' said Mattie. 'Mother of six, self-taught scientist, jointly the first female member of the Royal Astronomical Society. The Oxford college for women is named after her.'

On the stretched sheet that hung centre stage, a portrait of Somerville settled into focus.

'Florence Nightingale' – the picture changed – 'who asked the question: "Why have women passion, intellect, moral activity – these three – and a place in society where not one of the three can be exercised?"' The slide holder clicked and slid again as The Flea worked deftly in the dark.

'Frances Buss, pioneer of female education and founder of the North London Collegiate School for Ladies.

'Octavia Hill, housing reformer and saviour of Hampstead Heath.' A little sigh of appreciation went up from the audience.

'Charlotte Brontë, who once said, "I am no bird; and no net ensnares me; I am a free human being with an independent will."

'Dr Garrett Anderson, not only the first Englishwoman to qualify as a doctor and surgeon, but the first female mayor. And, finally, Grace Darling, oarswoman and heroine of the storm. Each of them barred from the franchise, each of them – I'm sure you'll agree – strangers to reason, liable to faint at inopportune moments and best employed in advising their cooks on the best method of preparing junket.' There was a hesitant titter. 'Meanwhile, after the extension of the male franchise under the 1832 Reform Act, vastly increased numbers of wastrels and drunkards, adulterers, wife-beaters and employers of child labour were able to stroll freely into a polling booth in order to ordain the governance of this country. Charlotte Brontë couldn't vote, but Branwell Brontë could. Dr Anderson stayed at home, while the Rugeley Poisoner, Dr Palmer, went to the polling booth. By 1903, when Mrs Emmeline Pankhurst founded the Women's Social and Political Union, over fifty years had passed since the publication of Harriet Taylor Mill's essay "The Enfranchisement of Women" – fifty years of petitioning, fifty years of discussion, fifty years of meetings, of canvassing, of promises made and of promises broken. The birth of militancy came after a long and painful confinement: sweet reason, it became evident, had changed nothing – sweet reason could safely be ignored by those in power. What was needed was a new approach, a shift from the genteelly audible to the boldly visible.'

Mattie swung her pointer towards the screen just as the WSPU motto replaced Grace Darling's rowing boat.

DEEDS NOT WORDS

'Deeds not Words,' she repeated, with ringing emphasis. 'And do not doubt, for an instant, that those deeds were called into existence not by reckless energy but by the stubbornness of those in power. Any questions, before I move on?'

She peered into the semi-darkness, hoping for a waving arm, a cleared throat; from her years on the stump, she knew that the real business of any meeting was not in the opening monologue but in the debate that followed: it was the difference between shadow-boxing and sparring.

'If you have questions, please raise your hand. I would much prefer to tackle points as they arise, rather than wait until the end. No? . . . Very well. Next slide. We see here Mrs Pankhurst holding a meeting outside the Houses of Parliament in protest at the talking-out of a women's suffrage bill. This was in 1904. If you have never seen a filibusterer at work, then imagine a small child trying to explain something important while his playfellow sticks his fingers in his ears and shouts, "La la la," and you will have some idea of the maturity of the tactic. Hand in hand with this inability to *listen*, the political parties at this time also demonstrated a marked reluctance to *speak*, a failing which led directly to the first arrests of the militant campaign. In October 1905, Miss Christabel Pankhurst and Miss Annie Kenney, pictured here' – bright young faces, hats like silk saucepan lids – 'attended a Liberal Party meeting in Manchester at which they enquired, both in speech and in writing, whether a future Liberal Government would give women the vote; not only did they fail to receive an answer, but they were also ejected, charged and imprisoned – and it is here that I wish to correct a long-standing and entirely false belief. I have heard it said that suffragettes received no sort of rough handling from the

LISSA EVANS

authorities until they themselves began to mete out physical protest, to which I would reply: *balderdash*. More injuries were received at the hands of stewards at political meetings than in any other theatre of protest – women asking questions of Cabinet Ministers at public discussions would be dragged from the hall, punched and kicked, shaken and indecently manhandled, often in full view of an unprotesting audience. I myself have a permanent depression in one calf resulting from a steward jabbing the ferrule of his umbrella directly into the muscle and, if anyone doubts this, then I would say, like Our Saviour to St Thomas, "Come thou and put thy finger in the wound!"'

There was a volley of gasps, followed by the rustle and creak of someone making their way along a row of chairs and thence out of the hall.

'For shame!' called a man.

'I use the phrase not in order to shock,' continued Mattie, mendaciously – that particular phrase had proved over the years to be a reliable method of gingering up a stuffy audience – 'but in order to convey the extraordinary forbearance of the suffragette movement in those early days; we received kicks and blows, and we returned with leaflets and speeches, newspapers, meetings and peaceful demonstrations. I myself was arrested for the first time when I arrived at the House of Commons as part of a deputation. I spoke; I may even have raised my voice, but I most certainly did not raise my fist – and for this, I and others were imprisoned in Holloway for over a month. You can see here a photograph of our release; the person holding the bouquet is Mrs How-Martyn and the person just beside her – wearing a headscarf beneath her hat – is me; what you cannot see in this photograph is the infestation of head lice that I carried out of the prison with me – yes, a question?' She had spotted a masculine handkerchief waving in the dark.

'Shouting in Parliament is all very well, Miss Simpkin, but what do you have to say about the acts of criminal arson carried out by the suffragette movement?'

It was a middle-aged voice, truculent. Mattie smiled.

'Could I ask you in return if you recall reading about the Reform Act riots of 1831, in which the gaol and the Bishop's House in Bristol were set on fire, with many deaths resulting, all in the name of representation? And yet no male reformer has ever been asked to apologize for this. Men have been allowed to use bloodshed and disorder to gain their freedom – have been celebrated for their passion in pursuit of the vote – and yet the suffragettes, who hurt not a single person with their fires, are condemned. As Thomas Fuller once said, "Abused patience turns to fury." By that point, we were furious, and justifiably so.'

'So you have no regret about these acts of vandalism?'

'If I have a regret, it's that no government buildings were burned to the ground, no electrical companies, no factories – we wasted our powder on half-built houses and tea pavilions, and were therefore seen as a private nuisance rather than a public threat. Do I see another questioner?'

'Did you say' – the elderly voice hesitated, tremulous with horror – 'did you say *lice*, Miss Simpkin?'

'Yes, I did indeed mention those persistent little blighters – I had to massage petroleum jelly through my hair and then comb out the corpses thrice daily for a month in order to rid myself of them. So let me say a few words now about the prison conditions that gave rise to such horrors . . .'

Over at the magic lantern, The Flea reached for the appropriate box. There were six altogether, each numbered in luminous paint, and the slides within were kept in an order that she had long ago memorized. Mattie's lectures rarely pursued a linear course, and The Flea often had to move back and forth between the boxes as questions flung up fresh subjects. She slotted a slide into the lantern and slid the frame across.

'This picture is not of an actual prison cell,' said Mattie, 'but of an accurate facsimile, assembled and exhibited by the WSPU at the Prince's Rink Exhibition in 1909. It all looks rather comfortable, doesn't it? – a decent-sized room, an adequate bed, a window, a wash stand, a chair, even a small table on which one might put one's belongings. One might almost be in an hotel, and I'm sure you're all wondering what those dreadful militant harridans were complaining about – however, I have withheld one vital fact: this is a *first*-division cell, of the sort occupied by the ordinary male political prisoner. If you were a Fenian, throwing bombs at English policemen, then this is where you would find yourself after conviction. By contrast, a suffragette found guilty of persistently ringing a Cabinet Minister's doorbell with the aim of receiving a simple answer to a simple question would be placed in one of *these* – a second-division cell.'

The slide changed; there was a murmur of consternation.

'As you see, it is half the size of the previous room, and singularly devoid of home comforts. And, as I can personally testify, were this one of the so-called punishment cells, which in Holloway Prison were situated in the basement, it would lack even a window. Lying on a plank bed with one's wrists cuffed together, one was reduced to staring at the irregular patches of black damp on the walls, trying to work out which of them looked most like a profile of Mr Asquith. Male political prisoners were, of course, allowed their own clothes, whereas I can best illustrate what we women were required to wear—'

(*Box 3*, thought The Flea: *Processions, fourth slide from the front.*)

'—by showing you a photograph from the 1908 march to Hyde Park. Of the 30,000 women and men who paraded that day, those who had previously been incarcerated wore their prison costume. You see the woollen dress – it was rather a strange shade of mustard – the apron with arrows, and the mob cap that possessed the singular attribute of making even the prettiest face look like a peeled turnip.'

There was a laugh, rather warmer than the one earlier, followed by a question from the audience about the march, and The Flea was able to stick with Box 3 for a while, which was anyway her favourite, though the photographs could never convey the true feeling of those processions – how, when the march had started, and the bands were playing, and the air was dense with cheers and song, it would feel as if a friendly wind had lifted you up and was carrying you along with a thousand friends – as if you could never be alone again, as if darkness had been outlawed, as if the world had already been won. And afterwards it took hours, days sometimes, for that wind to drop – so that typing at

35

her desk in the WSPU offices, or lying on her narrow bed in Archway, listening to Miss Sare filing her toenails on the other side of the shared bedroom, she would still feel like a swallow, skimming just above the ground.

And here was a slide of the Coronation procession: seven miles long, Joan of Arc on a white charger, pennants, floats, choirs, brass bands, societies of every kidney – the Actresses' League, the Theosophists, the Tax Resistance League – and somewhere towards the centre, the Pageant of Historical Women. 'We need nuns!' someone had called out at the office the day before. 'Christabel says that the Abbess Hilda really *must* have acolytes,' and The Flea had been herded into a fitting, and the next morning had found herself standing on the Bayswater Road, draped in black and white and awaiting the arrival of the abbess. Who had turned out to be Mattie Simpkin, the peripatetic speaker whose cross-country schedule The Flea had been organizing for the previous six months. 'How was Dorking?' she'd asked her, rather shyly. 'Dorking?' said Mattie. 'It was corking!' And the reply was so silly and unexpected from someone with such a weighty reputation that The Flea had actually giggled.

Mattie, wearing a headdress shaped like a cuckoo clock, had led her flock with dignity ('Though I'd rather hoped to be Boadicea'), occasionally blessing the crowds who lined the route. It had been the most thrilling day The Flea had ever known, the atmosphere not importunate but gloriously triumphal, and she could never forget, over the bitter, furious years that followed, her own bafflement that it *hadn't worked* – that the government had watched a display of such discipline, such civilization and culture and wit, and had then simply turned its back.

It was like the fairy tale that she'd read as a child, where the woodcutter's daughter was set task after task in order to free the prince from the witch's spell – first she'd had to find the magic egg, then the golden bird, then the blue heart of the mountain – and yet each time, when she succeeded, the promised freedom was denied and another task requested and, in the end, only violence and death were able to break the enchantment.

'The blunt fact,' said Mattie to the audience at the Drill Hall, 'is that we were betrayed, over and over again, by politicians who thought that because we were women we would accept high-handed duplicity as a hazard of our sex. We were left, finally, with no choice but to use the argument of the stone, and the hostage of our own mortality.'

And The Flea reached for Box 4: Hunger strikes. Three people exited the hall during the description of force-feeding.

The predictable question – asked at every single lecture and always with the air that the speaker was saying something tremendously original – came some twenty minutes later. 'But surely you must admit, Miss Simpkin, that the vote was ultimately granted only because of the sterling work by ladies on the home front, while their menfolk were away in the trenches? Surely it was responsibility, and not *irr*esponsibility, that won it for you in the end?'

'To which I would reply,' said Mattie, 'that it was, in my opinion, only the Government's fear that militancy would return after the war that forced the bill through. Sterling work is something of which women have *always* been capable: is not a mother raising seven children performing sterling work every day? Were not those ladies whose photographs opened this lecture all exemplars of sterling work? Is not a millhand who arrives home after twelve hours at the loom only to begin cleaning and cooking performing more than her fair share of sterling work? Is she not, in fact, the *essence* of responsibility? And yet such a woman, if under thirty, or failing the property qualification, may *still* not exercise her vote, while the devil-may-care youngest son of the mill owner, with a head full of silliness, has full possession of the privilege! Another question?'

'Yes, what did *you* do during the war, Miss Simpkin?'

'I neither abandoned my beliefs nor relinquished my aims.' Only The Flea noticed the slight hesitation that had preceded the answer. 'Any more questions?'

'I have a question,' said a woman from near the back of the hall; a deep voice, with a slight colonial accent. 'Does the name Agnes Bostock mean anything to you?'

Mattie started.

'Who *is* that?' she asked, peering into the darkness.

'Can't you guess?'

The audience were craning round now, curious.

'I'll give you a clue,' said the woman, and, astonishingly, she began to sing:

'Allons les femmes de la patrie,
Le jour de gloire est arrivé!'

'Good Lord!' crowed Mattie. 'It's Jacko!'

Jacqueline Fletcher looked altogether more elegant than when Mattie had seen her last, in the exercise yard at Holloway. Fourteen years on, studying the menu at the Sprite Café, she resembled a photograph from the society pages, hair artfully waved, a burnt-orange stole draped over a frock the shade of a conker.

'The gammon's good in here,' said Mattie.

'I think I'll have poached eggs,' said Jacko, closing the menu. 'I missed them in Queensland. No one can cook there; the national dish seems to be steamed bread. Richard and I had a cook who served it at every meal, even with roasts, and we were supposed to dance with delight whenever it appeared. You know, you look just the same, Mattie, apart from the colour of your hair.' Her eyes flicked down towards Mattie's blouse and cameo brooch, her tweed walking-skirt.

'Now please don't start talking to me about fashion,' said Mattie. 'The woman who makes my skirts keeps hinting that I'd be more *à la mode* in those dreadful narrow sacks that everyone wears nowadays, but I'm sure if I wore one I'd scarcely be able to walk, let alone run.'

'Do you run much these days?'

'No. But if I needed to, I'd rather not have to hitch my clothing up round my armpits.'

Jacko sniggered. 'Should we order for . . . I'm sorry, I've forgotten your helper's name.'

'Florrie. Florrie Lee, hence the fact that she's often referred to as "The Flea". No, she's packing the slides away, won't think of coming here before they're all perfectly arranged. In any case, she's rather like Shakespeare's chameleon – survives largely on air.'

'And she was in the offices at Kingsway?'

'Yes. And now she lodges at the Mousehole, with me.'

'I don't remember her. Never gaoled?'

'No, far too useful behind the scenes – mind like a filing cabinet. What, incidentally, did you think of the lecture?'

'Oh, I thought it was splendid. Quite brought back the old days.'

There was a whisper of dismissiveness about the comment. Mattie leaned forward.

'I'm not in the business of nostalgia, Jacko. The lecture is supposed to be a clarion call to those who think that feminism is safely in the past.'

'Well, isn't it? Aren't there other fish to fry?'

'But we still await *parity*. It was our most basic aim, and it's not yet been achieved. Do you know that The Flea has never voted? Forty-nine years old, a qualified sanitary inspector, a scrupulous taxpayer and yet still, by dint of her lacking a property qualification, denied the most basic right of the citizen. Doesn't that make you absolutely boil with the injustice?'

'You're lecturing me, Mattie. Though you lecture very well, of course. No, I know all this, and you're right, it's the absolute pip, but it'll be rectified sooner rather than later and then what are you going to do? There's a wider battlefield these days, and a younger generation to address. Do you think, incidentally, if I asked for a slice of lemon in my tea I'd be regarded as a dangerous troublemaker?' She beckoned to the waitress and was immediately supplied with a saucer of slices. 'Well, now,' she said, approvingly, 'that's something that's definitely changed since I've been away.'

'So what have you been doing in Australia?' asked Mattie. 'You've married, obviously.'

'I've married. A wonderful chap called Richard Cellini, he was a friend of the cousin who invited me out there. I felt a bit of a deserter, flitting off when the war started, but I was so *tired*, Mattie, absolutely wrung out – all those months of hide-and-seek with the police, I was a rag. I was twenty-six and felt eighty. I think I weighed seven stone and I simply didn't have the energy to start driving buses or making tanks or whatever it was we were all suddenly supposed to be doing instead of campaigning for the vote. And halfway across the world there was somewhere where the sun always shone and where women already had the vote, and . . . well, it was bliss.' She paused. 'Please don't tell me off, Mattie. I'm sure you drove ambulances or something equally valiant.'

'I went to the Balkans,' said Mattie. 'And worked with the Serbian Relief Fund.' Which was true, though in the partial way that one number out of a safe combination can yet be described as a number.

'Goodness,' said Jacko, 'did you really?' The food had

arrived and she began to eat neatly and quickly. 'And have you stayed in touch with any of the other mice? What's Alice Channing up to?'

'Oh, poor old Alice. She very nearly ran the Civil Service during the war and then was dropped in an instant when the men came home, and after that she had TB and spent half a decade in a sanatorium. She doesn't have a bean – in fact, I don't know whether you saw the legend on the poster, but the entrance money goes to the Suffragette Club, helping out needy ex-prisoners.'

'How about Helen Deale?'

'Teaching at Girton. We meet occasionally, but she's rather tiresome on the subject of theosophy – every subject leads inexorably into the immanentist theory of cosmology, so it's like trudging around a giant loop.'

'Brenda Tooley?'

'Mad for Ireland. Calls herself Briege and talks only of Home Rule.'

'Aileen?'

'Our dear hooligan? On and off the sauce, I'm afraid. It was always her weakness.'

'And that artist – what was her name? Chained herself to the statue in the British Museum.'

'Oh, you mean Roberta? Married after the war, domestic bliss in Ipswich, three children, paints song-birds. I travelled there for an exhibition last year and it was really rather good. I bought a wren and a robin for the drawing room.'

'And what about you, Mattie?'

'Me?'

'Yes, what do you do beside the lectures?'

'I write a weekly column for the *Ham & High* – it's called "Heath Musings", but it tackles the major issues of the day.'

'But are you actually involved in politics?'

'I'm a member of the Women's Freedom League.'

'But surely that's just the fag-end of the suffragettes? Isn't there a particular party you're digging in with?'

There was an intensity to Jacko's enquiry, palpable through the lightness of the phrasing. Mattie hesitated, rather as she'd hesitated in the polling booth in 1918, the ballot sheet before her, a pencil in her hand. The grand and glorious fight had shrunk to *this*: three choices on a scrap of paper, three parties who had consistently lied, prevaricated and backtracked on their promises to women, three potential governments who would make laws which she, Mattie Simpkin, would then be obliged to obey, under threat of further imprisonment. It was as if the sun had risen after an age-long night only to illuminate a landscape littered with traps. She had stood for ten minutes, unable to formulate a decision, and then her very soul had rebelled, and she had struck her X beside the fourth candidate, an Independent standing on a ticket of 'A Licence for Every Dog', and at the next election, four years later, she had stood herself, as an unaffiliated candidate for Equality In All Things, losing her deposit but gaining a stimulating few months of campaigning. She had toyed, since then, with the idea of labelling herself an anarchist, in the true sense of the word – ἀναρχία, 'without a head of state' – though The Flea had tutted at this: 'In other words, Mattie, you simply can't bear someone telling you what to do. "Contrarian" would be a far better description.'

Jacko was still waiting for an answer. 'I can't say that I have ever "dug in" with any party,' said Mattie. 'My fight has always been for the right of women to be treated as equal citizens.'

'And now they are, very nearly. Shoulder to shoulder with the finest of the men, they're beginning at last to address a world-wide—' Jacko broke off as Mattie waved a hand; The Flea had entered the café and was scanning the tables.

'Are you going to have something to eat, Florrie?'

'Just a cup of tea, if you don't mind. I have rather a headache from the lantern fumes.' The Flea removed her grey cloche and sat with it on her lap, stroking the velvety nap as if it were a cat. 'I didn't mean to interrupt,' she added. She had the peculiar sense that Jacqueline was not altogether pleased that she had arrived.

'You're not interrupting at all,' said Jacko, still smiling. 'Incidentally, I think I saw you give a little hop when I first spoke. Was the name Agnes Bostock familiar to you, too?'

'Of course. One of my jobs was to memorize the list of aliases. Agnes Bostock was Mattie's. You yourself were Thelma Harker for a few months, and then, after you left Aylesbury Prison, you became Gladys Freeling.'

'That's *right* – how extraordinary that you remember!'

'Florrie forgets nothing,' said Mattie. 'I've long thought that she should tour the Halls attired as a gypsy. "Challenge the Memory of Madame Lee!"'

'So,' said The Flea, inured to this sort of hyperbole, 'are you in England for a holiday?'

'No, not a holiday. Richard and I are forging international links; we've had great success at home with our youth section and, now that things are beginning to move forward in this country as well, I've been asked to help with a recruitment drive for younger women.'

There was a short pause.

'What "things" are you talking about?' asked Mattie.

'Have you heard of the Australian New Guard?'

'No.'

'It's a forward-thinking group, bringing together some of the finest political minds in our country. There are those who'd like to drag the country down, whereas we want to focus our gaze on a brighter future for citizens who are prepared to work for it, and we've been talking to an English organization with similar aims.'

'Which organization?'

'The Empire Fascisti.'

There was a sharp clink as The Flea set her cup down. Jacko must have heard it, but she surged onward, her voice as warm, her blue eyes as bright as if she were discussing a particularly gorgeous Christmas gift – a cashmere shawl, perhaps, or a jar of marrons glacés. 'There's a new spirit of the age, Mattie, that we need to capture and cherish before it's too late. Young people should be allowed to spread their wings, not to have them clipped by the shears of Communism. They need to be free to love their country unashamedly, they need to feel that their wonderful youth is valued by a strong leadership. Look at what's happening in Italy! Look at the pride that shines from the populace! And then look at this country, brought to its knees by strikes, by pinko weaklings stirring up the underclasses, by outside agitators poking their horrid great noses into British business. We need to inspire youth with a creed of unity and a sense of hon—'

The Flea stood up. 'Please excuse me,' she said, replacing her hat with unfussy speed. 'I simply can't listen to any more of this nonsense. Goodbye.' And then she was threading between the tables like an eel, her exit so rapid that a draught ruffled back along her path, swaying the tablecloth. The café door closed with a thump.

Jacko sat with her mouth open, her expression wavering between astonishment and affront. 'Well!' she said, turning to Mattie. 'What a reaction! I hope you're not going to do the same thing.'

'I shan't leave before my steak arrives,' said Mattie, 'but that's solely because I'm hungry. I mean to say, *fascism*, Jacko? Militarists covering themselves with gold braid and shaking their little bundles of sticks at one another? And lauding Italy, of all places, where women don't even have the vote yet! But then, of course, *no one* in Italy has the vote any longer, do they? It's equality of a sort, I suppose.'

Jacko coloured. 'Our version of fascism is rather different.'

'So you also eschew murdering political opponents? I'm happy to hear it. Ah, thank you,' she said, as the waitress arrived with the meals. 'That looks splendid.'

Jacko made a quick gesture towards the girl. 'Could you stay just a moment, please? I want to ask you something.'

The waitress looked worried. 'I'm sorry, ma'am. The cook said she'd never seen such small tomatoes.'

'No, it's nothing to do with that. How old are you?'

'Seventeen, ma'am.'

'Who's your favourite film star?'

'Douglas Fairbanks, ma'am.'

'And which politician do you most admire?'

There was a pause. The girl's eyes flicked uneasily around the room.

'Never mind. If you could vote tomorrow, who would you vote for? . . . Any thoughts . . . No?'

'My dad, he votes for the Labour Party.'

'I see. And are you proud of being English, dear?'

Another pause and a shrug. 'I suppose so.'

'And why are you proud?'

'Well . . . we won the war, didn't we?'

'Thank you, dear. You can get on with your work now.'

The waitress hurried away and Jacko leaned back with an air of triumph that Mattie found irritating.

'And what does that prove?' she asked.

'You know as well as I do, Mattie, that that girl wouldn't know what to do with a vote. She has no aspirations, no wider knowledge, no whisker of suspicion that the tentacles of Bolshevism are everywhere, and that foreign adventurers are treating this government like glove puppets. The war is over and the enemy is within.'

'Oh, nonsense,' said Mattie. 'The enemy hasn't changed in the slightest – this country's still run by stuffy old club-men who'll be rubbing their hands together at the prospect of women voluntarily forgoing their vote for the sake of patriotism.'

'I am not talking about forgoing the vote, I am talking about giving young women the wisdom to use it *correctly*. We need to educate them, we need fine speakers to inspire them and exciting activities to—'

'Oh, I see!' exclaimed Mattie.

'I beg your pardon?'

'That's why you came to the lecture. You want to recruit me.'

'Well, I was rather hoping that you'd like to lend your oratorical skills to a *living* cause. However, if you wish to retread old ground . . .' Jacko sat back with a little moue of frustration. 'You carry on dabbling,' she said.

'*Dabbling!*' The word was almost a shout; silence fell, and there was a rustle as the other diners turned to look at Mattie.

'Isn't that what you're doing? A little of this, a little of that . . .'

'I never *dabble*. *Dabbling* implies half-heartedness. I would hope that I bring the full weight of my beliefs to everything I do.'

Jacko smiled slightly. 'But your beliefs aren't reaching very far, are they, Mattie? How many young women were in the audience today? When was the last time you even spoke to one? Next week, the Empire Fascisti are giving a demonstration of horsemanship in Hyde Park, introduced by a film actress who also happens to be a staunch supporter of the cause. Which of the two events do you think that little Fairbanks-follower would rather attend?'

In the silence that followed, the other diners went back to their meals and Mattie sawed her steak into two halves.

'Perhaps you'll think about it,' said Jacko, in a more conciliatory tone. 'I can give you a pamphlet that Richard wrote which will explain more fully the philosophy behind the New Guard. You'll find it awfully interesting . . .'

༄

It was The Flea who actually sat and read the pamphlet, later that evening, tutting sharply as she did so. 'It's the usual hateful nonsense,' she said. 'Praising the strong and sneering at the weak and painting anyone on the left as mentally abnormal. And whenever they talk about the "enemy", they always mean Jews – "outside influences" means Jews, "Bolshevik" means Jews, "foreign" means Jews, "wealthy" means Jews. Wealthy! When I think of some of the families I see . . .'

'Please throw the damn thing away,' said Mattie, giving the fire a violent poke.

She had been uncharacteristically silent since returning from the café, and even half an hour spent chopping kindling – usually an infallible restorative – had failed to improve her mood.

The Flea crumpled the leaflet and tossed it into the fire, where it flared briefly.

'I think it's going to snow,' she said, resuming her careful transcription of work notes.

Mattie grunted. She'd long considered herself impervious to insult, but Jacko had delivered a stiletto to the

49

heart. The mimsy, ephemeral implication of *dabble* was almost unbearable; it was a word that walked hand in hand with *trifle* and *dilly-dally*, *flirt*, *toy* and *tinker* – terms that could scarcely be uttered without an enervated sigh. And, of course, the accusation was untrue, completely untrue. Was it possible, though, that she had lost a degree of momentum . . . ?

She selected a log from the basket and heaved it on to the fire, where it burned briskly.

'That's a pleasant smell,' said The Flea.

'Ash,' said Mattie. 'I found a dead branch last week, up near the Round Pond.' She'd dragged it back over a mile to the house – the grain of the wood was so pale and delicate that its heaviness always came as a surprise. She thought, with regret, of the ash club that had been in her handbag. There was another one somewhere in the house; she was sure of it.

∞

Everyone on the bus seemed to be coughing; some coughs were dry, some phlegmy, some so prolonged and explosive that they made you wonder if half a lung was going to end up, twitching, on the cougher's handkerchief. Ida kept her head turned away, squinting through the filth on the window. After a day of wet snow, it had frozen hard and the pavements were covered with a lacework of grey ice; pedestrians were picking their way along, holding on to garden walls and lamp posts. The bus was barely moving; at this rate, she would be late for work.

'Cold enough for you, Idey?' asked someone, plumping down on the seat beside her.

She turned to see who it was and then pulled a face.

'What's the matter?' asked Kenneth. 'Not pleased to see me?'

'Why would I be?' She tugged the hem of her coat out from under his buttock. 'I suppose you think it's all right to treat a person that way?'

'How do you mean?'

'You went off with someone else after I got hurt at the fair.'

'It wasn't like that.'

'Wasn't like *what*? You said, "Go home, you look a fright," and then you took Maud Beaman to the pictures.'

'Which was a mistake. She ate a bag of toffees and a whole box of chocolates. I had to roll her home.' He was actually laughing, which made his handsome face even more handsome. 'You look all right now, though,' he said. 'More than all right. Where are you off to?'

'Work.'

'Did you know I'd got a job at Clifton's?'

'No.'

'Carpet fitter. Nice money, nice houses, nice ladies admiring my backside when I bend over.'

He snaked an arm along the back of Ida's seat and she leaned forward so that his sleeve wouldn't touch her.

'Listen,' he said. 'I'll make it up to you. How about going to the Palais on Friday?'

She jerked her head round to stare at him. '*No.* I don't want to see you again. Your behaviour was monstrous.'

51

'Your *behaviour* was *monstrous*?' he repeated, incredulously. 'Ey say,' he added, in tones of mock-refinement, 'em I correct in thinking ey'm addressin' Lady Muck?'

Abruptly, Ida stood up and, at the same moment, the bus braked and slewed sideways; she shot out a hand for balance and found she'd snagged Kenneth's hair.

'Sorry,' she said, unhooking her fingers; a couple of dark strands drifted free.

He looked up at her furiously. 'That bloody well hurt.'

'We're stopping here!' shouted the bus driver. 'It's sheet ice all the way up South End Green, and there's an 'orse fallen over just ahead.'

It was a big old piebald, steaming in the cold, and it was struggling to its feet as Ida exited the bus, the smack and scrape of hooves curiously loud in the frigid air. The milk cart it had been pulling was blocking the road, shafts resting on the ground, the churns bunched together at the front, like interested spectators.

Ida started walking, not looking behind to see what Kenneth might be doing.

'Monstrous,' she muttered, out loud. Was that a posh word, or just an unusual one? The house on the Heath was full of words that she'd occasionally seen in print but never heard out loud, and it wasn't all to do with poshness; the first-class waiting room at St Pancras had oozed with money, but she'd never heard anyone there talk the way that Miss Simpkin did, producing sentences like a magician pulling silk handkerchiefs from a pocket. 'What you're holding is an ammonite,' she'd said last week, chancing upon Ida polishing a fossil shaped like a ram's horn. 'It was classified a cephalopod, from the Greek for "head-foot". Not what you might call a glamorous name, but they had staying power. The human race will be dust in a tenth of the time of the ammonites' reign on earth.' To which Ida had replied, 'Oh.' Which didn't matter, because Miss Simpkin hardly seemed to be expecting a reply – it was as if she just spoke for the pleasure of hearing the words.

Ida had been working there for nearly a month now. It was a big house, but half the rooms were unused and the others she was expected to clean, but not necessarily to tidy. 'Just leave those books where they are,' Miss Lee had said. 'Neither of us minds useful clutter.' Ida liked the way she was left alone to get on with it – no one hovered over her, no one followed her from room to room, waiting for her to do something wrong; Miss Lee was often away at work and Miss Simpkin blew in and out of the house like a gust of wind. When present, she was always audible, her telephone voice like someone shouting across traffic, her footsteps deliberate. She even *read* noisily, reacting to whatever was on the page with snorts and comments and scribbled notes, and when she wrote she used a typewriter which made every sentence sound like a box of bangers going off. 'What are the ladies like, then?' her aunt had asked her after the first week there, and Ida had thought for a moment before saying, 'They're not like anyone.'

It was only a quarter of a mile from the stalled bus to the Vale of Health, but it was all uphill and it took her an age, mincing along the icy pavement like a Chinawoman with bound feet. The Heath stretched away to her right, improbably vast. She'd never understood what it was *doing* there – a piece of countryside dropped into the middle of London, crows flapping above it, no signposts or street-lamps, a blank on the map by day, a black hole by night. It was all snow now, a tree-spiked sweep across which a small brown dog was zig-zagging, nose to the ground.

Despite its name, the Vale of Health was just a road – a lane, really, pushing into the heart of the Heath and lined with large houses. Ida picked her way past the gateposts: *St Ives, Braemar, Edelweiss.* Her employers' house was called Green Shutters. 'Though we usually refer to it as "the Mousehole",' Miss Lee had said, on the first day. 'Not because we have mice – though you might see the odd one; remind me to show you where the traps are – no, we call it that because it used to be a convalescent home for suffragette mice. When they'd been released from prison under the Cat and Mouse Act, you know.' Ida had nodded, though she didn't know. She opened the gate now, and took the path to the back of the house, aware that she could no longer feel her toes. Her first thought, when she saw the figure with the whirling arms, was that Miss Lee had bought a mechanical scarecrow to protect the vegetables.

Mattie had unexpectedly found the missing Indian club the evening before, wrapped in a balaclava helmet on the shelf of the coat cupboard. It still had the leather loop attached, and she'd given it a brief indoor twirl that had nearly taken a picture off the wall.

The next morning, she'd got dressed and gone straight into the back garden. It was at least a decade since she'd last practised callisthenics but, with the club in one hand and a rolling pin (for balance) in the other, she quickly picked up the rhythm of it again, standing legs apart on the frosted path, arms windmilling, puffs of breath rising as if she were the *Flying Scotsman* breasting a peak. Within a couple of minutes she was sweating fiercely, and she stopped to catch her breath and saw Ida goggling at her from the path.

'Callisthenics,' she explained.

'I'm sorry I'm late,' said Ida. 'The buses weren't going any further than Pond Street and the pavement was all icy. I can start out earlier tomorrow.'

'Cut across the Heath,' said Mattie. 'You'll knock off half the journey and it's far easier to walk through snow than on ice.' She glanced at Ida's feet. 'We have spare wellingtons.'

'The Heath?' repeated Ida. The idea was unimaginable, like taking a shortcut across Russia. 'I wouldn't know the way.'

'Directly up Parliament Hill, past the tumulus, then bear west across the viaduct and you'll come straight to the back of the garden here. You know the viaduct?'

Ida shook her head.

'What about the tumulus? No? But you know Parliament Hill, of course? Kite Hill, it's sometimes called.'

There was a pause. 'I think so,' said Ida, uncomfortably.

'Good Lord!' said Mattie. 'Well, I can draw you a map. It's quite straightforward.' She started to swing her arms again, and then abruptly stopped. 'As a matter of fact, Ida, I've been meaning to ask you one or two questions. Don't be alarmed, it won't take very long. How old are you?'

'Fifteen, Miss Simpkin.'

'And can you tell me the names of three great women of history?'

'Beg your pardon?'

'Three great women of history. There is no right or wrong answer, I'm simply interested in your response. The first three that spring into your mind.'

Ida, struggling for an answer, wondered fleetingly if she wouldn't rather be hit in the mouth with a miniature bottle of whisky. 'Queen Victoria . . . Queen Elizabeth . . .' She stared at the vegetable patch, as if the crossed pea-sticks might give her some inspiration. They did. 'The Virgin Mary.'

'I'm not sure that – no, never mind. What can you tell me about Dame Millicent Fawcett? Anything? No? What about Mary Somerville? She had a famous institution named after her.'

'You mean . . . the prison?'

'No, that's Pentonville. What about Mrs Emmeline Pankhurst? What do you know about her?'

'She threw a brick at the King's horse.'

Mattie absorbed the blow. 'And which politician do you most admire?'

'Politician?'

'Yes, is there a politician that you admire?'

Ida glanced around rather desperately, wondering when she was going to be allowed indoors. Which answer would get her into the warm? 'Mr Baldwin?' she suggested.

'The Prime Minister.'

'Yes.'

'And if you could vote tomorrow, who would you vote for?'

There was a pause. 'Mr Baldwin?' said Ida again, hoping it was a trick question. She was actually starting to shake now, partly from cold, and partly from the sense that, despite Miss Simpkin's assurance, she was somehow failing a test. Her employer's expression had the brooding, internal look of somebody with a large piece of meat stuck between their back teeth.

'Could I go in the house now, Miss Simpkin? I'm ever so cold.'

'Yes, of course. Run along.'

Mattie watched her go, and the memory of Jacko's complacent smile plucked infuriatingly at her memory. What could be done? How could these girls be rescued from the fog in which they were currently wandering, without recourse to the shallow sparkle of film stars?

Thoughtfully, she windmilled through another exercise, then tucked the rolling pin under one arm and lunged with the club towards an imaginary policeman, feinting and thrusting.

'Morning, Miss Simpkin.' It was her neighbour, Major Lumb, peering at her through the leafless thicket of the honeysuckle.

'Morning,' she said, crisply.

'Fencing practice?'

'Ju-jitsu, since you ask.'

He gave a mirthless 'Heh heh', as if she'd made a joke. 'Just wondering if your pipes have frozen? We're having a little difficulty with ours.'

'I shall check.' She gave the imaginary policeman an unexpected jab in the solar plexus and went into the kitchen; The Flea was filling the kettle.

'Not frozen,' shouted Mattie out of the back door, before shutting it.

The Flea looked up enquiringly. 'Major Lumb?'

'Can't stand the man.'

'Why the club?'

'I stumbled across it.' She weighed it in her hand, strangely reluctant to put it down. 'Over the last two weeks I have heard the opinions of two young women, and neither appears to know anything.'

'Know anything about what?'

'About anything. History. Politics. The geography of Hampstead Heath.'

'Have you been talking to Ida outside?'

'Yes.'

'I've just sent her to the drawing room to warm up a little; honestly, Mattie, her teeth were chattering, no wonder she couldn't answer your questions. She's actually a bright girl.'

'I wasn't impugning her intelligence; I'm talking about ignorance.'

'What on earth do you expect? She left school at fourteen and she's one of a very large family. I doubt they ever sit around the kitchen table discussing the *Times* editorial. If you talked to her when she wasn't frozen stiff, you might be pleasantly surprised.' Mattie grunted, and turned to stare out of the window, and The Flea took an orange from the bowl on the table and began to peel it. 'Do you eat fruit, Ida?' she'd asked the girl on her first day.

'Sometimes, Miss Lee.'

'I'm asking because I've noticed that the corners of your mouth seem a little sore, and that's most probably due to a lack of vitamin C. If you eat an orange every day, the soreness will disappear, and it will very likely help your styes as well. You may take one from the fruit bowl here if there are none at home.'

The girl had turned pink.

'Don't be embarrassed,' said The Flea. 'There were no oranges in the house that I grew up in. I was seventeen before I ate one, and I had no idea that you were supposed to peel it first. An apple will do just as well, but I suspect you don't eat those because they hurt your mouth.'

Ida had looked startled. 'How did you know, Miss?'

'Tender gums are another symptom. Vitamin C preserves the lining of the body, inside and out, and it's present in foodstuffs that are green, or red, or orange, or purple.'

'Like blackberries?'

'Yes, blackberries are a very good example.'

The girl had nodded; she'd actually been listening. Some women listened, some didn't, and to those that didn't you just had to offer clear and simple advice and repeat it when needed. The other sort, though, presented a type of chink, which with gentle persistence you could widen into a doorway. Ida's complexion had already improved.

The Flea broke the orange into quarters and left it on a plate on the table, together with a biscuit and a glass of blackcurrant cordial. 'I may be back rather late this evening,' she said. 'I'm carrying out a workshop inspection and I've asked to speak to the night-shift girls. There's cold lamb in the larder and I've scrubbed some carrots. Oh, and if you had any time, I'd be very grateful for some help addressing envelopes for the Mass Sanitation campaign. There's a pile of them in the morning room.' There was no reply. 'Mattie?'

Mattie was staring out at the view: the wintry garden, the ivy-clad back wall beyond which the Heath surged upward, so that the skyline was all bleak nature, unsullied by chimney or gable. Once over that wall, one might in an instant be Hiawatha, or Hawkeye, or Robin Hood, or even that sorely underwritten character Maid Marian.

'Mattie?'

'I've had an idea,' she said, and the idea, huge and splendid, actually emerged as she spoke the words, like a breaching whale. She gave the club a twirl, savouring her thoughts, already composing the advertisement. She would write the copy this morning and take it straight round to the offices of the *Ham & High*.

⁓

HAMPSTEAD HEATH GIRLS' CLUB
For girls aged 12–18
Healthy outdoor fun
Meet on Parliament Hill (also known as Kite Hill)
At 10 a.m. Saturday morning
Clothing: mackintosh, gloves, hat, sensible footwear.

Mattie was at Parliament Hill by nine thirty. There were no kites being flown. A gusty wind was flattening the long grass and tossing the rooks around like jugglers' balls. The only people she could see were dog-walkers.

She paced the top of the hill, unsure of the direction from which any girls might be arriving; she had rather imagined hordes of youngsters already waiting for her, eager to start. She had thought of beginning with a relay race; two teams, perhaps three, each named after a famous woman. Could Elizabeth Garrett Anderson beat Elizabeth Fry?

Time passed rather slowly. Mattie recited, 'O wild West Wind, thou breath of Autumn's being', and Hardy's 'Weathers', and counted and tried to name the church spires that poked like needles through the grey cloth of the city.

At nine fifty-five she was still alone, but now she could see Ida toiling up the hill from Parliament Fields, head down, The Flea's oilskin coat flapping round her wellingtons.

'Well done!' she called, as Ida came into earshot. 'Couldn't persuade anyone to come with you?'

'I asked my friend Vesta, but she says today's her only lie-in,' said Ida, trying to keep the resentment out of her voice, seeing as exactly the same thing applied to herself. Saturday was the day she got an extra hour's sleep, before going round to see her mother and the rest of them, and on Sundays she helped her aunt fold and deliver the ironing to a dozen different addresses. She hadn't wanted to come at all. 'Why not just attend the very first meeting and see if you enjoy yourself,' Miss Lee had suggested, sensing Ida's reluctance, not knowing that Miss Simpkin had already cornered her in the scullery and virtually

61

ordered her to turn up. And now she was out of breath from the climb, ankles aching from the unfamiliar weight of the boots, and looking like a fool in a mackintosh too long for her. 'Going fishing?' the bus conductor had asked, derisively, when she'd got on at Camley Street.

'And here are some others,' said Mattie, with satisfaction. Three figures, two very short and wearing matching tam-o'-shanters, and one rather tall, were walking up the more gradual incline from the tennis courts.

'Is this the girls' club?' asked the tall one, eagerly, when they were near enough for conversation.

'Indeed it is,' said Mattie. 'And you are . . . ?'

'I'm their nanny. This is Avril, and this is Winnie. What time should I collect them?' She was already backing away.

'How old are they?' asked Mattie.

'We're nearly eleven,' said Avril, as if Mattie had asked her directly.

'The advertisement clearly stated the parameters as twelve to eighteen. I'm afraid they're too young.'

The nanny's face fell. 'But they're quite advanced for their age.'

'Yes, we're quite advanced,' repeated Avril. 'Well, I am, anyway.' Winnie, rounder and plainer, retaliated with a jab of the elbow.

'Only I'd got something I have to do,' said the nanny.

'She's seeing her young man,' said Avril, 'even though she's just told our mother that she was going to take us to the boating pond. He's called Harold. He's a house-painter.'

The expression that flitted across the nanny's face was

one part anguish to three parts murder. She caught Ida's eye and a flag of fellow feeling flapped between them.

'If they stay, I'll look after them, Miss Simpkin,' said Ida. 'I know how.'

Mattie hesitated and looked around. It was starting to rain and there was no one else in sight.

'Very well,' she said, reluctantly. 'Meet us back here at twelve o'clock.' The nanny hurried away.

'Let us begin by finding the best shelter that the open air can offer,' said Mattie. 'Any suggestions, Ida?'

'Under a tree?'

'In summer, yes. In winter, less useful. Avril?'

'The bandstand.'

'Good suggestion, but it's nearly half a mile away. Winnie?'

'The Ladies' Convenience?'

'That's right next to the bandstand, you idiot,' said Avril. Winnie hit her on the hip with a clenched fist, and Ida inserted herself between the two of them, like a copper separating brawling drunks.

'Let me show you where I mean, rather than standing here becoming gradually damper,' said Mattie. 'Follow me, and as we walk, perhaps someone could tell me why there is an area of untamed heath and woodland very near the centre of one of the great capital cities of the world? Anyone? No? Well, which wild animal might have lived here in the past? In herds? With antlers?'

'Deer,' said Avril.

'Very good. Hampstead Heath was none other than the place where King Henry the Eighth came hunting.'

'I'm in the top set at school,' said Avril. 'I can name all of his wives, in order.'

'And now this wonderful wilderness has been preserved to enable us city-dwellers to breathe fresh air and feel the grass under our feet. As Wordsworth said, "Come forth into the light of things, let Nature be your teacher." Not far now.' Mattie led them into a stand of dripping beeches. The furthest and largest had been scooped out by age and disease to form an irregular dark cave. A large white dog was sniffing delicately around the entrance; as Mattie approached, there was a distant whistle and it loped away.

'And in we go.'

Winnie held back. 'Are there spiders in there?'

'Not in winter,' said Mattie. 'Have you heard of hibernation, Winnie?'

'It's when animals go to sleep when it's cold,' answered Avril. 'I'm afraid it's no good asking *her* anything. Our father calls her Witless Winnie.'

Ida, following Avril over the jagged threshold, managed to give her a sharp kick.

'Ow!'

'Sorry.'

'And now we are perfectly dry,' said Mattie, savouring the richly fungal smell of the interior. 'And we can proceed with the inaugural meeting of the Hampstead Heath Girls' Club, although I've decided, since placing the advertisement, that the name is rather a mouthful and we should have a snappier title. Why don't we each think of one and the winner shall get a prize.'

'I won seven prizes at last speech day,' said Avril.

'And were any of them for inventing a new name for a girls' club?'

'No.'

'Then you are under no particular advantage in the current situation,' said Mattie. 'Ida, do you have a suggestion?'

'No, Miss Simpkin,' said Ida, who was wondering if she'd ever in her life spent a more dispiriting Saturday morning. She was standing inside a *mouldy tree*.

'Any thoughts, Winnie?'

'No. But honestly, Miss, I'm sure I just saw a spider.'

'Avril?'

'The . . . the . . .' Avril was clearly thinking hard, desperate to win the competition. 'The Healthy Heath Girls.'

There was a pause, during which Winnie tittered.

'My suggestion,' said Mattie, who'd actually thought of it the day before when re-reading Herodotus, 'is the Amazons. The Amazons were a legendary race of female warriors, renowned for their athleticism and skill in archery and imbued with a spirit which I would like to kindle in this group – a spirit encompassing self-reliance, knowledge of the countryside and a daring approach to physical exercise. Any other suggestions from anybody? No? So who votes for the Healthy Heath Girls?'

'I do,' said Avril, putting up her hand.

'And who votes for the Amazons? Excellent. Carried by a clear majority.'

'So does that mean you win the prize?' asked Winnie, daringly.

'The prize is a bar of chocolate and we shall all share it later on. Now, what I would like to start with is—'

'What on earth are you doing?' asked a dark-haired girl of about Ida's age, peering into the hollow trunk.

'Conducting the inaugural meeting of the Hampstead Heath Girls' Club,' said Mattie, with dignity.

'Is that like the Girl Guides?'

'No.'

'In what way isn't it like the Girl Guides?'

'Do you learn to use weapons in the Guides?' asked Mattie.

'No.'

'Well, there's a difference, for a start.'

'*Weapons?*' repeated Avril.

'Like the Amazons of old, we shall be learning archery, and also use of the slingshot.'

'Whizzo. If I join, can my dog come, too?' asked the dark-haired girl.

'I can think of no activity that cannot be improved by the addition of a dog,' said Mattie. 'What is your name?'

'Freda.' The girl turned, and shouted over her shoulder. 'Billy! *Billy!* Come here!'

'Girls can't use weapons,' said Avril, primly. 'Only boys.'

'And why should that be?' asked Mattie.

'Women aren't strong enough.'

'Strength is not the sole criterion for their use. A woman who can unerringly thread a needle can accurately throw a stone.'

'But why would she need to throw one?'

'As a protest; as a means of defence; as an exercise in

coordination. Weapons are not only for those who begin disputes, they are for those who wish to end them.'

The dog had returned, panting, and Freda tied him to a nearby hawthorn before climbing into the hollow tree; the number of elbows in the narrow space seemed to double.

'We always start Guides' meetings with a prayer,' remarked Freda.

'We shan't be doing that, either,' said Mattie. 'However, I am happy to begin with a quotation. John Stuart Mill wrote, "I consider it presumption in anyone to pretend to decide what women are or are not, can or cannot be, by natural constitution." In other words, one can assume nothing about a person's capability until one gives that person the freedom to attempt the new, the bold, the untried. When I was your age, women were scarcely considered capable of levering themselves from a chaise longue, and yet, even then, there were women crossing India, and conducting electrical experiments, and climbing the Matterhorn. While we wait for the rain to stop, I would like to hear each of you name a personal ambition – a career or an achievement that might currently seem to you no more than a daydream. Something beyond the conventional, something not defined by your sex, something with *grandeur*. Freda?'

'I'd like to own a trout stream and fish every day.'

'That would require only money. Can you think of an aspiration for which you would have to strive?'

'I'd like to catch a record-breaking fish after a day-long

struggle, then, and have it in a glass case with my name beside it.'

'Very good. Winnie?'

Even within the darkness of the tree, Winnie's blush was visible. 'I'd like to play Wendy in *Peter Pan*.'

Avril snorted.

'That sounds most exciting,' said Mattie, ignoring her. 'I believe that Wendy is one of the characters who flies?'

'Yes.'

'Hope the wires are strong,' said Avril. Ida managed to grab Winnie's hand in mid-air.

'And you, Avril?' asked Mattie.

'My father says I would make a very good headmistress. But I would like to sculpt statues.'

'Is there a particular sculptor you admire?'

'Magua in *The Last of the Mohicans*,' said Winnie.

'She's trying to make a *joke*,' explained Avril, loftily. 'But that's only because she doesn't know the difference between "scalp" and "sculpt".'

'And what about you, Ida?' asked Mattie swiftly.

'I don't know,' said Ida. She was, by this time, grasping a twin's wrist in each hand, but the urge to leave them tussling, to step out into the daylight and walk away, was almost overwhelming. These children with their piping, poking accents, their certainty that they were worth listening to, the fairy-tale nonsense they were talking (sculpting! Mohicans! trout-fishing!) were making her clench her jaw so hard that her teeth were aching; she kept thinking that she could have still been asleep – in fact, *that* was her grand ambition: to lie in bed for the whole of a Saturday.

'No daydreams at all?' asked Mattie.

'No.' Ida relaxed her grip on the girls, and Winnie instantly leaned round the back of her and yanked her sister's plait so hard that Avril's head jerked backwards. The interior of the tree erupted into a congested scuffle that reminded Mattie of certain scenes in Parliament Square.

'Violence should always be a last resort and have a purpose,' she called over the melee. 'Let us adjourn to the open air, and there will be a reward for those who renounce fisticuffs.'

The sky between the trees was beginning to brighten. Freda untied Billy and he bounded across to where Mattie was handing round chocolate; Ida flinched away.

'Don't you like dogs?' asked Freda.

'Not really,' she said, looking at Billy's pale blue eyes. It was a colour she associated with unpredictability.

'*My* nursemaid didn't like dogs, either.'

'I'm not a nursemaid.'

'Oh.' Freda's gaze, not unfriendly, darted from her face to her clothing. 'A nanny, then.'

'Ida is neither a nanny nor a nursemaid,' said Mattie, over-hearing. 'She is a fellow *Amazon*, who brings her own array of knowledge and ability to add to our commonwealth. We shall pool our strengths and divide our weaknesses, and the whole shall be greater than the sum of the parts.'

'Like a Trades Union,' said Freda. 'My people are social-ists,' she added. 'I'm already *persona non grata* in the Girl

Guides, after I told Brown Owl that I thought Great Britain should be a republic. Did you know that you could win an Empire Badge by naming Crown colonies?'

'Can we have badges in the Amazons?' asked Avril.

Mattie nodded. 'If that is the wish of the majority.'

'All right,' said Avril. 'Who votes for badges?'

No one put their hand up.

'You might wish to enlarge and deepen your case,' said Mattie. 'What advantage would a badge confer? How would it be earned?'

'What would it look like?' added Winnie.

'Why don't you prepare a speech for the commencement of our next meeting?' said Mattie. 'And if you manage to win the vote, then you will earn the very first badge. For public speaking.'

'But what are we going to do *today*?' asked Winnie. 'It's stopped raining. Nearly.'

Mattie took a small notebook out of the pocket of her coat and thumbed through to a page ruled into closely written columns.

'I propose that we divide each meeting into three parts: firstly, discussion or debate; secondly, recreation; and thirdly, training.'

'Training for what?' asked Avril.

'For your lives as twentieth-century women, to enable you to take your places as equals in society, in Parliament and in the professions. In future, we shall vote upon our itinerary but, for today, I propose a lively game of forty-forty, followed by a lesson in ju-jitsu.'

'But how will ju-jitsu help our lives as twentieth-century women?'

'Thereby hangs a tale,' said Mattie. 'As we pivot and lunge, I shall tell you of its place in the struggle for equality. And we shall end with refreshments at our Heath headquarters, to which Ida will guide us, demonstrating the use of the magnetic compass.'

Ida looked up, horrified. 'But I don't know how to!'

'Those who are prepared to argue about geography should also be able to navigate,' said Mattie. 'An intelligent girl such as yourself won't find it hard to learn.'

Ida felt her face grow hot; Avril was looking at her with the expression of someone who'd just bitten into a meat-paste sandwich and found it full of ham.

'All right,' she said. 'I'll give it a go.'

'Excellent,' said Mattie. 'As Thomas Fuller said, "An invincible determination can accomplish almost anything and in this lies the great distinction between great men and little men."' She smiled suddenly, and Ida was surprised to see a row of regular, well-shaped teeth, like the illustration in a dental-powder advertisement. She didn't know what she'd expected. Fangs, perhaps.

Tentatively, she smiled back.

⁓

'I'm meeting Pomeroy at the Criterion so I shall be passing Fortnum's,' said Mattie to The Flea. 'Should I buy a tin of those Highland oatcakes you're fond of?'

'No, thank you.'

'Or the butter shortbread with the imprint of a cow?'

'No. If I wish for biscuits, I can make some.' The Flea was rolling pastry with what appeared to be unnecessary force. Mattie paused to look at her.

'Are you feeling quite the thing?' she asked.

'I'm in perfect health, I'm simply busy.'

'Very well. I imagine that I won't want anything beyond toast this evening.'

'I'm sure that's the case, but *I* should like something to eat, so if you don't mind I shall carry on making this pie.'

'Of course,' said Mattie, attempting an emollient tone. Moodiness had always baffled her – the way that it placed the onus on the other person to gauge which breeze of circumstance was the cause of this particular weathercock twirl. If one were cross about something, then one should simply say so; conversation should not be a guessing game.

'I'm going to ask Pomeroy's advice on this business with Major Lumb. He may see an angle which might help us. His instincts are invariably decent, as you know.' There was no response. The Flea draped the oblong of pastry across the pie dish with the visage of someone easing a flag over a coffin.

'I shall see you later, then,' said Mattie.

In the front hall she paused beside the large Georgian mirror, whose dappled reflection had followed her from her childhood bedroom to her current home. She removed and then repositioned a hairpin, and gave her hair a satisfied pat, before fastening her cloak and leaving.

The Flea heard the front door close. She finished

trimming the pastry edges then bundled the trimmings into a soft ball and threw it at the larder door.

'You're a silly woman, Florrie,' she said, out loud, but saying it didn't dissipate the jealousy. Nor did reminding herself that Mattie had known Pomeroy for nearly half a century, nor that she saw him only once or twice a year, nor that the man was, in any case, married. She had seen the way that he looked at Mattie, eyes like melting chocolates.

She picked up the pastry ball and dropped it on the scraps plate that Mattie kept for the birds. She felt almost sick; when one could say nothing, *do* nothing, then the slightest trickle of bad feeling stayed and stewed like a bitter marinade.

Untying her apron, she went into the garden and shook out the folds of cloth until flour hung in the air like talcum powder and the parcel of sparrows who'd been squabbling in the currant bushes had long since scrambled clear and dived over the wall into the wilderness beyond.

Mattie bought the shortbread anyway (The Flea's moods seldom lasted for long) and then continued on foot to the restaurant, swinging the package by its striped ribbon. She enjoyed her lunches with Arthur.

She had been ten, and he thirteen, when they'd first met: 'Pomeroy's going to be staying with us for the summer,' her older brother Stephen had written from school; 'You'll like him, he's a splendid fellow,' although Mattie had actually been annoyed at the prospect, since she hadn't wanted to share Stephen with anyone. But Arthur

73

Pomeroy, a boy with sandy eyelashes and a face that looked vaguely unfinished – as if the sculptor still needed a day or two in order to refine the features – hadn't attempted to annex Stephen, nor to dominate the days with his own wishes; instead, he'd seemed content to be an acolyte, just as Mattie had been.

'This is my sister,' Stephen had said on their introduction. 'She is cleverer than I am.'

'Though not so good at needlework,' Mattie had added, and Pomeroy had laughed – a loud, schoolboy 'Ha! Ha!' – a reaction both unexpected and rather gratifying. The needlework remark had been a reference to Stephen's attempts at taxidermy the previous summer, starting with a grass snake and culminating with a labelled mallard (*anas platyrhynchos*), whose limp, crisply feathered corpse had proved tricky to restore to a living shape and which had undergone a rapid, maggoty disintegration just a fortnight later. Further experiments in that direction had been forbidden, but by then Stephen's brain had already been teeming with fresh ideas – growing crystal forests in alum, keeping an indoor ant-colony, lighting a fire using the friction method employed by Hottentots – for while it was true that Mattie was the quicker study, it was Stephen who always reached wider and further, a gibbon swinging through the tree of knowledge.

The summer of Pomeroy's first visit had been devoted to hydraulics. With Stephen as chief engineer, and utilizing the steep-banked stream that skirted the wood beyond the kitchen garden, the three of them had built a series of dams of increasing sophistication, incorporating parapet walls, sluice gates and spillways and inadvertently flooding the back lane to a depth of three feet. 'Every dress *ruined*,' her mother had said, faintly, after Stephen and Pomeroy had returned to school and Mattie was once again under the tutelage of a governess, who taught her the French for 'button hook' and thought that grass snakes were poisonous.

'My dear Mattie!' He stood as she approached the table; a short, square, blunt-featured man in a mustard tweed suit, its left sleeve empty and pinned in a loop to the shoulder. 'You look extremely well,' he said, a little too loudly, an eardrum as well as an arm having been lost at Vimy Ridge; the head waiter had, as usual, tactfully placed them at a corner table, where other diners would be less affected by the volume of their conversation.

'Thank you, Arthur. Whereas you look as if you need a dose of fresh air, closeted in that office – there's a rather pasty look to your complexion; almost nacreous.'

'Nacreous?'

'Pearly. Desirable in a painting of a sea-nymph, less so in a Wimbledon solicitor.'

'Heavens. I hadn't thought I was looking quite that bad,' said Arthur, attempting to examine his reflection in a spoon.

'Nothing that a brisk daily walk wouldn't restore. Perhaps you should get a dog.'

'They make me wheeze. Especially those with long hair. Surely you remember – the worst was that animal you once had that looked like a snowball. Bismarck.'

'Boswell.'

'Boswell. I could scarcely breathe when he was in the vicinity.'

'He was highly intelligent – do you know, I taught him to distinguish between three different types of cheese? Unfortunately, once, when Angus was toddling, he grasped Boswell's tail for balance and ended up with a nasty bite on the chin – he had a permanent scar.'

'I don't remember ever noticing it.'

'It was exactly central, so looked like a natural cleft.'

'Good Lord!'

'Yes, extraordinarily lucky. Did you ever see Boswell's party trick? If one shouted, "Johnson has spoken!" at him, he would run and fetch a pencil.'

Pomeroy tipped back his head and laughed – the same loud, well-spaced 'Ha! Ha!' that had marked their first meeting, and every encounter since; 'I always thought you were a card, Mattie,' he'd said, the first time he'd proposed to her.

The sommelier was holding a bottle of claret for inspection.

'The lady will taste it,' said Pomeroy. 'So why don't you have a dog of your own at the moment? What was the name of the most recent?'

'Susan B. Anthony. A beagle.'

'And what happened to her?'

'I'm afraid she swallowed a tennis ball. In answer to your question, I tend to wait for the dog to find me – living on the Heath, I've discovered that, sooner or later, another stray will always land on the doorstep. Yes, thank you, this is excellent, almost as good as the '21.'

She waited until both glasses were filled, and then raised her own.

'Cheers, Arthur.'

'Your very good health, Mattie.'

'And how is Eliza?'

'She's very well.'

'And the boys?'

'Flourishing.'

'Good. I'm glad to hear it.'

Courtesies over, there was a short, comfortable silence while they studied the menus.

'I shall have my usual,' said Pomeroy, to the waiter.

'And I shall have the quail followed by the Dover sole,' said Mattie. 'Now, before we talk of anything else, I need legal advice. You've heard me speak of my neighbour, Major Lumb?'

'Several times, and never kindly. The motor-car again?'

'On this occasion, no. He is threatening to prosecute me for criminal damage.'

'Good God!' said Pomeroy, leaning forward. 'Whatever have you been doing?' For all that he was a solicitor, his expression was one of someone eagerly watching a cinematic thriller.

'I am running a girls' club – rather successfully, may I say – and for two out of the last four weeks, our activities have accidentally resulted in various injuries to Major Lumb's greenhouse. For which, I hasten to add, I have instantly offered financial compensation. However, he won't be satisfied unless I promise not to use my garden for training, and I'm simply not prepared to do that. Until the girls are proficient, it would be careless in the extreme to practise in the public spaces of the Heath.'

'Practise what?'

'Javelin throwing. Archery. Use of the slingshot. And before you say anything, Arthur, I am not teaching these skills with violence in mind – they are exciting activities, which the girls relish, and which nicely balance the brain work which is also part of the club regime. The third leg of the curriculum involves a great deal of noisy running around, for which, of course, we use the Heath.'

'And how many girls are in the club?'

'Four the first week, seven the second, and now – eight weeks in – there are twenty-nine.'

'Twenty-nine javelins!'

'*Three* javelins; the girls take turns. And I also make certain there is no one at all in the next-door gardens during our practice sessions. I'm not a fool, Arthur.'

'No, I'm sorry. You know that I have never – *would* never – think you a fool. So tell me precisely what happened.'

'The Major sent me a letter, indicating that he would contact his lawyer if the garden activities continued.'

'And did you respond?'

'I told him that I had no intention of complying.'

'Was that in writing?'

'No, we spoke.'

'Formally?'

'Over the garden wall.'

'When you say "spoke" . . .'

'I may have raised my voice,' said Mattie, rather stiffly. 'There is something rather dreadful, rather *low* about someone who overhears youthful high spirits and desires only to quash them.'

The quail had arrived, and she began, energetically, to dismember it. By contrast, Pomeroy took a single mouthful of his soup, and then laid the spoon down.

'Mattie.' The tone was delicate, as of someone tapping on a slammed door.

'What is it, Arthur? Do you have some advice for me?'

He paused, evidently to consider his phrasing. 'I suppose I'm wondering why it is that your neighbour earns quite such a degree of opprobrium. You're not the sort of person who would normally care very much about a carelessly parked motor-car, or a scraped wall, or even a threatened prosecution – in fact, were it anyone else, your first instinct would be to find the incidents amusing. But when it comes to Major Lumb, you appear entirely to lose your sense of humour. Which makes me wonder whether there is another aspect to this particular story.'

Mattie carried on carving for a moment or two, and then dropped her knife on to the plate with a clatter that turned heads.

'Damn it, Arthur,' she said. 'You should have been a barrister.'

'No, I'm far too dense. I barely matriculated.'

'You would make up with shrewdness what you lacked in examination technique.'

'All right, then.' He attempted a stern expression, leaning forward on his single arm. 'Will the witness please answer the question?'

She tried to smile, but the acuteness of his observation still smarted. She fortified herself with a mouthful of claret.

'Just after I bought the Mousehole, I rather recklessly invited the neighbours for a glass of Christmas punch. A friendly gesture, I thought. I cannot describe to you the almost unremitting ennui of the resulting afternoon. Are your neighbours dull?'

'Yes, quite dull, but then I'm rather dull myself.'

'Nonsense. False modesty on your part, I have never once been bored in your company. Whereas listening to Mr and Mrs Wimbourne on the topic of their grandchildren is akin to being chloroformed. And servants – do you have any idea of how much the average middle-class woman has to say on the subject of servants? Mrs Wimbourne, Mrs Holroyd, Mrs Lumb – all *ululating* on the difficulty of keeping a housemaid. So out of self-preservation I began to talk to Major Lumb – the alternative being to hang myself with my own stockings. It transpired that he's a magistrate and we began to have quite a meaty discussion on the subject of prison reform.' It was strange, now – painful, even – to recall that she'd rather taken to him: a sharp little man, intelligent and sardonic. Their conversation had twanged and thrummed like a vigorous tennis match.

'So is that the reason for your antipathy? His opinion on prisons?'

'No.' Mattie paused. 'No. It dates from Wimbourne joining us.' Conversation had instantly withered; the man was a garden roller, flattening all before him. 'He said that his son was thinking of the Army and, as Lumb had been a regular, he wanted to sound him out about regiments. And, of course, talk turned to the war. As it always does. Wimbourne had been in the Pay Corps.'

'And Lumb?'

'A staff officer for Ferrier-Brown.'

And, as she spoke, she was once again standing there, the sting of brandy on her tongue, the reddish winter light giving spurious warmth to the high-ceilinged room, Mrs Holroyd shrieking, 'My dear, they're not like you and I. These girls simply have *no* loyalty,' and the slow, dreadful realization – a creeping agony, as if she were being peeled and salted – that the man in front of her had issued the orders which had trapped her younger brother and his battalion behind enemy lines at Mons, barely a fortnight after the war had begun, fighting a hopeless action that only a third of them had survived. Shrapnel had sheared away a triangle of Angus's skull and a wedge of brain matter beneath; a mortal wound that had nonetheless taken almost two years to kill him. He had lost his speech and his ability to walk, and most of his sight, but his charm had remained intact – not the gimcrack variety, that coat of gilding over a cheap material, but a charm that seemed woven into his very substance. To put it simply, one had wanted to be with him. And when he had been moved to an army hospital for incurables on the south coast, Mattie had followed, taking a job as a history teacher in a nearby girls' school so that she could visit as often as the hospital allowed, and this, then, was what she had seen of the

81

Home Front: ward after ward of splintered, hollow men, who writhed, screamed and died, and were replaced.

'So there we have it,' she said, the bright dining room dropping into view again like a theatrical backcloth. Pomeroy's features, unsuited to displaying the subtler emotions, were clenched in sympathetic understanding.

'Tell me,' he said. 'Is Lumb a Major or a Major General?'

'I've only ever heard him referred to as "Major".'

'So, quite junior. You do realize it's likely that the orders at Mons originated from a far more—'

Mattie made a sudden gesture that knocked her fork halfway across the table.

'To be frank,' she said, restoring it to its place and ignoring the swivelled heads of other diners, 'I would rather not discover the true extent of his culpability. You may be right, but what if you are not? It is only the slight uncertainty that keeps my responses within the bounds of legality.'

For in the half-decade since the housewarming, in their quotidian encounters she had only managed to speak to her neighbour with anything approaching civility by looking past his right ear and addressing whichever tree, gatepost or trellis he was standing in front of.

'Speaking of legality . . .' said Pomeroy.

'Yes, back to the subject. And do, please, eat. Though I always find consommé a dreadful disappointment; one might as well add gravy browning to tap water.'

'I shall make sure I pass your compliments to the chef. So tell me more about this club. For instance, what possessed you to start it?'

'An encounter with an old colleague and the realization

that I was no longer swimming steadily upstream but treading water.'

He listened intently as she explained.

'And what sort of girls are they? Ladylike? Rough? High-spirited? Hoydenish?'

'You are asking – are you not – which class the girls are from?'

'I suppose I am.'

'We have a mixture. I altered the time that we meet from Saturday morning to Sunday afternoon, so that those who work for a living are more likely to attend, but we also have a large contingent of schoolgirls.'

'And did you say there's an element of education in the proceedings?'

'It ingrains everything. The other activities are, if you like, the Trojan Horse in which the education is smuggled.'

'Well, there you have it!' said Pomeroy. 'No magistrate could be seen to oppose a scheme to educate the working classes – all you need to do is to make sure that your aims are publicized. Why not write about it in your column? Or, better still, let someone else praise you – the paper must be able to send a journalist along. You could even mention the tolerance of your forward-thinking neighbours.'

Mattie snorted. 'But a very good suggestion,' she said. 'Really rather cunning.'

'Thank you.'

'Should we order another bottle of this? Did I ever tell you, incidentally, the name of the Wimbournes' house? Bear in mind that they are teetotallers.'

'Temperance Towers?'

'No.'

'The Locked Cabinet?'

'Ha! Very good – no, it's called Many Waters.'

'I think that's quite poetical.'

'Yes, but doesn't the name remind you of someone? Every time I walk past I find myself humming "Take a Pair of Thparkling Eyes".'

'Minnie Waters! Your room-mate at Somerville! "I am thtudying Thocrateeth."'

The waiter, approaching with the next course, flinched at the blast of laughter.

'Good Lord!' said Pomeroy. 'I've not thought of her in decades. Did you stay in touch?'

'No,' said Mattie, sobering. 'She was firmly against votes for women. Possibly because she could not pronounce the word "suffragette".'

Pomeroy, a piece of steak halfway to his mouth (the meat discreetly sliced in the kitchens before serving), had to lower the fork again, in order to wipe his eyes, and the gesture and its cause seemed to encapsulate all Mattie's pleasure in the friendship: both the simple fact that it was flattering to be found so consistently entertaining, and the more complex truth, troubling yet comforting, that Pomeroy was the only living person who spanned her memories: he had known her as a child, a student, a campaigner, a prisoner; he had wept when Stephen, by then a surgeon with the Red Cross, had been killed by a Boer sniper; he had stood bail for Angus after his arrest in Parliament Square; he had wired money to Mattie in Serbia; he had dragged her father's tangled will through the thorny hedge of probate, enabling her to buy the Mousehole; he had been as much a brother to her as Stephen or Angus – this being one of the reasons (and the one she had chosen to give him) why she had refused his proposals. For she would never have wanted him to know that, for her, a husband would have required not only steadfast kindliness but actual brilliance, or a rare magnetism; her brothers had spoiled her for more ordinary men. And neither did she choose to share the reason that underpinned it all – a kind of horror at the idea of standing still, of choosing a single existence, as if life were a sprint across quicksand and stasis meant a slow extinction. Long ago, as a child in a pinched and stifled century, she had seen her own mother gradually disappear.

'I shouldn't mock,' she said. 'Minnie Waters could hardly help the gaps in her teeth. I instruct the Amazons both to refrain from and to rise above petty teasing – there are a number of youths on the Heath who follow us around with catcalls – and here am I succumbing to exactly the same urge, solely for the purpose of making you laugh.'

'We're all human,' said Pomeroy, cheerfully. 'It's one thing the Papists get right, in my opinion. Regular forgiveness for trivial transgressions.'

'In my own case, it's what Fuller termed a constitutionary sin, riveted in my temper and complexion. Do you still attend church, Arthur?'

'Yes, every Sunday.'

'And do you still believe in a supernatural creator?'

'I believe in . . . *something*. I don't think I'm capable of defining precisely what it is. I believe that we go on.'

'But go on doing *what*? Singing praises? Paddling in the glassy sea? Buffing our crowns with Brasso? Imagine the terrible, terrible boredom – an eternity of agreement, an infinity of nodding heads. Without grit, Arthur, how can there be pearls?'

'I say, that's rather good. Is that your own aphorism?'

'No, I'm afraid not.'

'So what do you think happens to us after death?'

'Nothing at all. We blink out like brief candles. Again, not one of mine.'

He smiled, rather sadly. 'It seems an awful waste, Mattie – all that knowledge, all that experience, gone for ever.'

'Which is why one should try to spark a few fresh lights along the way. To be a tinderbox rather than a candle.'

'Yours?' asked Pomeroy.

'Mine,' she said.

∽

There was no clock in her parents' flat, but Ida had just heard St Pancras striking the half-hour, and if she didn't leave soon to catch the bus, she'd be late for the Amazons. 'I've finished these,' she said, pushing the darning needle back into its felt sheath, and balling the socks to add to the pyramid she'd already completed. 'I'll have to go in a minute or two.'

'What, already?' Her mother looked wounded.

'I've been here two hours, Mum. Nearly.'

'Oh dear, Danny, d'you hear that? It sounds as if your sister's been counting the minutes.' Her mother gave the baby's head a stroke; he was sitting on her lap, sucking one of the buttons on her housecoat. Even in the faded print wrap, her blonde hair twisted into a knot, she looked pretty; a soft, quilted prettiness, though there were pins in the fabric.

'No, I mean – it's just that Miss Simpkin doesn't like us to be late.'

'Ooooh, Miss Simpkin doesn't layke us to be leet,' said her older brother Charlie, in a rotten impression of someone posh.

'She doesn't layke it,' chimed in ten-year-old Frank. Ida ignored them.

'I'll be back again next week,' she said.

'Why can't you drop in of an evening?'

'No, I told you Auntie says I'm to help her in the evenings, she's rushed off her feet.'

Her mother's mouth tightened. 'Well, that doesn't seem fair, does it? Can't you tell her your mum and dad want to see you?'

'But she doesn't ask me for any keep. That was the agreement, wasn't it? That's what we said – I'd help her out sometimes and then I could give you something from my wages.'

She'd been at her aunt's six months now, swapping a bedroom full of brothers for one pillared with stacks of newly folded laundry – a bleached palisade that blotted out all sound so that, for a week or two, she'd kept waking, listening for the sound of Jerry grinding his teeth, Frank muttering about the bicycle that he was saving to buy, her father's snore audible through the wall.

'Well, it still seems selfish,' said her mother, 'having you all to herself. But' – she gave a sigh that was more like a wince – 'maybe you like being with her more than you like being with us.'

'No, of course I don't. But—'

'The thing is, Ida, your auntie's a little bit jealous. Never had children herself. Never had a lovely little bundle like *this* lad.' She nuzzled Danny's neck, making him laugh before abruptly scooping him off her knee on to the rug. 'Well, if you're going, I'd better get on with lunch.' Danny's eyes widened with the shock of sudden abandonment, and he let out a wail. 'Look, he's upset now. You have to say tata to Ida, Danny. She can't stay and play, she's got important things to do.'

'Oh, I forgot . . .' Ida felt in the pocket of her coat and took out a little packet. 'I got something for you, Danny.'

Her brother reached up for it, tearing off the paper and staring at the pink object inside.

'That's a funny old present,' said her mum. 'You usually bring him a sweet.'

'Well, I thought I'd make a change. Keep his teeth nice. I thought he'd like the bright handle – it's made of celluloid.' The new word felt awkward in her mouth, like an outsized lozenge.

Danny turned the toothbrush over in his hand, looked up at his mother with eyes of exactly the same pale blue as hers and then, sensing some unspoken cue, swivelled his gaze to Ida.

'Sweets,' he said, mouth puckering.

'I'll bring you some next time.'

'Sweets!' He threw the toothbrush on the floor.

'Oh dear, oh dear,' said Mum, picking it up and dusting it. 'He's disappointed now. Never mind, Danny, Ida meant well. But I keep your toothy-pegs nice, don't I? I put a little bit of tooth powder on a flannel, just like I did with Ida when she was a baby, and her teeth are all right, aren't they?'

'I know, Mum, but toothbrushes are even better, they get into all the little gaps, Miss Lee says. And you know, don't you, you can take Danny to the baby clinic in Drummond Street for them to look at his teeth and it won't cost you nothing?' She paused. 'Cost you anything, I mean.'

'Corst you anytheeng,' said Charlie. Frank sniggered.

'I'm sorry, sweetheart,' said her mother, lifting Danny's solid little body on to her hip, 'but Ida says I've been looking after you all wrong.' He was crying hard now, arching backwards over her supporting arm.

'I didn't mean that, Mum, I just meant—'

'I thought I was doing my best, but I let you down, didn't I? . . . No, don't cry, little lad. Can you take him for a second, Ida?'

Reluctantly, Ida tried to comply, but he batted her away with sticky hands, his mouth a roaring hole.

Her mother smiled sadly. 'It's because he hardly sees you now. You're a stranger to him.'

'I'm not. He's just in a mood.'

'Well, I can't cook when he's upset like this, you'll just have to do the potatoes for me. The others'll be back any minute.'

She whisked off into the bedroom, and Ida banged the pan on the stove, smeared it with dripping and lit the gas, tears pricking her eyes. Outside in the world, with other people, she could *talk*, give answers, be quick off the mark – too quick, her mouth sprinting away with her thoughts – but here at home with her mother it was as if the floor was always shifting, so that she never got her footing, could never fix her aim. It was almost as bad at her aunt's; they were both on at her at the moment; she felt like a pencil sharpened at both ends.

Charlie was reading the funnies at the kitchen table. 'Corst me anytheeng,' he said again, not looking at her.

'Oh, shut up,' she said, wearily.

There was supposed to be someone coming from the Hampstead newspaper today, to write an article about the Amazons, and she'd been stupid enough to get excited at the idea – 'As senior founding member, Ida, I would particularly like you to talk to the journalist,' Miss Simpkin had said. And now she was going to be late. She'd ironed her shirt specially, and embroidered another gold star on to her green sash; this one was for 'making pertinent points during discussions'. Ida suspected that Miss Simpkin made up some of the star awards as she went along – Winnie had recently got one for 'avoiding retaliation when provoked' – but there were more standard categories as well: navigation, tree identification, Great Women of History, voice projection. Ida had more stars than anyone else. If Freda and the others could have seen her nearly crying over a panful of spuds, they wouldn't have believed it.

She glanced across at her brothers, and Frank stuck his tongue out at her. 'Don't be cheeky,' she said, automatically, as if to a lad she was passing in the street. Her friend

Vesta came from a very big family – fourteen children – but they seemed to like one another, teased without malice, went out together of an evening. Being with them was like being with a basketful of puppies, whereas her own family was ... what? ... a row of watchdogs, all waiting for a pat from the owner. Rivals, checking on one another out of the corners of their eyes. And it didn't help, of course, that she was the only girl.

'You could do this, Charlie,' she said. 'Anyone can fry potatoes.'

'I've been working all week.'

'And I *haven't*?'

'Men don't cook.'

'Yes, they do. Sailors when they're at sea. Hotel chefs. There's a man called Escoffier who's a better cook than anyone in the world.'

'I wouldn't eat French food.'

'Well, you're going to,' she said, triumphantly, 'because these are called sauté potatoes, and that's a French word.'

'You turning into a snob, Idie?'

'*No!*' she said, stung. 'Learning new things doesn't make you a snob. Learning new things is part of being a human – it's why we've ended up with bigger brains than monkeys.'

'Who are you calling a monkey?'

She turned away, to avoid Frank's chimp impersonation.

'Here's a sweet chestnut,' Miss Simpkin had said last week. *'Long, serrated green leaves, fissured trunk, little different to any other tree, you might think. But its Latin name is* castanea sativa, *and its light pale wood is used to make the Spanish dancers' hand-clappers, which is why they are called castanets. The species was brought to this*

91

country by the Romans, who wanted a large supply of chestnuts, not
to roast over the fire in winter, as we do, but to dry out and grind into
flour. When a Roman said "bread", he didn't think of wheat fields
but of this tall and splendid tree. Look up at it, girls, and think of
twirling flamenco dancers, and those poor homesick legionaries eating
sweet, yellow loaves that reminded them of their mothers' kitchens.
Now, doesn't that make the world feel wider?'

There was a scuffling on the outside landing, and then
the door opened and the flat was suddenly full, brothers
everywhere, Ted back from his shift as a porter, Harold
and Jerry carrying a bag of small coals between them,
picked from the road beside the goods yard.

'Got me a present?' asked Jerry, the second youngest
and dreadfully jealous of the baby.

'Not this time.'

'I bet you got Danny a present.'

'Just a toothbrush.'

'A *toothbrush*?'

'Don't disturb Ida, she's sooootying the potatoes.'

'She's what?'

'It's nothing fancy,' said Ida, irritably. 'It just means fry-
ing potatoes that you've already boiled, and there isn't an
English word for it. And I've finished now.' She jerked a
pile of plates from a shelf.

'Idie, I forgot, there's a couple of rashers on a dish by the
window,' called her mother from the other room. 'Can you
do those for Ted? And put on the kettle after, will you?'

'Oh, Mum—'

But, as she spoke, the station clock chimed the hour,

which meant that she was so certain to be late, now, that another five minutes would scarcely make a difference, and she fried the bacon with such vehemence that the plate she slammed in front of Ted was covered in tattered scraps. Clattering down the area steps, the frown tightened across her forehead like a bandeau.

'Give us a smile, girlie,' said the bus conductor.

She could have bitten him.

᪄

'Paper's here,' said Mattie, dropping the *Hampstead & Highgate Express* on to the kitchen table and straightaway beginning to search through it.

The Flea was standing beside the sink, reading a letter. 'This came this morning,' she said.

'What came?'

'It's from Ida's aunt, the one she lodges with. Mrs Beck. Lilias Beck. She asks if I can visit her.'

'Does she give a reason?'

'No. Well, not precisely. She says it's about her niece, but gives no details.'

'Odd.'

'Yes, it is, rather.' The handwriting was surprisingly elegant: *I would be obliged, Miss Lee, if you don't tell my niece I sent this.*

'Here's the article!' said Mattie, smoothing flat an inner page of the newspaper. 'Quite a spread. Though rather a peculiar headline.'

The March of Progress
Heath Activities for the Youth of Today

Gleeful shouts mark the weekly meeting of 'The Amazons', a girls' club founded by Vale of Health resident Miss Matilda Simpkin. Free of charge, and open to all young ladies between the ages of eleven and eighteen, it offers healthy and hearty fun to schoolgirl and factory lass alike. The sight of these coltish creatures in their weekend clothes and green sashes, kicking up their heels and frolicking 'cross the sward, is becoming familiar to Heath walkers.

'Good God, I should have insisted on writing it myself,' said Mattie, elbows planted on the table. 'The style is frightful.'

'But factually correct,' said The Flea, reading over her shoulder.

Last Sunday, more than thirty girls were gathered 'neath a hollow tree, their voices raised in gay chatter as the plans for the week's meeting unfolded. 'I say, can we have a crack at Fox and Hounds today?' called one pig-tailed girl. 'Bags I the fox!' called another.

A register was taken, Fox and Hounds agreed upon, and then soft, young faces became serious as the weekly discussion topic was broached. 'What is Freedom?' was the subject of the day, and rosy foreheads, more usually harbouring visions of matinee idols and hair ribbons, were wrinkled in donnish thought.

Mattie snorted. 'One would think they'd employed Ethel M. Dell as a copy-editor.'

'Well, *I* think it's first rate,' said The Flea, whose well-thumbed copy of *The Way of an Eagle* was wedged between the hygiene textbooks in her bedroom bookcase. 'Any girls reading this would be longing to join.'

After the discussion, and the eventual capture of 'the fox' (a speedy Doris Elphick, of Grafton Terrace, whose stated ambition is to be a games mistress), the girls gave a display of self-defence techniques, carried out with creditable vigour, before the meeting ended with cocoa and biscuits back at 'Headquarters'. Pink cheeks and bright eyes abounded, and many biscuits were eaten! 'When I'm bored in lessons, which is almost all of the time, I just think of the fun we're going to have on Sunday,' said Miss Freda Solomons, aged fifteen, who has been to every single club meeting. But 'fun' is not the sole aim of The Amazons:

'Several of our members left school before matriculation and have little time for further study,' Miss Simpkin told the *Ham & High*. 'This club gives them an opportunity to develop and maintain fitness of both body and brain. The Equal Franchise Bill has just had its first reading, and it is more than likely that, by the end of this year, every British woman of twenty-one and over will be allowed to vote. Our girls need to learn to question and to analyse, so that they can step up to the ballot box with confidence and knowledge.'

Elsewhere on the Heath, recent Saturday mornings have been presenting a contrasting approach to youth education.

'Oh, no! Oh, Heavens *above*!' exclaimed The Flea, reading ahead.

Smart in tan uniforms and gleaming belts, a mixed group of boys and girls march past the bathing ponds, the parade headed by a flag-bearer holding aloft a Union Jack, while a drummer and a trio of fife players mark the beat. Admiring glances follow the progress of these young members of the Empire Youth League as they assemble beside the boating lake and wait in respectful silence for their orders. There are no shouted suggestions here, and no horseplay; marching drill, running practice and semaphore are the activities of the day, and they are carried out with impressive energy and discipline. Young faces shine with pride at the praise from their leaders, Mr and Mrs Richard Cellini, of Highgate, and after a short address on the subject of duty, followed by a rousing song ('The Empire's Flag Raise We with Pride'), they are dismissed for another week, with the stern admonition to keep their belts polished!

'Richard and I recently arrived from Australia, where we have spent many years working with young people, and what struck us on reaching these shores was that not enough is asked of the youth of this great country,' says Mrs Cellini. 'British boys and girls are capable of tremendous feats – just think of the patriotic youngsters who defied the reds and pressed themselves into the nation's service during the iniquitous General Strike. The aim of the League is to treat young people as citizen soldiers, as junior guardians of our island realm. Rather than encouraging them to play childish games, or engage in classroom debate, we urge them to stride into the future, using their strength and commitment to drive back the sickly tide of foreign

interference. In unity, and with pride, they will take this country forward.'

'What utter spinach,' said Mattie. 'What an essentially
meaningless succession of sentences!' She felt winded, as if
she'd just received an unexpected blow to the solar plexus.

'And also quite spiteful,' said The Flea.

'Rhetoric without content has always been the trade-
mark of the charlatan. Twenty years ago, Jacqueline Fletcher
was a good egg, but it is clear that she is now *addled*.'

She rose abruptly; irritation always goaded her to physical action, and she unhooked her gardening apron from
the scullery door and removed a pair of secateurs from the
pocket. 'If you want me, I shall be pruning the dogwood.'

'But do you think that she did this deliberately, as competition?' asked The Flea. 'Had she seen the Amazons on
the Heath?'

'I have *no doubt* that that is the case. And I believe I told
you that we had recently been tailed by a group of boys,
and at least two of those were wearing some species of
uniform.'

And as she stamped outside into the mildest of early
spring days – nature perceptibly stirring, an early bee
fumbling among the grape hyacinths, catkins twisting on
the hazel – it was the appropriation, and perversion, of her
idea that rankled most. To take airy freedom and turn it
into military drill, to sprint across the paradise of the
Heath in the name of patriotism, to prohibit spontaneity
and sneer at the notion of 'fun'; these seemed as good a
definition of fascism as any she had come across. She knelt

by the *cornus alba* and began to cut back last year's blood-red stems, pausing only to shy a clod of earth at the Wimbournes' tabby (a vicious thrush-killer), who was watching her from the rail of the summer house. It fled into the near-perfect camouflage of a clump of raspberry canes and, after a moment or two, Mattie knelt back on her heels and felt in her skirt pocket for the miniature notebook and pencil that she always carried. Thumbing through, she added the words '*stalking/camouflage*' to a list of possible Amazon activities.

Her annoyance was already subsiding; really, one could almost pity the narrowness of Jacko's vision. What girl alive would want to stand to attention for a lecture on duty when she could be sneaking through the woods with a hat made of leaves? Why hold a flagpole when you could hold a javelin? Still, it might be expedient, from now on, to interview new Amazon recruits rather than let them simply turn up; she would not put it past the Empire League to send a single spy creeping across the lines . . .

In the kitchen, The Flea read the article again, her lips compressed into a thin seam of disquiet. She would not, in honesty, ever have classified Jacqueline Fletcher as 'a good egg'. The phrase implied solidity and kindness, both qualities rather lacking in the glamorous figure who had occasionally visited the WSPU offices in a coat worth more than an organizer's annual wage, and a trailing tippet which had once knocked two hours' worth of filed paperwork from The Flea's desk. ('Shall I help you to sort it out?' Jacqueline had asked, making no move to do so, 'though I might not be a great deal of use – I'm awfully stupid about that type of thing . . .') And yet one could never forget that she had been just as brave, just as dedicated to the cause of equal franchise as Mattie, as Aileen, as Roberta – possessed of the same iron backbone that seemed to have been issued to all the militants, however disparate their characters and backgrounds, so that stoics and mystics, contemplatives and workhorses, the robust, the cheerful, the imperious, the shy had all been transformed into troops who could be thrust, again and again, into the fray, at hideous physical cost.

'We were a battering ram,' Mattie was wont to say. 'Together, we broke down the door,' but beyond that splintered door had been a dozen more doors and, scattered by their momentum, some women had tried one and some another, and some had given up and turned away, and it seemed to The Flea that all that unity and passion, all that wild energy, had dissipated. And she herself and her ilk, trudging soberly behind, had somehow ended up in the vanguard . . .

'Miss Lee?'

It was Ida, glass-cloth in one hand, looking around the kitchen door with a faint air of excitement.

'The telephone was ringing and ringing, Miss Lee. I thought maybe you hadn't heard, so I answered it.'

'Thank you – you're right, I hadn't. So who is it?'

'It's for Miss Simpkin, Miss Lee.' Ida left a tiny dramatic pause. 'It's the police!'

Mattie followed the constable on the familiar route down to the cells – not that she had ever been incarcerated in the basement beneath Hampstead police station, but the maroon-glazed brick, the broad staircase (wide enough for the passage of a prisoner between two escorts) and the trill of carbolic that failed to mask an ammoniacal bass note were all so reminiscent of the interior of Bow Street or Havant Row that one almost expected to hear a polyphony of female voices, all bellowing slogans or singing as they awaited their appointment with the magistrate.

'When are you lot going to shut up?' a Bow Street policeman had once enquired, and from every cell had come the shout of '*Never!!*'

But there was no noise at all here, save for the clank and swish of someone mopping the floor.

'Are you all right, Miss?'

Mattie found that she had paused, gripping the rail. She inhaled sharply. 'Yes, I am perfectly well,' she said, resuming her descent.

'The witness is here, sir,' called the constable, knocking on a door at the foot of the stairs, and the man who exited the room was the sergeant who'd visited the Mousehole. Beal. An intelligent face, though not a friendly one.

'Thank you for attending, Miss Simpkin,' he said; his tone was dry.

'I wasn't aware that there was an element of choice.'

'No, that's correct, though it's not something we usually have to enforce. Most honest citizens are pleased to be able to help us catch criminals.'

'But as I mentioned on the telephone, I scarcely had a glimpse of the thief.'

'You might surprise yourself,' he said. 'People think they're not going to remember, and then they see the perpetrator and it's like spotting an old friend. In a manner of speaking.'

'And how did you catch him? Has he committed another crime?'

'I can't tell you that.'

'And what would happen in the event that I recognize him? Will the case go to court?'

'I can't tell you that, either. Are you ready? You don't need to say anything when you're in there – each of the men will be holding a number, and when you've decided, give me a nod and we'll come back out.' He opened the door halfway and then realized that Mattie was making no move to follow him.

'Through here, please.'

'Yes, I'm coming.' And yet she could not unglue her feet. Above her head, a bulb emitted a soupy yellow glow.

It was the lack of windows, she thought; one always needed a glimpse of sky, however grey, and a horizon on which to fix one's gaze. In her subterranean cell in Holloway, the weak electric light had made her feel purblind. Her prison dreams had been not of food, or of home, but of shutters prised open, of daylight spilling in. She still couldn't abide a closed curtain.

'Is something the matter, Miss Simpkin?'

'No, nothing at all.' And as she spoke, she was already

starting the process of gathering herself together again, tucking in weakness, trussing herself like a parcel, just as she had done twice daily on hearing the approaching rattle of the feeding trolley, the purposeful footsteps of the doctor and the wardresses. By the time her cell door had been opened, by the time she'd been pinned down, the core of her had been unassailable.

'I am quite ready,' she said.

'On your feet, eyes ahead!' shouted someone as she entered the narrow room – no more than a section of corridor, really. Ten or twelve men, sitting on a long bench, stood up and formed a loose line; each held a square of cardboard bearing a number. They were all working men. Sawdust speckled the trousers of one, another had ink smudges on his hands, another smelled marvellously of horses. The youngest was a pimpled beanpole of sixteen or so, the oldest a man in his fifties with a soldier's bearing, a frayed collar and a nose that he hadn't been born with – a soft, pale sausage of a nose, conjured up by a surgeon to cover God knows what battlefield horror. He alone was disobeying the instruction to look straight ahead, his gaze flicking around the room. Briefly, his eyes met Mattie's, and they seemed to be relaying a bitter joke: *What a farce, eh? Is it likely that a man who looks like me would commit a public crime? I'm ruined but I'm not a fool.*

'Are these men volunteers, or are they being paid?' asked Mattie, turning to the sergeant.

Before he could speak, there was a cough from behind her that seemed to conceal the word 'neither'.

'Or have they been coerced?'

'I'd be obliged, Madam, if you could continue to look along the line,' said the sergeant, evenly.

'I was merely enquiring,' she said.

'This isn't the time or place to discuss the matter.'

'Ah! – familiar phrase. I have discovered over the years that there is *never* a correct time or place to question those in authority. As in Tennyson's *Ulysses*, the "margin fades, forever and forever when I move".'

Sergeant Beal's face remained expressionless, but a certain blotchiness was creeping up the skin of his neck. 'To repeat my request, can you continue to look along the line and see if there is anyone you recognize.'

'Very well. If only to release these men from an unasked-for, unrewarded and somewhat humiliating task.'

'Attagirl,' muttered the soldier.

There was actually no need for further scrutiny on Mattie's part since she had seen from the moment she'd entered the room that the person who had robbed her was standing fourth from the right. Nevertheless, she walked to the end of the row, pausing for a moment in front of Number 12, a man with olive skin and a narrow moustache.

'*Buon giorno*, Signor Fazio,' she said.

'*Buon giorno*, Signora.'

Sergeant Beal opened his mouth to speak.

'Signor Fazio delivers our laundry,' said Mattie. 'I have met him only under strictly legal circumstances. Now, I think I have seen everything that I need to.'

The sergeant led her out into the corridor.

'Well?' he asked, when the door was closed once again. 'Apart from the Italian, did you recognize anyone?'

She hesitated for a second, searching for a strictly truthful answer. 'I saw no one that I would be prepared to swear in court was the thief.'

'You're not in court now.'

'Indeed.'

'So if there's someone who rings a bell, you should say so.'

'Most of these men, I imagine, live or work in the vicinity – as do I. It's quite likely that I have seen several of their faces before.'

'But not in the act of stealing your bag.'

'You forget that I didn't see him until he was running away. The back of a man's head is rarely distinctive.'

'Dark hair, you said in your original statement.'

'That's correct.'

'A young man with dark hair.'

'I don't believe that I used the word "young".'

Beal jerked his head impatiently. 'This isn't a debating club, Miss Simpkin. You were robbed and the police force is trying to bring the perpetrator to justice. Why won't you help us?'

'You truly wish to know?' And, though, judging by his face, he didn't, she couldn't stop herself now; half an hour in a police station had primed the fire and pumped the bellows. 'Because I have suffered – and have seen many others suffer – repeated and unprovoked violence at police hands. I have been punched, kicked and vilely assaulted while engaged in the democratic right of taking a grievance to the doors of Parliament. I have seen burly officers throw women half their size to the pavement – women whose crime was to carry a banner no bigger than a handbag. I have seen unarmed men hit across the face with truncheons, their hands stamped on as they crawled away. On the many occasions I was arrested, I never once offered resistance and yet was treated like a dunghill cur, with nary a protest from the officers in charge as their men acted like hired thugs. I have seen the so-called upholders of justice, and I have realized that the word "justice" is simply and only that: a word.'

A sudden noise made her turn: the constable had opened the interior door and was peering through. 'Sorry, sir,' he said, 'but some of the men are asking if they can go.'

'One minute,' said Beal. The door closed again.

'I, too, would like to leave,' said Mattie.

'Where would you draw the line, Miss Simpkin?'

'I beg your pardon?'

Beal looked like a dog at a foxhole, his gaze fixed and bristling. 'If your house was burgled or if you saw a murder or a kidnapping, would you call the police then? Or would you prefer anarchy – criminals roaming the city, everyone taking the law into their own hands? What if the man who robbed you has robbed other ladies as well – ladies less able to defend themselves? What if he goes and does it again? What if he's a nasty little thug who deserves to be convicted? Where's your justice then? You have to put your prejudice aside. For the public good.'

Mattie snorted – a Peeler lecturing her on her debt to society!

'Prejudice implies an unfair bias. My views are based on facts.'

'Facts from twenty years ago, at a time when you were deliberately and repeatedly breaking the law.'

'Laws upheld by those who were apparently beyond the reach of it themselves!'

The words – a declamatory near-shout – hung in the air for a second or two, and then Beal stepped back and rapped sharply on the door.

'Let them out,' he said.

'So I'm free to go now?' asked Mattie.

Beal looked at her for a long, hard moment and then nodded. 'And I hope you never find yourself in urgent need of our assistance, Miss Simpkin,' he said as she turned to mount the stairs, and the chill of the words stayed with her as she emerged on to Haverstock Hill.

'Please, Mattie, do *try* not to give them your impression of a mule with a sore hoof,' The Flea had said before she'd left for the police station, but once again the visceral had overridden the expedient, and now she appeared to have made an enemy. An enemy who had actually fought rather well – there was, she was forced to acknowledge, a certain uncomfortable truth at the core of his argument. Those who preyed on the weak should not go unpunished.

A fine rain was falling, and Mattie opened her umbrella and took inadequate shelter beneath a leafless plane.

Yards away, the police station door opened, and the men from the line-up began to file out, the beanpole breaking into an immediate sprint after the 168 bus as it laboured up the hill. Signor Fazio tipped his hat at Mattie and the man with the nose gave her a nod. She waited. Ten minutes passed, and then the door opened again, and Number 9 walked down the steps. He paused to light a cigarette, flicked the match away and saw Mattie standing beneath its trajectory. His eyes widened.

'A word, please,' she said.

'What?' He turned away and started to walk down the hill. She furled her umbrella and hurried after him.

'I would like a word with you.'

'You're bleeding joking.'

'I'm bleeding not.'

He looked round then, the view of his face directly comparable to the one she'd seen on the Heath.

'You're a thief,' she said.

'And you're mental.'

He broke into a run. Mattie did the same. The Amazons had had a splendid effect on her muscular fitness.

Passers-by were beginning to watch and point.

'Stop now,' she called, 'or I shall continue to follow you, intermittently shouting the word "Thief!"'

'Christ *Almighty*.' The man halted so abruptly that Mattie almost cannoned into him. 'What?' he asked. 'What the fuck do you want?'

He was young, no older than eighteen, his clothing cheap and flashy, his expression one of angry bafflement. Close up, the sharp cheekbones looked not so much Slavic as undernourished.

'You stole my bag,' she said.

He looked at her as if she were speaking in Swahili.

'You can't pin it on me now, you stupid cow, you had your chance.'

'Nevertheless, we both know the truth.'

'Says you.'

'Presumably I was not the first that you robbed, nor the last, though perhaps I was the only one to see your face.'

'I haven't done nothing. The rozzers are always trying to pin stuff on me, you'd think I done every bleeding crime in Camden.' He spoke the words with practised outrage, glancing back at the police station as he did so.

'What did you do with the contents of my handbag?'

'I never took your fucking handbag.'

'Besides the purse, and various other items, there was a volume by Thomas Fuller.'

'Dunno what you're talking about.'

'I presume that you immediately recognized its value and took it to a book dealer?'

His gaze swivelled towards her.

'It was a third edition,' she said. 'I imagine worth at least fifty pounds.'

He looked suddenly shorter, a tent-peg hit with a mallet.

'Possibly more,' said Mattie, wielding her weapon again. The boy's lips moved involuntarily, as if essaying the word 'more'.

'Do you still have it,' she asked, 'or did you throw it away? If the latter, then I'm afraid that you threw away both wisdom and profit.'

'Shut up.'

'If, in future, I hear of any similar robberies – and I shall read every crime report in the *Ham & High*, the *Euston Observer* and the *North London Mercury*, scouring them for a modus operandi that matches your own – I will go straight back to the police and tell them I was mistaken.'

He tried to laugh at that. 'They won't take no notice of you.'

'I am not easily ignored.'

The laugh died.

'Fuck off,' he said, succinctly, turning away. This time, she let him go. He walked off down the hill with an attempted cockiness that struck her as pathetic, an ambulatory version of swearing; the rain, heavier now, was moulding his jacket to shoulders as narrow as a girl's. She thought of the relish with which she'd informed him of his mistake, and felt discomfited. He was Ignorance and Want personified – one should pity and not gloat; one should think of volume two of Fuller's *Worthies of England* lying in a dustcart, covered in tea leaves and rancid cheese-parings, and wince at the symbolism.

Raising her umbrella, she set off for home. There was much to be done.

∽

Flats were being built at the end of Croker Road, and The Flea paused to watch a man push a brick-filled wheelbarrow across a plank that spanned the gap between an open-backed lorry and the first floor of the new building. He took the angled journey almost at a run, the plank bowing beneath the weight, his boots dislodging dust that sifted slowly to the pavement, eight or nine feet below. The barrow wheel thumped on to a solid surface, and The Flea breathed again. An unskilled labourer, she thought, doing a job that required the precision of a circus artiste.

She crossed the road and turned along a narrow passage between a rag shop and a butcher, skinned rabbits hanging above the sawdust, and emerged into a square. There was a railed garden at the centre – a sparse lawn and a few shrubs, and a bench, currently unoccupied. One end of the bench was in sunlight, and she sat and took out her notebook.

'I would advise you never to fill in record cards during the visit itself,' her tutor, Miss Beering, had been wont to say, on the health visitor certificate course at Bedford College. 'Do not forget that, in many households, producing a notebook is suggestive of the policeman collecting evidence. Rely on your memory and make your notes afterwards. Similarly, call out when you visit, rather than use the door knocker. To many people, a "rat-tat-tat" means only the rent-collector or the bailiff.'

The King family, basement flat, 14, Hatfield Road.
Alfred King, 41, labourer; Dorcas King, 27; Alice, 10; Enid, 9; Raymond, 5; James (Jimmy), 2; 3 other infants died shortly after birth.
5/4/28 Mr King suffering from TB. Clear decline since last visit, now bedridden. Mrs King worried about Enid's cough and has heard of the Sunshine Homes. Asked me to enquire about Enid and Raymond getting a place. The

children receive free milk from the Needs Fund, but Mrs King says she cannot afford meat, and they share potatoes for two meals a day. All four children appear ailing. Mrs King is taking in sewing but is behind with the rent, and is awaiting a Relief Committee decision.

The children were as pale as porridge. On a visit last autumn, The Flea had – very softly, and in the course of listing sources of possible help – mentioned the Mothers' Clinic in the Tottenham Court Road, and had seen Mrs King give a start and glance over at her husband, who was sleeping in a chair. 'He won't have none of that,' she'd muttered, barely moving her lips. 'Says it's all wrong.'

'I see. There are . . . I'll just mention this, for your information . . . there are methods now which are the . . . the sole concern of the wife.'

Dorcas King had glanced at her husband again, and this time her expression had been hopeful. 'He wouldn't have to know?'

'No. Perhaps you might want to think about it? The clinic is open every morning and there's no charge. And you may be absolutely certain of their discretion.'

Sitting on her bench in Adam Square, The Flea sighed.

Mrs King is expecting again, and thinks she is four months pregnant. I will enquire about the lying-in grant, and have strongly recommended she attend the Drummond Street mother-and-baby clinic.

The outside convenience, serving all the inhabitants of the building, is currently blocked (this is the fifth time in a

111

year), but Mrs King asked me not to serve a notice on the landlord, as she is afraid of being evicted if she—

'Hello, Florrie!'

Etta Kirby waved to her from the edge of the square, and walked across with her usual India-rubber step. She was in her early thirties, all bounce and bonhomie, curly hair springing from beneath the brim of her health visitor's hat.

She dropped on to the bench with an impact that sent The Flea's pencil skidding across the page.

'Golly, I could do with some fresh air,' she said. 'Been visiting a family in Bloemfontein House, and the grandfather was busy sticking new soles on the children's boots with fish glue. There was a pot of it bubbling in a pan the whole time. I might as well have been *bathing* in the stuff – can you smell it?' She offered a sleeve to The Flea, who sniffed, recoiled and nodded.

'Oh Lord . . .' Etta gave a crow of laughter and leaned back with her eyes closed, face up to the sun. 'Five-minute break,' she said. 'Tell me if anyone comes by – remember Miss Beering? – "Comport yourselves with dignity, ladies. To be respected, one must look respectable."'

'"And behave respectfully, however alien the situation."'

'Good old Beery.'

'Etta, have you recommended any children for Sunshine Homes lately?'

'I have, as a matter of fact. Couple of kiddies who'd survived whooping cough and were living in a room that was as damp as a . . . a *sponge*. I didn't have much luck – the home in Watford was full and the one in Barnet's been converted into a hospital for infantile paralysis; they've had heaps of cases lately, they say, and some of those poor mites stay in for years. The only thing I could do in the end was get them sun-lamp treatment. Oh, Florrie,' – she straightened up and opened her eyes – 'did I tell you that Gresby proposed to me?'

'That's splendid. Congratulations!'

'I haven't said yes yet.'

'Why not?' The Flea had met Gresby, briefly – a pleasant, slightly built young man who looked as if Etta might be able to fold him up like a carpenter's rule and stow him in her handbag.

'Oh, I don't know. If I say yes, I'll have to marry him, and then I shan't be able to work any more, shall I, and I'd hate that. On the other hand, I *would* like a couple of babies, and time's ticking on and he's quite a decent chap and . . .' She shrugged, smile fading. 'Well, I'm jolly lucky to have found anyone at all, aren't I? Most don't. I went to a school reunion last month, and out of thirty girls in my class, nineteen of us are spinsters – apparently, the newspapers are calling us "the surplus women". "Like a drawer full of forks," my friend Minnie said, "when all the knives have been stolen."'

There was a moment of bleak silence, and then Etta slapped her knees, like someone knocking dust from a cushion. 'So yes,' she said, 'I shall probably consent to become Mrs Leadbetter. *Don't!*' she added, clocking The Flea's expression. 'It's ridiculous, isn't it? Henrietta Leadbetter. Like a character from a nursery rhyme.'

'I thought he seemed very nice when I met him,' said The Flea.

'Yes,' said Etta, more soberly. 'Yes, he is. I'm wicked to complain, especially when . . . Were you ever engaged, Florrie?'

'No.'

'You don't mind my asking?'

'Not at all. I wasn't one of those poor girls who lost a fiancé at the Front.'

'Just never found the right fellow?'

The Flea shook her head. 'But I'm sure that you have, and I hope you'll be very happy.'

Etta leaned across and gave her hand a clumsy squeeze. 'You're a chum,' she said. 'And I'll expect you at the wedding. Now, I have to go and weigh some nice fat babies at the clinic – at least, I hope they'll be nice and fat. You?'

'I'm seeing someone in Wilson Road.'

'Oh, bad luck.'

It had seemed to The Flea as a child that there was something akin to a miracle about the process of ironing – the way that black metal, hellish heat and the violent hiss of steam could turn crumpled cloth into an angel's raiment. Sitting now in Mrs Beck's kitchen, she marvelled all over again. Outside the front door were soot and sparrows, the very air full of smoky filth, and inside were folded snow-drifts; the striped linen cloth in front of her might have been draped across the table straight from the loom.

'Thank you,' she said, as Mrs Beck set down a tray. Two delicate gilt-edged cups and a matching teapot stood on a cross-stitched mat. The sugar bowl and the milk jug were plain.

Lilias Beck nodded and took a seat opposite, lowering herself stiffly, as if the act of sitting were unfamiliar. She clasped her hands on the table-top, fingers grinding against the reddened knuckles. There was no bend to her, thought The Flea – she was like a chess queen, upright and severe, her tautly handsome features somehow at odds with the boiled-bacon complexion of someone who worked perpetually in steam. 'It's a beautiful teapot,' said The Flea.

'It was my grandmother's.'

There was a pause. In the silence, a child could be heard crying drearily in the next-door flat, and beyond was the perpetual dull thunder of the trains. The Flea cleared her throat; formality was a killer to confidences – she was always glad when the women she visited were sewing or holding a child.

'So . . .' she began.

'You've been giving Ida lessons,' said Mrs Beck, abruptly, 'about the human body.'

The Flea hesitated, struggling to gauge what her response should be. Was she being accused of wasting Ida's time? Of introducing indecent subjects? Of giving the girl ideas above her station?

'We've had some little chats about vitamins and general health,' she said, cautiously. 'I showed your niece one of my textbooks, with a diagram of the digestive system. It wasn't exactly a lesson . . .'

'She told me you'd talked about her going back to school.'

'Continuation school? Yes. Yes, I mentioned the idea. Perhaps you know about the scheme?'

Mrs Beck said nothing, but her hands continued to move, kneading and twisting each other.

'The service is provided by London County Council, and it's free – Ida could go for two afternoons a week, or even three. She could come to work a little earlier on those days, and we'd make no reduction to her wage.'

Her voice, bright and conciliatory, hung in the air like an offered handshake.

'And then what?' asked Mrs Beck, smacking it aside.

'Well . . . if Ida were also able to study in the evenings, she could matriculate, and maybe go on to a training college.'

'A training college?'

'To be a teacher. Or perhaps she could go to nursing school. She really is a bright girl, Mrs Beck – she has great curiosity and an excellent memory. I think that, given the chance, she could do very well.'

The aunt's hands stilled, and she leaned forward slightly, her eyes fixed on The Flea.

'I'll tell you what Ida is,' she said, fiercely. 'She's a pearl. A *pearl*.'

She sat back again, as if she'd just issued a challenge.

'Oh!' said The Flea, startled. 'Well . . . yes. I think she is.'

'She's always had character. She's always been the best of that family. My brother-in-law's not much of a man and his wife's a prize—' She clamped her mouth shut over the letter 'b', before it could escape. 'I don't like to use the word, Miss Lee, but if you met Violet, you'd be using it yourself. You've not met her, have you?'

'No.'

'She's like the Queen of the May. They all dance round her' – she flapped a hand in a parody of airy deference – 'she's got the whole family on reins and none of them will hear a word against her, but she holds them back, Miss Lee. I've watched her. Ida could have stayed on at school, there's enough money coming in, two of the boys are earning now, but Violet couldn't stick that – couldn't have someone making more of themselves than she'd ever done. I know it's men that hold women back, Miss Lee, but there are women who hold women back as well. It's jealousy, my own mother was the same . . .' She paused for a moment, her lips moving silently, as if reprising old arguments. 'I didn't get any chances in life,' she said, matter-of-factly, 'nor any luck. I don't want the same to happen to Ida. The end of last year I told her parents she ought to come and live with me, and I'd pay for her keep – they've got no space; a growing girl sharing with her brothers, it's not right. And I found Ida that job at the station waiting room – they send their table-linen to me – and I thought it might lead to something better, but then she got the push. You know about that, Miss Lee?'

'The geography question?'

'Sacked for being too clever. And when you offered her work I wasn't happy at first, what with her just being a daily, but then you and Miss Simpkin took an interest. First the Sunday club, and then the lessons. Ida comes back from the Amazons and she's a foot taller.'

'I'm glad,' said The Flea, smiling at the image.

'But what I want to know is this.' She fixed The Flea with an unblinking gaze. 'Will you stick with her, Miss Lee?'

'Stick with her?'

'You can't raise her hopes and then drop them again. It doesn't take much to knock back a young girl. I knew of one who had a school prize for penmanship and thought she could be a clerk at the Post Office, and then someone turned round to her one day and said, "You've got hands like a navvy. No one would believe you could do copperplate," and that was the end of it. I don't want that for Ida.'

'I promise you,' said The Flea. 'We shall go on helping your niece. You haven't met Miss Simpkin, but she is, perhaps above all else, a . . . a *sticker*. She is staunch, Mrs Beck. And good-hearted, and utterly reliable. And you've met me now, and I hope you can see that I'm sincere.'

Ida's aunt held her gaze for a moment more, and then gave a grudging nod.

'You're not what I expected, Miss Lee.'

'No?'

Her hostess lifted the lid of the teapot and gave the contents a stir, and poured them each a cup before she spoke again. 'I thought you'd be one of those ladies who works just to give herself something to do.'

'No, I've always needed to earn my living. But I think you're being a little unfair, Mrs Beck — a great deal of good has been achieved by people who could have spent their lives doing nothing.' Her tone was sharper than she'd intended (as always happened when she found herself defending Mattie, however obliquely), but Mrs Beck

appeared not to take offence – the tone seemed, if anything, to brighten her, as if she relished a clash of swords.

'That's as may be,' she said. 'But you can always tell. If
someone's never had to think about money, you can see it
in their faces. They haven't ever had that worry, dripping
away year after year. It wears a groove in you. Stains you.'

'And you can see that in me?'

'I can.'

The Flea nodded. 'My mother took in laundry, Mrs
Beck.'

Ida's aunt gave a huff of grim amusement. 'But you got
a chance,' she said.

'Yes, I was quick with figures, and my teacher suggested
that I go to a commercial school for a year – it was near us,
in Northampton – and my parents agreed. I learned short-
hand and book-keeping and that led to . . . many chances.'

'So your ma and pa did their best for you?'

'Yes, always.'

'Brothers and sisters?'

The Flea shook her head; impossible to explain that she
hadn't seen her brother for more than twenty-five years.
'And you, Mrs Beck?'

'I have a sister who's a defective – she lives in the country with my cousin. I send money for her.'

'That does you credit.'

'She never did anyone any harm. Smiles at everyone.
Not many people you can say that about.'

'No indeed.'

Mrs Beck laid her hands flat on the table and looked
down at them. They were large, the fingers splayed with

arthritis. 'Another few years, I won't be able to grip the iron,' she said, 'and I'll be finished.' There was no self-pity in her voice, just truth and a flat bitterness.

'Perhaps . . . perhaps you have a widow's pension?'

'I'm not a widow. He was a beast. He walked off one day and I never saw him again, and good riddance.' She reached for her cup, and tilted it so that the gilt rim caught the light. 'This was a full set of china when I married him. He'd get in a temper and *bang*, *crash*, all my nice things.' She rocked it gently back on to the saucer. 'I was a fool to marry. I've told Ida to stay away from men, but they won't stay away from *her*, will they? She'd be better off the way that you are, Miss Lee.'

That raw, unblinking stare again.

The Flea had to swallow before she could speak. 'The way that I am?'

'Independent.'

She could feel her cheeks burning. Quickly, she drank the remains of her tea, and stood up. 'Thank you, Mrs Beck, I'll have to go now, I have another visit to make. And I hope that you're reassured that our – that my interest in Ida is genuine, and that I'm aware of the responsibility of . . . of encouraging your niece to further her education.'

And then she almost fled from the flat, hurrying down the outside staircase, stopping only on the last flight in order to button her coat and straighten her hat, so that she emerged on to Wilson Road looking composed, and professional, though she could still feel the heat in her face. She crossed the road and started walking briskly in the direction of Silverdale, glancing back once at Alma

Buildings, as if expecting to see Lilias Beck leaning out of a top-floor window, pointing accusingly.

Had Mrs Beck guessed? *Had she guessed?* And yet what was there, actually, to guess at? The Flea lived with a friend, as did countless other women; what could be more sensible or more pleasant – or expedient, for that matter, with rents so high and no men left to marry? Neither Ida, nor any visitor to the house, could ever have heard a syllable or witnessed a gesture that conveyed more than innocent companionship.

No, thought The Flea, there really was nothing to guess. And if the certainty of that thought lacked comfort – if, in fact, it felt like a door slamming on an empty room – then there were other thoughts against which she had learned to balance it. While there was no one she had ever loved with more passion than Mattie, and nothing she could do with that passion except carry it around like a wrapped parcel, there was also no one who had ever interested or entertained (or, occasionally, infuriated) her more, or for whom she had greater admiration, or who had proved more able at dispelling loneliness, or who stood more in need of protection – because Mattie would never take a shortcut that might avoid the battlefield; she simply couldn't dissemble, couldn't mute her own reactions, couldn't turn a blind eye. She needed a shield-bearer.

Long ago, The Flea had loved another friend: Agnes Hines, an old schoolfellow. They had shared a desk at the offices of Northampton Town Hall, as well as a room in lodgings and – on one cold night of astonishing happiness – a bed. The next morning, Agnes had refused to speak or even look at her (and how terrible that had been, how icy, after waking to the brief warm bliss of another body curled around one's own), and that evening her room-mate had packed and left the lodgings. Something had been said at work, something nebulous perhaps, but hateful, so that all around The Flea were averted heads and the sound of scraping chairs as their occupants edged away, and Mr Sopwith, in charge of the office, had drawn her aside – as if with tongs – and suggested she make a fresh start elsewhere. No reference had been offered. The Flea's own brother, who worked at the Midland Bank and who was a member of the Conservative Club, the Temperance League and the Lodge of St George (accumulating respectability as a farmer bags rooks), had somehow heard the rumours, and sent her a letter saying that she was no longer welcome at his house, nor was she to see his children again; that was the one thing that had made her weep; she had cherished her little nieces. After that, given that her parents were dead, there was no reason to remain in Northampton, and she had moved to London, feeling not shame – she had never felt shame – but fear, since her own inclinations had proved to have the power to remove her from those she loved.

And she loved Mattie. Living with her in simple friendship might be akin to dancing the Charleston when what you really ached for was a slow waltz – but the music still played; it was, in its way, still a dance.

'Afternoon, Miss Lee.'

'Oh – hello, Mrs Chase,' said The Flea, gathering her thoughts and stepping out of the way of the dilapidated baby-carriage that was blocking the pavement, 'and hello, Cyril.' Cyril had a stick of rock in his hand, which he had evidently dropped and retrieved several times, judging by its dense coating of grit.

'He's got pink-eye again,' said Mrs Chase. 'I told him not to play by the bins but he won't listen.'

'How are the twins?' asked The Flea, ducking down to peer under the hood of the perambulator. A total of three babies stared back at her, one of them with a cluster of weeping yellow scabs on its chin.

'I'm minding the one in the middle for a friend.'

'I'm afraid that the one in the middle has impetigo. Which is extremely contagious.'

'You mean it's catching?'

'Yes, very.'

'I heard you get it from tinned milk, and I never give my babies tinned milk.'

'Unfortunately, you get it from touching the affected area. You should bathe your two little ones very thoroughly with soap and hot water when you get home.'

'We're just on our way out. My sister's had a baby girl and we're visiting. Bit of a party.'

The Flea opened her mouth and then closed it again. The phrase 'And some fell on stony ground' might have been written with Ruby Chase in mind; years of delicate suggestion – *Perhaps start baby off with a little mashed carrot, rather than kippers? I happen to have a bottle of Jeyes Fluid with me – might you find it useful?* – had made no difference at all to the sticky chaos of her home or the random mixture of whim and superstition by which she lived. And yet she was cheerful, her husband grimily affectionate, her children hugged and dandled.

Occasionally, though, it was necessary to be blunt.

'Mrs Chase, I really think your friend's baby shouldn't go with you. The infection could be very dangerous for a newborn. It would be wrong to bring him.'

'Oh. Well, I don't know . . .' Ruby Chase looked around helplessly. 'His mum's out and his grandma's all the way up at Mornington Crescent, Orgreave Road. I can't go all the way there with this to push.' She paused, and fixed The Flea with a hopeful gaze. 'She's at number 6, I think. Mrs Rains.'

'I'll take him,' said The Flea, resignedly. 'What's his name?'

'Edgar.'

'Come along, Edgar.' She extracted him from the carriage, a stiff little figure, dressed in a petticoat over layer upon layer of knitted garments, his face pink and damp. 'Let's get you to Grandma.'

'There's a definite *whiff* in here,' said Mattie, that evening, pausing in the hall with her sherry.

'It's my coat. I had to carry a baby rather a long way. I shall steep it in soda.'

'The baby?'

The Flea managed half a smile. 'As a matter of fact, the baby wasn't terribly well. Impetigo, but also, I think, a temperature. I had a word with the grandmother about giving him a luke-warm bath, but she was horrified at the idea, you'd have thought I was suggesting an ice-bucket –

the last I saw, she was wrapping him in a blanket. I sometimes wonder if I make the slightest difference.' There was,
unusually, a note of frustration in her voice. Mattie reached
for an antidote.

'Small sherry?'

'No thank you.'

'Or a toddy? Buck you up a bit.'

'It always gives me a thick head.'

'Glass of crème de menthe?'

The Flea wavered; she had a weakness for peppermint.
'A very, very tiny one, then. I must write up my notes
before bed.'

'I shall pour you a measure that Thumbelina would deem
inadequate. And then I'd like to read you my latest column
for the *Ham & High*; I have given Mussolini a roasting.'

'Should you? You know they keep on asking you to
limit yourself to strictly local affairs.'

'And what could be more local than a military bugle
drowning out the duck-calls by the Upper Pond?'

'Oh, you're going for Jacko?' said The Flea, visibly
brightening.

'Did you think I might not?'

The Flea smiled; a proper smile this time.

'I've lit the fire in the drawing room,' said Mattie. 'Let's
vamoose.'

✍

Ida stood by the exit of Westminster Underground station, and counted heads.

'I have ten,' she called.

'Ten in my group,' said Freda.

'Ten in mine,' echoed Bessie.

'Six,' said Hildegard Collings-Waverley, in the startled squeak of a voice which always made her sound as if she'd just been jabbed with a pin. 'But I'm *meant* to have six,' she added. 'I didn't have ten to start with.'

'So are we fully present and correct?' asked Miss Simpkin. 'No one still on the Northern Line, rattling towards the fleshpots of Tooting?'

'We're all here,' said Ida.

'Excellent. Good work, group leaders – bullseyes all round. Now, before we make our way to Parliament Square I suggest we cross the road and examine the magnificent statue on the Embankment.'

'Could I take a photograph of us all first?' asked Freda, who had received a Box Brownie for her fifteenth birthday, and had appointed herself documentarian of the Amazons' Especial Outing.

'How would you like us arranged?' asked Mattie.

'You in the middle, please, and the group leaders flanking you, like a bodyguard, and all the others surrounding. The little ones could kneel at the front.'

'Kneeling on stone gives you housemaid's knee,' said Winnie.

'You've already got housemaid's knees,' said Avril. 'Big, puffy ones.'

'You could *crouch*,' said Ida, rustling the bag of bullseyes under Winnie's nose. The twins always seemed to end up in her charge; the most recent star on her sash had been awarded for 'commendable diplomacy'.

'You all need to squash together a bit more,' said Freda, peering down at her camera. 'That's it. And then I'll count to three and everyone should say, "Cheese".'

'Or maybe we should say "Amazons",' suggested Hildegard.

'But you hardly have to open your mouth to say "Amazons". We'd all look po-faced.'

'We could shout it,' said Mattie. 'With brio.'

'All right then. One. Two. Three.'

'AMAZONS!'

The pavement was suddenly a frieze of startled faces, all pointing in their direction.

'That was a noise all right,' said Avril, giggling. 'Like the trumpets at Jericho.' And the giggle swept through the whole group because there was something almost intoxicating about making a racket on a public street, and not having to worry about being told off; being *praised* for it, in fact.

'A splendid effort,' said Mattie. 'Now, let us cross the road towards the Embankment. If we all look both ways, it's just possible we may return to Hampstead with the same number of girls as when we left.'

Elsie O'Brien, a recent recruit from the Wilson Road flats, held on to Ida's hand as they crossed; she was a wizened little thing in a coat too large for her, gloveless, despite the cold wind, her fingers lumpy with chilblains.

'Is that the sea?' she asked.

'The *sea*?' repeated Avril, derisively.

'It's a river. The Thames,' said Ida, giving Avril a pointed look. 'And anyway, it goes down to the sea, doesn't it, so Elsie's half right.'

'I think I knew that,' said Elsie, blushing. 'But I forgot. I never saw it before.'

'*Never . . . ?*' This time, Ida got the look in early, and Avril subsided.

'When *I* seen the Thames the first time I thought it was going to wash me away,' said Bessie Pritchard, who worked on the manicure counter at Bourne and Hollingsworth, and who had won the recent Amazons' wood-chopping competition without breaking a single nail. 'I didn't know water ever moved fast like that – I'd only seen the canal before.'

'Oh,' said Avril, who was slightly in awe of Bessie.

'So let us contemplate one of London's most famous statues,' said Mattie. 'And unlike Nelson, who stands so high above the spectator that he appears as a mere dot on a pedestal, this subject seems almost to gallop among us. We are looking at Boadicea, Queen of the Iceni, scourge of the Romans, a gallant fighter, a martyr for freedom.'

'Who are the other girls in the chariot?' asked Winnie.

'Her daughters, cruelly ravished by the Romans.'

'What does "ravished" mean?'

'Treated brutally,' said Mattie, after a slight pause.

'*You can see their bosoms*,' whispered Winnie.

'The Britons fought gallantly under her command, but were finally routed by the general Suetonius Paulinus, whom, as a child, I always imagined having a face like a steamed pudding. Rather than be captured alive, Tacitus records that the Queen and her daughters took poison. Would anyone care to comment on the chariot wheels?'

'There's daggers sticking out of them.'

'Traditionally, scythes,' said Mattie. 'But yes – sharpened blades, very good. Just imagine those whirling through a cluster of Roman legs. Like an axe through rhubarb.'

There was a shriek of delighted horror.

Winnie put up her hand. 'But in the battle were they in the actual nude?'

'I think it unlikely,' said Mattie. 'Just as I deem it improbable that David felled Goliath of Gath while dancing around in his birthday suit. Sculptors, like painters, seem to prefer the depiction of naked flesh, rather than, say . . .'

'Drawers,' suggested Elsie.

'Indeed. No, I think Boadicea and her daughters would have had armour – at the very least a breastplate, to protect the most vulnerable areas of the body. I have, in the past, when anticipating rough handling, fashioned my own out of cardboard, and it has proved quite effective – we should go, now, to Parliament Square, the very site of such bruising encounters. Are you taking another photograph, Freda?'

'I wanted one of the statue,' said Freda, 'but the sky's too bright – all I can see is a silhouette.'

'What about re-creating it as a tableau?' asked Hildegard. 'I was cast in one at school, as Brutus killing Caesar. I held a kitchen knife covered in crimson lake and I had to maintain an expression of implacable hatred for nearly a minute, and people clapped an awful lot and said it was exactly like the real thing.'

'Can we do that, Miss Simpkin?'

'I think it's a rather good conceit. Would you like to be Boadicea, Hildegard?'

'Didn't Ancient Britons have red hair?' said Freda. 'I think it should be Ida.'

'What? Oh no . . .' said Ida.

'Yes, I'm more of a Roman type,' said Hildegard, rather complacently. 'You'll need to let your hair hang loose, Ida, to match the statue – and what about Winnie and Avril as the daughters?'

Winnie went scarlet. 'I won't take off . . .' she began.

'Miss Simpkin, could we borrow your mackintosh for Boadicea's cloak?' asked Freda. 'There's a bit of a breeze, and if we face the right direction, it'll fly out behind and look just right.'

And thus, Ida found herself standing on Westminster Bridge with a rolled umbrella for a spear, arms raised, hair streaming out in a wild halo, Winnie (fully dressed) to one side, Avril to the other and Miss Simpkin's oilskin rattling in the gusts. It was the most public, the most embarrassing, the most *exhilarating* thing she had ever done.

'It looks absolutely topping,' said Freda. 'Hold steady, I'll take one more.'

'Remember – fierce and commanding,' said Hildegard, just as a fat man stuck his head out of the cab of a passing lorry and shouted, 'Oi, oi, Ginger, fancy a lift?'

'A Queen with her own chariot has no need of lifts,' called Miss Simpkin.

'So, what was my name?' asked Winnie afterwards, as they walked towards the Houses of Parliament.

'I don't know,' said Ida. 'Miss Simpkin, what were the names of Boadicea's daughters?'

'I don't believe they were ever recorded. Innumerable are the unnamed women of history. Which brings us very tidily to the reason why we are here today – gather round for a moment, girls. Tomorrow, in the House of Lords, there will be a second reading of the Representation of the People Act. If it is passed, then its recommendations will almost certainly be framed in law before the year is out. And, if you remember, those recommendations are . . . ?'

'All ladies older than twenty-one will be able to vote,' said Bessie. 'The same as the men.'

'That is correct. Regardless of whether they are . . .'

'Tenants or property owners.'

'Yes.'

'Spinsters or married,' said Ida.

'Very good.'

'Tall or short,' suggested Elsie.

There was a shout of laughter. 'That, too,' said Mattie, kindly. 'But let us not forget the efforts it took to get this far. I can recall occasions – one in particular – when merely seeking to cross Parliament Square towards the Commons was enough to provoke violence or arrest.'

'Were you smashing windows there, Miss Simpkin?'

'Not on the day I am thinking of. I was part of a peaceful deputation attempting to speak to the Prime Minister. So great were the number of police officers that it took upward of an hour to cover ten yards, and there were many, many injuries – it became known as Black Friday.'

'Was you hurt, Miss Simpkin?'

'I was, though not as severely as others. And my younger brother, Angus, who was in the Men's Political Union – supporting the aims of the suffragettes – had all the fingers of his left hand broken, when a policeman repeatedly stamped on them.'

'Bloody coppers,' muttered Elsie, under her breath.

'So,' said Mattie, 'perhaps we should think of an activity that might symbolize our current freedom to pass unimpeded not only across the square, but also to the polling booth. Any suggestions?'

∽

'Three-legged relay races,' said Mattie.

'Across Parliament Square?'

'Yes. Four teams. In a closely fought final, Marie Curie pipped Elizabeth Fry at the post. I was informed that it was a "ripping" outing and Decima Cornish has decided that she would like to be the first female Prime Minister. Shall I put the kettle on?'

'Yes, please,' said The Flea. 'There is, actually, a girl here to see you about joining. I popped her in the conservatory, and I presume she's still there – I've been writing a report on the Parson Street overall workshop – the owner hasn't acted on a *single* recommendation – and I have to confess I completely forgot about her until you came back.'

It was more of a lean-to than a conservatory, but on sunny days it stored the heat wonderfully, and the girl had fallen asleep on the window-seat, her head resting against the glass. She had an unusual face, almost wider than it was long, the cheekbones very marked, the eyes aslant, like a faery from a Richard Dadd painting. Angus (still bobbing near the surface of Mattie's thoughts) had looked rather similar; they had called him Elfie as a child.

'Good afternoon,' said Mattie.

'Oh, hello.' Far from looking discomfited, the girl stretched and yawned before standing. 'Golly, I must have been here hours,' she said. She had strikingly light blue eyes, with a dark ring around the irises.

'I'm Miss Simpkin,' said Mattie, indicating a chair and herself taking a seat on the sofa. 'And what is your name?'

'Inez Campbell.'

'And how old are you, Inez?'

'Fourteen.'

'And why do you want to join the Amazons?'

The girl sat and looked at her patent-leather shoes, apparently admiring their shine, tipping her feet from side to side to send reflections scuttling across the conservatory walls.

'I don't know, really,' she said, at last. 'My stepmother said I needed to find a hobby. And I do quite like nature.'

'Excellent – we spend a great deal of time on the Heath. And what is your favourite tree?'

There was a pause. 'Laurel?'

'That's a domesticated shrub, rather than a tree.'

'Oh. Do I need to know about trees to join, then?'

133

'Not necessarily. Though, as a member, you might find yourself climbing one and you wouldn't get much of a view from the top of a laurel!'

Inez nodded inattentively, her gaze drifting around the room. If she were a horse, thought Mattie, one would advise blinkers.

'Do you like sports? Running, for instance, or swimming?'

'No, not really. We play lacrosse at school but I have weak wrists so I'm allowed to do Grecian dancing instead.'

'Do you enjoy that?'

'I think I might enjoy it more if we didn't have to wear these awfully stupid tunics. And the dance teacher is a pill.'

'What about your wider interests? Is there an ambition you cherish?'

'An ambition?'

'Yes. An achievement or career that you aspire to.'

Inez appeared to give the question some thought, using her shoes as inspiration.

'Well, in the shorter term, I've never been to Harrods; and in the longer term, I'd rather like to go on a sea cruise.'

Mattie felt as if she were trying to sharpen an India-rubber pencil.

'Could you name three women you admire?'

'I like Louise Brooks. And Dolores del Rio.'

'Perhaps someone who isn't a film actress?'

'Gladys Cooper?'

'She's a theatre actress, isn't she?'

'Yes. We saw her in *Lights over Leicester Square* last Christmas. She's very pretty. Could I ask something?'

'Of course.'

'There isn't a uniform in the Amazons, is there?'

'Not as such. The girls wear green sashes over ordinary clothes. And shoes they can run in,' she added, pointedly.

'You see, my brother's in the Empire Youth League and he has to polish his belt and buttons every week. I wouldn't like that at all.'

'I see,' said Mattie, stiffening; she had long been awaiting a spy from the other camp, though this colourless creature seemed an unlikely choice for the role of Mata Hari.

'And are there any other reasons why you would rather join the Amazons than the Empire Youth League?' she asked, dangling the bait.

'Yes, actually – they start awfully early in the League. Ralph has to leave the house at eight o'clock to be on parade. I don't get up till eleven, usually, at the weekend.'

Mattie brooded for a moment. She had never yet turned down an applicant for the Amazons, however unpromising, but there was usually *something* about the girl – a glimpse of backbone, a flicker of originality – that offered hope.

'What I'm going to suggest,' she said, 'is that over the next fortnight or so, you spend a little time deciding whether you truly wish to join a club that is dedicated to open-air activities and enthusiastic conversational interchange, or whether, perhaps, there is another hobby that might suit you better. The Amazons are a very . . . *energetic* group of girls.'

Inez nodded, apparently unruffled by the rejection. 'Actually,' she said, looking directly at Mattie for the first time, 'there was another reason why I came here.'

'And what was that?' asked Mattie, standing up and waiting for the girl to do likewise. Instead Inez leaned back in her chair.

'I just wanted to meet you,' she said.

'Why?'

'Because I know one of the Amazons from school and she told me that you were a suffragette. And so was my mother.'

'Really? What was her name?'

'Venetia Campbell.'

And all the breath seemed to leave Mattie; she gazed at the girl and for a moment she simply couldn't speak.

'Did you know her?' asked Inez.

'Yes,' said Mattie, the word emerging as a little flake of sound, like a crust of paint scratched from a wall.

'She died when I was a baby, you see, so I don't remember her at all.'

'I heard, yes . . . I heard that she'd died.'

'Did you?'

'It was not long after the war started. But I didn't know . . .'

But she couldn't possibly say what it was that she didn't know. 'I really have to go now,' she said, glancing at her wristwatch without actually seeing it; she wanted to look at Inez again, and yet could hardly bear to.

'Oh. Can I talk to you about my mother another time?'

'Come on Sunday.'

'To the Amazons?'

'Yes.' Mattie felt, for the first time in her life, as if she might faint, the edges of her vision peeling away, the centre shimmering.

'I thought you said that you wanted me to go away and think about it.'

'I've changed my mind. Please see yourself out.'

She turned her back on the girl, and left the room.

'What on earth's the matter?' asked The Flea, standing so hastily that her pen rolled across the table; Mattie's face was the colour of clay. 'Are you ill, are you in pain?'

'No.'

'But you look dreadful!'

'I've had a shock.' She gripped the back of a chair, steadying herself.

'Good God, Mattie, what's wrong? What's happened?'

'Wait.' She took a couple of deep breaths. 'Wait.' She felt dislocated, battered; the past had roared into the present and knocked her down.

'At least sit down. I'll pour you some tea.'

The cup shook in Mattie's hand.

'That girl,' she said, 'the girl you showed into the conservatory. She's the daughter of Venetia Campbell.'

'Venetia Campbell!' The Flea clapped a hand to her mouth. 'But . . . but I thought she had a son – a little chap with blond curls, I met him once.'

'And this child, too. She was only a baby when her mother died.'

'I remember hearing about the suicide. I think it might have been Aileen who told me,' said The Flea, 'but there was no mention of a baby. Of course, no one had seen her for months by that point.' She shook her head. 'What's the girl's name?'

'Inez.'

'Do you think she knows her mother actually stayed in this house?'

'I don't know. I wasn't . . . I wasn't thinking of that.'

Mattie's expression was unfamiliar to her, an inward gaze, like that of someone struggling to keep their balance.

'What is it?' asked The Flea. For it was clear that there was something more to come. Venetia Campbell had been young, and spirited – and married – and after three hunger strikes, her husband had decided she should take no further part in WSPU activities. And in 1914, she had swallowed poison, and died.

'What *is* it, Mattie?' The Flea sat down, so that she could look directly into her friend's eyes. 'Please tell me,' she said.

Mattie lifted her cup and drank its contents in one steady pull, and then set it down with such accidental force that the saucer cracked clean across.

'How stupidly clumsy of me,' she said, and then: 'Angus was her father.'

'What?'

'She's my brother's child. The second I saw her, before we had exchanged a word, I thought how much she looked like him. The shape of her face, her eyes – the resemblance is very marked. But of course, I would never have thought it anything but a coincidence if she hadn't told me her mother's name.'

'Was there . . . I mean, did you know that they . . . ?'

'I believe that they met during one of the Hyde Park assemblies and I know he came to see her later on, when she was recuperating here. I must, I'm afraid, assume they were lovers.'

'So . . .'

'Inez Campbell is my niece. Great *God*!' Saying the fact out loud seemed to treble its force — a scion, flesh of her flesh, a hand from the past, reaching out to grasp hers! Before, there had been no one, Stephen dead in one war, Angus in another, all that brilliance, all that spark and charm—

'What's she like?' asked The Flea.

'Utterly vapid,' said Mattie, euphoria punctured. 'As zestless as a marzipan lemon — goodness knows what her upbringing has been like; anti-progressive, I would imagine, any potential clearly untapped. I was, to be frank, on the brink of turning her down for the Amazons.'

'Intelligent, do you think?'

'Hard to tell. She wanted to find out more about her mother and I've asked her to come back on Sunday.' She rubbed her eyes. 'Angus's daughter,' she said, and the phrase was so new, so unlikely, that she stumbled slightly over the words.

'Do you think that your brother knew?' asked The Flea, abruptly.

'I don't know. I suppose that they may have exchanged letters.'

'And do you think she . . . ?' The Flea stopped talking and began to gather the cups.

'Do I think she killed herself because she heard about Angus's injury, and realized that he would never be capable of meeting his daughter? Or perhaps because her husband knew that the child was illegitimate?'

'It's not my place to speculate.'

'Oh, nonsense, Florrie, of course you can speculate, you have opinions and a brain. Perhaps I should have speculated myself. If I'd known there was a child, I could have . . .'

She paused. Could have *what*? Arrived at Campbell's door and demanded to inspect his new offspring? Spied on the baby-carriage? Disguised herself as a governess and infiltrated the household? No, if she had known there was a child, she could have done nothing at all.

Florrie, evidently reaching the same conclusion, busied herself at the sink.

'I'm going for a ramble,' said Mattie.

It had started to rain, and the Heath was almost empty of people. She walked fast, not stopping as she usually did to check for signs of spring unfurling at the woodland edge, or for the emergence of cygnets from the nest beside the East Pond – in fact, she scarcely looked around at all, using the uphill path as if it were a treadmill. It wasn't until a green woodpecker called from a clump of grass nearly at her feet and then shot upward like a vivid firework that she realized that she had reached the tumulus. She stopped to catch her breath; the thickly wooded mound acted as a frequent staging-post for Amazon expeditions, and also as a favourite spot for Red Indian stalking. A chosen victim (and Mattie herself had taken this role only last week) would take a random route between the trees, while a team of trackers attempted to follow soundlessly, with the aim of extracting one of the three feathers that the victim had stuck in her hair. There had been a debate as to whether Ida's brilliant team strategy – deliberate loud blundering from two team members providing distraction for silent robbery from a third – was allowable. 'Since when have Red Indians had to follow a rule book?' Avril had asked, pertly.

'Or thieves,' Ida had added.

Spindles grew around the edge of the tumulus, and Mattie reached for a branch, running her thumb over the tight green fruits; in autumn each would be a shocking pink, splitting later to reveal scarlet seeds, but they were already fully formed – winter presaged before spring had even begun, Omega and Alpha.

She let the branch whip back. No, if she had known about Inez fourteen years ago, there was nothing she could have done. But *now*, she thought – *I could do something* now.

PART 2

'I've been made a leader,' said Inez to her brother, round the half-open bedroom door. He'd been frowning over his prep, but he put the pen down and stared up at her.

'What on earth are you talking about?'

'In the Amazons. Miss Simpkin's made me one of the leaders.' She took a step or two into his room. It smelled faintly of socks, though he was a fiend for bathing. His Youth League uniform was hanging from the wardrobe door, buttons polished, their reflections freckling the opposite wall.

'So what do you have to do as leader?'

'Oh, encourage my team, and think up ideas and all that sort of thing.'

'And why were you chosen?'

'I haven't the foggiest. I'm no good at all.' She sat down on the bed, hands on her lap. 'It's silly, really,' she said.

'Nothing silly about being given responsibility. But if you don't enjoy it, you'd do better to join the League.' He was already turning back to his books. His concentration was fearsome – an hour's prep meant an hour's prep, whereas Inez found her own schoolwork stretching thinly across entire weekends.

'Miss Simpkin's always talking about our mother,' she said, 'but it's only things like "You should have seen her at such-and-such a deputation," or "She heckled the Minister for this-and-that." None of it's interesting.'

'What do you want her to say?'

Inez shrugged. Through the open window, she could hear the shouts of her half-siblings in the garden. One of them had a watering-can and was chasing the others; she could hear her stepmother laughing.

'Miss Simpkin says she'll try and find some magic-lantern slides of Mother.'

'We already have photographs of her,' said Ralph.

'Yes, but I've seen those, I know them off by heart. I want some new ones.'

She took off her shoes and lay flat on the counterpane. Above her, a strand of cobweb stirred in the warm breeze.

'Collins isn't cleaning properly,' said Inez. 'I'll have to tell Mama.'

Her gaze wandered across the ceiling, noting odd flaws in the plasterwork, a fine crack in the cornice. She had pored over the few images of her mother to the same obsessive degree, to the extent that she could no longer register the whole, only tiny details: a gilt clock in the background of the wedding picture, the blur of her brother's foot in his christening photograph. In each, her mother's expression was as formal as an engraving on a coin; one could learn nothing from it.

Miss Simpkin, by contrast, had a face as readable as a penny newspaper, enthusiasm and exasperation, encouragement and the odd gust of rage chasing across her features. 'Thar she blows!' some of the bolder girls would whisper, as Mattie sounded off about Mussolini, or dogs with docked tails, or vegetarians. She had visibly never taken the oft-repeated advice of the 'Ask Althea' page of *Health and Beauty* (to which Inez always turned first) that, if you wanted to avoid wrinkles, you should eschew both laughter and frowns.

There had been occasions, though, when Inez had caught Mattie looking at her with a very odd expression; some of the other girls had spotted it, too. 'It's as if she's met you before but can't remember where,' Hildegard had said. It was peculiar; but then, of course, Miss Simpkin *was* peculiar. Normal people stayed indoors when it rained, and thought that nice stockings were important; they didn't sing in public, they didn't pick up frogs and tell you about Greek plays.

Inez rolled over and lifted her arms. 'I wonder if our mother had slim wrists?' she said, admiring her own. That was the sort of thing she wanted to know: the detail, the filling-in of blanks. She thought of her mother as one of those paper ladies that she'd cut out as a child, standing in their underwear on a cardboard base, waiting to be coloured and dressed. Her father wouldn't ever discuss her in any detail ('It wouldn't be fair on Mama') and all that Miss Simpkin offered were speech balloons. 'No taxation without representation,' said the paper mother. 'I'm a thoroughly committed member of the cadre.'

There was a shout from somewhere in the house, and then footsteps taking the stairs two at a time.

'It's Simeon,' said Ralph, and Inez sat up quickly and smoothed her skirt. She liked Ralph's friend.

147

'Hello, people,' said Simeon. 'Been polishing your buttons, Ralph? They're absolutely blinding me.'

'Let the outer man reflect the inner man. Yours were a disgrace last week – didn't RC make you run twice round the lake as a punishment?'

'A punishment for me, a treat for all observers – as I'm sure you're aware, when I run, I look exactly like a gazelle.'

'You talk such rot,' said Ralph. 'Give me five minutes to finish this and then I'll be with you.'

Simeon exaggeratedly put his finger to his lips, and then sat on the bed quite close to Inez. The whole side of her body seemed to change temperature.

'How are you, Eeny?' he asked.

'Quite well,' she said, tilting her head down so that she was looking up at him through her lashes (another tip from 'Ask Althea').

'What's wrong? Have you hurt your neck?'

'No!' Quickly, she straightened her head again and tried to assume an expression of rapt interest (*Widen the eyes and lean forward slightly*). 'Are you two going out somewhere?' she asked.

'Thought we might head off for a swim.'

'I've just come back from the Amazons. Ralph thinks I should stop going and join the League instead. What do *you* think?'

'Oh Lord, don't ask me for an opinion,' said Simeon, leaning back against the wall with his hands behind his head. 'I only go because my father said it might help me get into Cambridge. Ralph's your man of politics.'

'He thinks Miss Simpkin's a Communist sympathizer.'

'What, the old baggage? I tell you what, if she storms the barricades, they'll certainly stay stormed. She's a one-woman battalion.'

He really was ridiculously good-looking, thought Inez – like the hero of a romantic novel, hair the requisite colour of ripe wheat, eyes a proper, deep blue, not the washed-out shade of her own.

'I wouldn't like to wear a uniform, though,' she said. 'I think perhaps uniforms don't suit girls very well.'

She'd been hoping for a compliment ('Depends on the girl') but Simeon only nodded. 'As a matter of fact, I saw some of your lot on the Heath last week,' he said. 'Waving flags on Parliament Hill.'

'We were supposed to be learning semaphore,' said Inez.

'I gathered that. I stopped to tell them about the wonders of the modern telephonic system and one of the girls was awfully snappy with me.'

'I wonder who it was?'

'She had red hair.'

'That's Ida,' said Inez. 'She's another one of the leaders.'

'Bit of a looker, I thought.'

Inez felt as if she'd been kicked.

'She's Miss Simpkin's char-lady,' she said, stiffly.

'Really?' he seemed amused rather than shocked. 'Goodness, how very *socialist*. And what's she like?'

For once, he was looking straight at her, and with interest, but only because he wanted to know about *Ida*.

149

'Common,' said Inez. 'She ties her plaits with string.'

'Right. Done,' said Ralph. He carefully screwed the lid back on his fountain pen and then stood and stretched. His profile, silhouetted against the window, looked exactly like that of their father. 'Shall we go?' The invitation was to Simeon only. The boys clattered off downstairs and Inez could hear them talking to Mama in the hall; there was chaffing and laughter.

'Inez, the little ones are going to bathe the puppy, do you want to help?' called Mama.

'No thank you. Maybe later.'

'But they're not going to do it later, they're filling the tub now!'

As ever, her stepmother's voice bounced with good humour, all set for the type of child who giggled and cheeked; she had never grasped that some people were different, that some people preferred to be left alone.

'I have a bit of a headache,' called Inez.

'Would you like me to bring you up a powder?'

'No thank you.'

'Or some lemonade?'

'No, I'll just . . .' She lay back on Ralph's bed again. She often had days like today, days when she thought she might literally die of boredom and yet could think of no event or encounter that might alleviate the condition, days when she felt entirely hollow, like a plaster cast – or a ship without ballast, heeling slowly on a windless sea. 'Draw on your passions, girls,' urged the school drama mistress, a woman who wove her own scarves. 'Close your eyes and think of a time when you were burning with rage, or bubbling with delight,' and Inez, eyes half shut, could recollect nothing stronger than the irritation occasioned by a mislaid brooch, or the mild satisfaction of finding it again.

Linking her hands behind her head, she lay and listened to the shrieks of the children.

≪∽≫

'And in biology we watched a rat being cut up,' said Ida, pausing with the silver polish in one hand and a fork in the other. 'Dissected,' she added. 'One of the boys nearly fainted, they had to lean him up against the wall.'

'And what did you think?' asked The Flea.

'It was so *tidy*,' said Ida, a sense of wonder still adhering to the memory. 'The way the insides fitted in, there was no gaps. *Were* no gaps. And it looked just like the inside of humans in the classroom picture, only smaller. I hadn't expected that. I thought it would be . . . I don't know . . . a mess, like blood and worms.' She looked up, sharply, in case she'd shocked Miss Lee, and actually caught her smiling. 'I haven't told my auntie,' she said. 'If she knew I was looking at rats she'd have me bleached. And in English we're reading *The Merchant of Venice*.' Her tone was suddenly glum.

'I always found Shakespeare terribly difficult to understand. Miss Simpkin is the one who – ah, Mattie!'

'Yes?' said Mattie, entering the kitchen at speed.

'Ida's reading *The Merchant of Venice* in her continuation class.'

151

'I had to stand up and be that Shylock last week,' said Ida. 'I had to pretend the blackboard rubber was a knife.'

'Very good. Now, Ida, could you help me find something?' asked Mattie. 'I'm looking for a notebook bound in red morocco. Foolscap. Though I think the spine may be cracked, so it might be difficult to spot on a shelf. It's not in the study or the drawing room, so could you check the bedrooms while I look in the conservatory?'

She sped out again, clipping the kitchen door as she went so it smacked against the cupboard. There was a short, surprised pause.

'What's foolscap?' asked Ida, standing.

'It's a reference to the size of the paper.' The Flea gestured a dimension, and then stood frowning as Ida left the kitchen. There had been several occasions lately when she had witnessed Mattie missing a chance to educate or to quote or explain; her friend's focus seemed to have narrowed, as if previously she had scanned the horizon with the naked eye and was now using a telescope.

Last week, she'd not responded to a call to supper, and The Flea had found her sitting in the darkened study, torch in hand, the lecture boxes on the desk in front of her.

'I'm searching through the procession pictures,' she'd said, tilting a slide so that a swathe of white-clad figures blossomed across the wall.

'That's Emily's funeral.'

'Yes. I'm almost certain that Venetia Campbell was one of the lily carriers. Do you remember if that were the case?' She placed the slide on the desk and reached for another.

'Mattie, you're going to get them mixed up!' The exclamation came out as a reprimand; The Flea took a breath. 'I have a precise order for the slides; I sometimes wonder if you fully appreciate how difficult it is to keep up with your continual changes of topic.'

'Then I shall try to be more careful,' said Mattie, unoffended. She picked up the discarded slide, and slotted it back into place.

'So are you coming for supper?' asked The Flea.

'A cold collation?'

'Brawn and salad.'

'In that case I may carry on here for a while. Now that I've started.'

The Flea had ended up eating alone, a book in front of her. She had checked the slides the day after, and discovered several out of place.

'Found it!' shouted Mattie. 'Ida? I've found it.'

She heard a distant acknowledgement, and then the girl's rapid footsteps coming down the stairs and heading back towards the kitchen.

The notebook had been hidden among piano music on the lowest shelf in the conservatory, tucked between 'Folk Songs of Ireland' and 'White Lilacs: A Rhapsody'.

It was years since she had re-read its contents – or even thought of them – but lately she'd been having dreams of her childhood home, vivid and surreal; she had woken this morning from one in which Inez had walked into the nursery with fourteen-year-old Angus by her side; twins, separated by time. The image had clung to her for hours

153

afterwards, muffling the present. Still kneeling beside the shelves, she opened the book. The black ink had dulled to brown, but the handwriting was firm and legible.

My first words were 'I sha'n't.'

She had written it at Angus's bedside. The world had been at senseless war, the rooms around her filled with blinded, blunted youth, and her own fight, that single decent cause, that decade of fierce comradeship, had been thrown aside by the very people who'd initiated the struggle. She'd felt unable to look ahead; instead she had turned back.

My first words were 'I sha'n't'. This was according to my older brother, Stephen, and since, from an early age, he possessed the meticulous observational skills and rigorous honesty of a born scientist, there is no reason to doubt the memory. I will say on my behalf that the words were spoken as a correction rather than a defiance.

The occasion was a rural walk in search of blackberries; it was a cold day in early September, and the nursery-maid who was pushing my baby-carriage soon tired of the keen wind. 'Master Stephen,' she said (bear in mind that we are talking about that long-ago decade, the '70s), 'we can go and get blackberries tomorrow. If we stay out any longer, your sister will start crying.'

'I sha'n't,' I said – the sentence was apparently spoken with great clarity and conviction. The expedition continued and I remained placid and tearless.

My words were prescient. Cold winds never did make me

cry; nor bee stings, nor blisters, nor purulent tonsils, nor (as I grew older) scoldings, nor smackings, nor the forbidding of treats nor the cancellation of rewards. A familial physical strength (inherited from my father), together with the conviction of my own beliefs (at this point, limited to schoolroom affairs and the strained pursuit of 'fairness'), always sustained me, like a splint on an injured limb. If I ever cried, I cried about other matters.

The writing had come easily; she had not had to delve for memories – the past had seemed to sit all around her, waiting to be plucked.

Stephen and I read constantly and indiscriminately, moving through the contents of our father's small library like pigs in an orchard. There are children who believe that their own house is the world, but we were the opposite – we strained to look beyond the walls, and we peopled the dull, flat Bedfordshire countryside with imagined marvels.

Even our Sunday reading (which was required to be 'improving') could be searched for plums. Besides the Bible, and a child's guide to the Psalms, there was a thrillingly bloody Lives of the Saints, *a hymnal, stuffed with marvellous language ('the horned moon doth shine by night, mid her spangled sisters bright'), and a queasily virtuous collection of stories entitled* Little Emmie and Her Dollie, *in which Little Emmie explained to her toy why she should not procrastinate, dissemble, contradict, rage or covet, in such a way as to make that collection of vices appear peculiarly attractive. There was also a volume by Thomas Fuller. The title of this*

(Sermons) was not tempting, recalling the watery weekly homilies of the local parson, but the prose within was clear and vigorous. One could chew on its content, as on a mouthful of good steak. I loved one parable in particular:

> The Sidonian servants agreed amongst themselves to choose him to be their king, who, that morning, should be the first to see the sun. Whilst all others were gazing on the east, one alone looked on the west. Some admired, more mocked him, as if he looked on the feet, there to find the eye of the face. But he first of all discovered the light of the sun shining on the tops of the houses.
>
> God is seen sooner, easier, clearer in His operations than in His essence, best beheld by reflection in His creatures.

As a young girl, this story suggested to me a second meaning, beyond the religious. One of the servants had chosen to do the opposite of all the others, and that servant had been right. Like the thin vibration of a pane of glass chiming with the thrumming note of a piano, the action rang something within my heart.

In the mornings, we shared lessons with our governess, Miss Gibbons. In the afternoons, Stephen was tutored in science and mathematics by an elderly doctor of our family's acquaintance, while I was instructed in more ladylike arts. Sitting with my mother in the drawing room, we awaited visitors; amidst the vividness of my childhood memories, these afternoons are a series of blank pages. Time crawled, as if treacle had been poured into the clock. Ladies came, they drank tea, discussed matters of dreadful blandness (servants figured largely) and then went away again. In that era of Mayhew, Nightingale, Bell and Burton, no wider issues or broader horizons were ever mentioned; there might have been no world beyond Bedford. I was encouraged to speak, but vehement opinions were frowned upon, nor was I allowed a book or a toy as a way of passing the time — my only permitted activity was sewing, for which I lacked the slightest talent. I remember my mother sadly examining a hemmed dishcloth, which sported a blood spot for every stitch.

I use the word 'sadly' without facetiousness — my poor mother was infused with sadness, though a badly sewn dishcloth hardly ranked beside the other tragedies of her life. Stephen was her second child; her first-born son had died of a fever and, in the years following my own appearance, she lost three more infants, all born prematurely. I was allowed to see one, a girl, who had lived just long enough to be christened. She lay in her basket, bonneted and beribboned, a pathetic waxen miniature. I never cared for dolls after that.

This, then, was my mother's life: a drawing room and a series of little hopes, each quickly snatched away, each eroding her already weak constitution, and when, at last (many years later), my brother Angus was born, robust and blooming, she did not long survive the birth.

To Stephen and to me, she was kind, but distracted, as if perpetually listening for those other children, whose voices she would never hear. I wondered sometimes if she could quite see me, and I'd court her gentle protest by talking loudly or 'galumphing' around the room, just as a proof of my presence. It was difficult for me to believe that in her youth she had ridden and sailed; her spirit had dwindled, so that what Stephen and I saw was like a candle stub – a wisp of smoke, where once there had been a flame.

My father would generally return home very late in the evening, long after we children were asleep; he was a private banker who managed the money of some of Bedford's more affluent inhabitants, and on his rare holidays, he seemed vaguely disconcerted by our presence, as if he had forgotten, in the interim, that he had any children.

'And what have you learned this week?' he would ask Stephen, snapping open his newspaper as he spoke, and nodding absently at the subsequent answers. 'Mattie has learned things, too,' Stephen would say, loyally. 'She knows all the battles in the Wars of the Roses.'

But demonstrations of my knowledge were rarely requested, and we would soon drift away from the study, our departure unremarked. It was hard for either of us to please my father, not because he was harsh or exacting, but because he was one of those beings (surprisingly common) for whom infants are only poorly formed adults, creatures that require full growth before they are recognizable. He took no pleasure in childishness.

So my brother and I were left largely to our own devices, a family within a family, building our own traditions and enterprises, sui generis. We were the best of friends, the jolliest of companions – twin flints, striking sparks off each other, never lonely and never bored. It did not occur to me that this might ever change.

Then, when I was nine, and Stephen twelve, he was sent away to school.

The words began to judder and blur, and with a start, Mattie realized that her nose was almost touching the paper; the sun had shifted, leaving the conservatory in shade. She stood up, a noise like that of a pepper grinder emanating from both knees, and pulled the basket chair over to the French windows. The grass was in need of its first trim of the year; lady's mantle frothed over the edge of the beds and the leaves of the spent daffodils were waiting to be looped and knotted. Small tasks were accumulating.

I don't think that I fully believed that Stephen was leaving for school until the station dogcart disappeared from view and at that moment I felt as if my heart had been replaced with an anvil. I fell into a dark, flat mood that evened out all pleasures and sorrows; everything I saw, from a goldfinch to a firework, seemed filtered through the same grey lens. Stephen wrote to me but I had nothing to write in return; sorrow makes for dull prose.

I was told that Miss Gibbons would be leaving (it not being deemed economical to retain her for the sake of one pupil), and that henceforth I would be sharing lessons with two sisters who lived nearby, and whom I knew slightly from Sunday School. Both girls were younger than me and neither had the slightest interest in any subject beyond the colour of their hair ribbons. Our conversations contained as much mutual comprehension as those between an Alpine goatherd and a South Sea Islander and incomprehension

*quickly led to dislike. I, who had never quarrelled, became
quick-tempered and defiant. I was set the same tasks as the
sisters, but would finish my work long before them and then
sit with my arms folded and my eyes shut, trying by sheer
force of will to project myself elsewhere. I do not know where
I stumbled across this idea – many years later, when I read
the short stories of Mr H. G. Wells, I recognized the same
fictive device – but I fancied that if I could picture another
place strongly enough, then when I opened my eyes I might
find myself there.*

*One day I was sitting thus, imagining the sea at Herne
Bay – the water foaming over my bare feet as I paddled with
Stephen, the cold sting of the wind, the sharp sands underfoot, the shock of one's sole landing on the sliding dome of a
jellyfish; all these sensations combining to give a feeling of
the most spectacular vitality – and then I opened my eyes to
see the little schoolroom and the somnolent faces of my fellow
pupils. Something seemed to crack within me, and what
emerged was the nearest to a waking vision that I have ever
experienced. The world seemed to shrink, to tighten around
me like a straitjacket, restricting my breathing, blackening
my vision, and I ran from the room, through the sisters'
house and out into their orchard, flailing at the air.*

*It was Miss Pett who followed and caught me: Miss Pett,
the girls' governess, a woman I had scarcely considered until
then. Dusty in appearance, spare of speech and lacking Miss
Gibbons' firm invigilation, she read when not instructing
us, the book held close to her face.*

*She sat me down in the wooden summer house at the bot-
tom of the garden and extracted my story in the manner of a*

dentist removing a tooth, before applying therapeutic wadding in the form of literature. 'I believe that you are bored,' she stated, adding, 'Boredom corrodes the soul, and the will.' Before this moment, I had chosen my reading at random; Miss Pett drew me up a list, the bulk of it the finest English prose and poetry, though with entertaining novels scattered like cherries among the good bread. A few of the books she owned, but the majority she borrowed from the public library; when I had read a volume, I would be required to memorize the first and last pages, and to write a summary of the contents. A tick would then be applied to the list and the next book substituted.

As a method of teaching it lacked variety, but it pummelled my intellect and meant that I dreamed no more during lessons.

The other half of the cure was effected by myself. I craved fresh air, as a sailor craves tobacco, and since, as a young lady, I was not permitted to roam alone, I dragged our bulky and placid collie from its place on the mat and walked it into sleek health, via every path that I had ever roamed with Stephen. And all this gave me subject matter for my letters to him, so that when he came home for the holidays we had no unfamiliarity to steer through, but could resume our conversation as if the gap of a few months had merely been a pause for breath.

And what of Miss Pett, who loosed me from that stifled nightmare, the interpretation of which scarcely requires the skills of Dr Freud? The truth is that I never knew anything about her; that first confidence did not lead to others and, *after another year, she left for a position on the south coast, supposedly for her health's sake; as a farewell present she left me a copy of* Middlemarch *(then quite recently published), inscribed with no more than her name, Sophia Pett. But I have no doubt that her job as tutor bored her, that she had a brain fit for greater things, that she was lonely, that she lived on very little and faced an old age of desperate penury, and that her prospects had been hobbled since birth as a consequence of her class, her background, her appearance and − most of all − her sex.*

I know this because England was then awash with Miss Petts; women with the ability − and the desire − to achieve far more than their position allowed. Below her in social rank were the mill-girls and servants, condemned to menial and relentless labour, and above her were the wives and daughters of gentlemen, condemned to do precisely nothing at all. In a mighty industrial and scientific power, where every means was harnessed to the pursuit of progress, the brains of fully half the population were allowed to wither. It is hard to think of a more terrible accusation to level against those in power.

'You'll strain your eyes,' said The Flea, snapping on the light. 'I've brought you tea and a scone.'

'Thank you.' Mattie straightened up; for a few seconds, the conservatory seemed less familiar to her than her childhood home.

'So what's in the notebook?'

'My memoir.'

'Your memoir?' The Flea was astonished. 'I had no idea!'

'Started long ago and never completed.'

'But why ever not?'

Mattie hesitated. 'I found the task . . . counterproductive.' She could remember the precise moment that she had stopped writing. Angus, propped up on pillows, had slipped sideways, and she had risen to help him and had seen, revealed by his disarranged pyjama jacket, the burn on his shoulder incurred by a childhood accident. She had written about that accident just days before, her recollection of it both detailed and panoramic, but now, she realized, *now*, she could recall it only from the single angle of her prose; in a moment of horrid clarity, she saw that each memory she had pinned to the page had become fixed and lifeless, the colours already fading. She was narrowing her past to a series of sepia vignettes, her brothers as footnotes to her own life.

'Well, I think it's a shame,' said The Flea.

Mattie began to leaf ahead through the remaining pages. 'It has occurred to me that I should see what I wrote about Angus when he was a child.'

'Do you have a particular aim in mind?'

'A direction, perhaps, rather than an aim. Inez is not easy to engage in conversation; to be frank, I have yet to ascertain where her interests lie.'

'Well, you can hardly regale her with anecdotes about her real father!'

The Flea's voice was shrill; Mattie looked up in surprise.

'Obviously not. I'm merely wondering if I might find a resemblance beyond the visual. A connection. A chink in the wall through which I could whistle.'

She saw the word 'Angus' on a page, and started to read. When she looked up again, The Flea had gone.

∽

'You don't look quite the thing,' said Alice Channing to The Flea. 'She doesn't look quite the thing, does she, Ethelwynne?'

'What's that?'

'The Flea! She doesn't look *quite* the *thing*.'

Ethelwynne Cripps broke off from unscrewing a Thermos and gave The Flea a long, professional stare.

'Pale,' she said.

'I had a bout of illness a few weeks back,' said The Flea. 'I caught rather a nasty fever from a baby I was looking after, but I'm better now.'

'I hadn't noticed the pallor,' said Alice. 'It's more your expression.'

'What's wrong with my expression?'

'You look as if you're under strain, dear. Worried. Is anything wrong – is Mattie quite well? I'm disappointed she couldn't come this evening.'

'Yes, perfectly well. We're both perfectly well. She's taking advantage of the weather to camp out with her girls' club.'

'It's certainly glorious.'

Within the sheltered brick box of Soho Square it was as balmy as midsummer, boys lying on the grass in their shirtsleeves, girls in bright weekend dresses, an ice-cream cart beside the gates. Alice had bagged a bench at the centre, and the three of them were sitting in a row, rather as they had once done in the offices of the WSPU, Alice, now as then, bright-eyed and bursting with gossip, Ethelwynne more taciturn, her long, heavy-featured face reminiscent of an Easter Island statue.

'What's the title of the lecture?' asked The Flea, hoping to change the subject.

'What's that?' asked Ethelwynne, cupping a hand to her ear. A straw-hatted girl, sitting on the grass close by, nudged her friend, and they both giggled.

'The title of the *lecture*,' repeated The Flea, more clearly, aiming a chilly look at the girls.

' "The Future of Civilization",' said Alice. 'To be honest, I'm not certain it'll be up to much, but I was given free tickets. Tea?'

The Flea tried to drink without tasting; Alice routinely dried and re-used tea leaves, reflecting both her tiny income as writer of leaflets for the Radical Thought Society and her life-long commitment to frugality. Ethelwynne, who had always spurned tact, and whose voice had been loud even before she was deafened by a shell burst while nursing on the Western Front, said, 'Bilge water,' and tipped the contents of her mug into a flower-bed.

'Before you arrived,' said Alice, 'we were talking about Mrs Pankhurst. You have heard that she's been dreadfully unwell, haven't you?'

'Yes.'

'Well, I'm afraid that the news is very bad indeed, there really isn't any hope . . . I was told by Annie Taylor yesterday that there's already talk of funeral plans. Rather morbid, but I suppose necessary – it would be an historic occasion.'

'I shan't be going,' boomed Ethelwynne.

'I know that, dear.'

'She betrayed us. Turned on a sixpence when the war began, one moment equal franchise, the next handing out white feathers.'

'But Ettie, dear, without her fire and her gung-ho, where would we be? Still signing petitions. Still writing letters. Still waiting to be noticed.'

'And *then* she joined the Tories,' said Ethelwynne, undeflected. 'And opened a teashop. In France.'

'Nevertheless . . .' said The Flea, thinking of that frail figure, already in her fifties at the height of militancy, who had yet survived repeated arrest, assault and starvation; it seemed almost miraculous that she had gone on to live any sort of life beyond the cause – it was still, in fact, hard to think of her without a surge of anxiety; one had always wanted to protect her, to rush to her aid, to carry her to safety . . .

'Nevertheless, I would want to pay my respects,' she said, 'though of course I can't speak for Mattie.'

'No one ever could,' said Alice. 'That's part of her splendour. How are we for time? Ah! A quarter of an hour.' She dipped into her bag and took out a piece of scarlet-and-blue tapestry-work, and re-threaded a needle. 'It's going to be a firescreen for a sale-of-work,' she said, at The Flea's enquiry. 'I've found I can charge as much as a guinea if I choose a patriotic theme. So do tell Mattie that I'm managing very well, and there's really no need for her to keep sending me brandy and hams, as if I'm the parish pauper.'

'Which patriotic subject in particular?' asked Ethelwynne, tilting her head to try to identify the design.

'Britannia,' said Alice. 'Who else?'

❧

'I say!' called an elderly man with a querulous voice and a Pomeranian on a lead. 'There's no camping allowed on the Heath.'

'I see no tent,' said Mattie, lifting a straw palliasse from the handcart that she'd borrowed from the greengrocer. 'Hands up any girl who is concealing a tent about her person. No? Winnie, is that guilt I see writ large on your features?'

'It's chocolate, Miss Simpkin.'

Hildegard, unrolling a length of oilcloth beneath the trees, gave a shriek of laughter.

'There we have it,' said Mattie to the man. 'No tents here.'

'You're splitting hairs. You clearly have the intention of spending the night in this copse.'

'And since *sleeping* on the Heath is not an offence, I fail to see wherein lies the problem.'

The man turned rather red, as men so often did when faced with unassailable logic. 'You're a very disputatious woman,' he said, as if that were a slur.

'I am merely countering your allegations.'

'There are Heath by-laws.'

'Which I know by heart. I assure you we shall be breaking none of them.'

Her accuser made a noise which sounded remarkably like 'Harrumph,' and then turned away, the dog staring at Mattie for a moment longer before its head was jerked round by the lead.

'Incidentally, his collar is too tight,' called Mattie.

There was no reply.

'What sort of dog *is* that?' asked Freda. 'It looks like a feather duster.'

'A Pomeranian – a German breed. I believe that Queen Victoria owned one. Inez, you take this one,' she said, holding out another palliasse. 'The straw inside is rather impacted, I'm afraid.'

'Did you ever meet Queen Victoria, Miss Simpkin?'

'No, Bessie, though I once saw her in the distance, travelling in an open carriage.'

'But if you ever *had* met her, what would you've said to her?'

'That's a remarkably interesting question,' said Mattie, pausing. 'And a good discussion point. Let's give these mattresses a thorough shake – take one between two, girls, and try not to breathe too deeply – and while we do so, let's each think of an historical personage to whom we would like to have spoken, and decide what we would have asked them. To Queen Victoria, I would have said, "Your Majesty, as indisputably the most powerful woman in the world, please explain to me your unswerving opposition to the female vote."'

'What, she was against it?'

'Implacably. She referred to Women's Rights as a mad, wicked folly, to which I would have replied, in the words of Dryden, "Great wits are sure to madness near allied, and thin partitions do their bounds divide." And what would you have asked her, Bessie?'

'I would've said, "How do you keep that tiny little crown on top of your head?"'

The laughter startled a pair of wood-pigeons; Inez ducked as they clattered past.

'I'm afraid I can't sleep on this,' she said to Mattie.

'Keep shaking it, and you'll find it softens. So, which historical figure would you most wish to have spoken to?'

Inez shrugged. 'I've no idea. It's not so much the hardness' – she let her end of the mattress drop, leaving Ida supporting it on her own – 'it's the awful smell that comes out when you shake it. I shan't be able to lie down on that.'

'Once it's covered with a blanket, you won't notice. Perhaps you'd like to start collecting kindling instead? I'm sure you'd enjoy building the fire.'

'*I'd* talk to Florence Nightingale,' said Ida. 'I'd ask her—'

'But I don't have anything to put the sticks in,' said Inez.

'Here, take this.' Mattie handed her a basket. 'And now, the rest of us should start arranging these mattresses in a semicircle.'

'I'd choose Henry the Eighth,' said Freda. 'But I wouldn't talk to him, I'd just kick him in the shins.'

The applause at the end of the lecture was muted, and the audience began to disperse in near-silence.

'I'm certainly glad the tickets were free,' said Ethelwynne loudly, re-pinning her hat. 'Were you actually asleep, Alice?'

'No, not asleep. Mentally composing my next leaflet. What did you think, Florrie?'

'I'm certainly a little disappointed that the Future of Civilization promises to be quite so dull.'

Alice gave a hiccup of a laugh. 'Yes, a flying motor-car or two might have been welcome.'

'Also a speaker who didn't repeatedly swallow the end of his sentences,' announced Ethelwynne, pursing her lips in imitation of the lecturer's. '"My talk will be divided into two parts – firstly, the likely form of universal governance and, secondly, the *mimble mimble mimble mimble*."'

'How awfully rude,' said a man in the row behind. 'Professor Adams is *highly respected* in forward-thinking circles.'

'More likely semicircles,' said Alice, 'if only half of what he says is audible.'

Ethelwynne's laugh, a wild staccato, rarely heard but never forgotten, turned every head in the hall, and The Flea put a hand over her own mouth in a vain effort not to join in and almost ran, hunched over, towards the exit, faint squeaks escaping between her fingers. A dishevelled Alice joined her shortly, puce in the face, and then Ethelwynne arrived too, dabbing at her eyes, her voice a quavering ghost of its usual self.

'Oh, good *Heavens*, just look at us! Professional women

behaving like hooligans. If any of my probationers saw me now . . .'

The Flea shook her head, her lips still wobbling – she felt as if she'd been turned inside out, like a glove; unfamiliar muscles twanged. 'It's a long time since I . . .'

'Yes, me, too – years,' said Alice. 'Years and years.' She let out a sudden, final whinny.

'I would like a *proper* cup of tea,' said Ethelwynne. 'Shall we go to the Lyons on New Oxford Street?'

'And yet,' said Alice, straightening her coat, 'I used to laugh like this all the time – even in Holloway, that's the extraordinary thing. Mattie would sometimes have me howling, I'd have to throw my apron over my face so that the warders wouldn't see . . .'

'Mattie hasn't been quite herself,' said The Flea, the words taking advantage of her weakened state and emerging before she could stop them – though she felt instant relief, as if a boil had burst.

'Really? Not herself in what way?'

'A new girl called Inez Campbell has joined the Amazons, and it transpires' – The Flea paused for a second, steadying herself so that she wouldn't blurt out the impermissible – 'it transpires that she's Venetia Campbell's daughter.'

'Venetia! One of the Young Hot-Bloods! Oh, that was terribly sad, of course. She was a suicide at the start of the war, wasn't she? So does the daughter take after her?'

'No. And she's not at all like the other Amazons, either. She has no enthusiasm – no spirit – and yet Mattie's so determined to make something of her. Inez *preoccupies* her;

she seems to think of little else. The effect is . . . is . . .'
Like the banking of a fire, she thought, or the muffling of
a bell. 'The effect is deadening.'

There was a short silence.

'Odd,' said Alice.

'Am I my brother's keeper?' said Ethelwynne, sonorously.

'Whatever do you mean?' asked The Flea.

'Mattie's brother Angus – Venetia Campbell was one of
his many conquests. It may be playing on her mind.'

'Oh yes, *Angus*,' said Alice, with significance.

The Flea looked from one of them to the other.

'You didn't know?' asked Alice. 'He was a fearful
womanizer.'

'No – I never met him. And Mattie hasn't ever hinted
that he—'

'Oh, I don't suppose she ever saw that side of him. Or
perhaps she was simply blind to his behaviour – she doted
on him. Of course, one mustn't forget that she almost
brought him up.'

'I didn't know that,' said Ethelwynne.

'I suppose it was because we were locked up together,'
said Alice. 'We all knew one another's life stories – gassed
non-stop whenever we got the chance, which wasn't
often. And then, of course, since the war, Mattie doesn't
have any family left, does she?'

'She has a distant cousin,' said The Flea, 'in Kentish
Town.'

'Really? Is he *simpatico*?'

'He's a rate collector and a member of the Conservative
Party.'

'Ah. Well, to get back to the gist, their own mother died shortly after giving birth to Angus, when Mattie was already quite grown-up – sixteen, I think – and all set to fly the nest, though her parents didn't know that. She was secretly studying for a scholarship, you see, to follow her older brother to Oxford – terribly daring in those days – and then suddenly there was a motherless babe in the house and no question of Mattie leaving. I think she was in her mid-twenties when she finally went to Somerville – Angus was away at school by then. And her older brother was a physician, wasn't he?'

'A surgeon,' corrected The Flea. 'With the Red Cross.'

'Killed in the Boer War, another awful tragedy – and he was a fine man, an exceptional man, by all accounts. So then only Angus was left. Her baby brother.'

'Young women fell for him like *nine-pins*,' said Ethelwynne. 'Simply toppled over.'

'I mean, he wasn't entirely a bad lot,' said Alice. 'He helped the cause. Adored his sister. Was sent to the Scrubs after Black Friday. But one couldn't help wondering . . .'

'. . . if he were actually on the side of women, or merely in a place where he could meet a great many of them,' said Ethelwynne, with severity. 'I think Venetia fell for him awfully heavily.'

There was a pause.

'This daughter,' added Ethelwynne. 'When was she born?'

The fire had died down a little and the sausages were being digested when a white shape, swift and formless, moved at head height across the clearing.

'It's not a ghost!' shouted Mattie, over the screaming. 'And there is an extra sausage, only very slightly burned, for anyone who can accurately name the creature.'

'It *was* a ghost.'

'No, Elsie, I promise you it was a bird.'

'An eagle?'

'No, an owl.'

'But owls are brown.'

'Tawny owls are brown. This was a barn owl, otherwise known as—'

A thin shriek, suggestive of a small child being murdered, pierced the air.

'—a screech owl. As you can hear. And, of course, it's one of the easiest bird calls to imitate. Shall we all attempt it?'

A banshee chorus swelled monstrously and then died away and, for a moment, only the barking of every dog in Hampstead was audible. A branch cracked in the fire, sending up a bloom of sparks.

'I'd still quite like to go home,' said Inez, for the third time. Ida, sharing her mattress, muttered, 'Why don't you, then?', but quite softly, so that Miss Simpkin wouldn't hear.

In the firelight, Mattie was thinking, Inez's profile was more than ever like that of Angus. And yet, in this situation – a fire, the stars, a wild freedom – her brother's face would have been animated, full of mischief. He had loved building fires, had loved spectacle and danger – in fact, it had been an experiment with a home-made Roman candle that had resulted in the scarring to his shoulder. (Mattie had never forgotten the horror of glancing out of the window and seeing green-and-pink flames spurting from Angus's shirt.) But despite having been put in charge of the fire, Inez was looking bored; as Mattie watched, she listlessly dropped a dried pine cone into the flames, barely glancing as it spat and curled, the air suddenly resinous.

'I saw a ghost once,' said Hildegard. 'In our school.'

'Please describe exactly what you witnessed,' said Freda, who had recently decided that she wanted to be a barrister, and was practising courtroom technique whenever possible.

'Well, I didn't actually *see* it. I was in the sick room, waiting for Matron – I had a ghastly sore throat – and all of a sudden the door slammed shut, with no draught and nobody there to slam it, and somebody told me afterwards that it was the ghost of a girl in the Lower Fourth who'd died.'

'Died of what?'

'No one knows, though someone said that the Matron they had then was a drunkard, and she locked the girl in the room when she was blotto and then completely forgot about her, and it was the school holidays, and the girl starved to death.'

'Doesn't sound very likely.'

'And if the girl got locked in, wouldn't the ghost try to *open* the door and not slam it?' asked Ida.

'Good point,' said Freda. 'I don't believe in ghosts.'

'I do,' said Elsie, her face solemn. 'Have you ever seen a ghost, Miss Simpkin?'

'No. Like Freda, I have no belief in a corporeal afterlife. I do, however, have a ghost *story*, which took place in my very own house. And it may interest one of you in particular.'

Hildegard rolled her eyes and mouthed, 'Inez,' to Bessie, and they both smirked. Ida, lying on the mattress, her head resting on one elbow, could find nothing to smile at. Everything seemed to be about Inez now, as if the rest of them were only there to smooth her way, like ladies-in-waiting. *Can someone help Inez with the blankets? Can you teach her how to work the flint? Inez, if you're finding that difficult, I'm sure that Ida will give you a hand, she's a tip-top wielder of the penknife.* And then, when Ida helped, Inez would simply stop what she was doing and watch her. 'You try it now,' Ida had said, handing over the penknife. 'Oh, I can't,' Inez had said, with absolute certainty. There was something wrong with her, thought Ida; she was like a clock with a cog missing, so that the hands never moved round the face but just twitched on the spot, and it was always five to four but never teatime.

'It happened in 1913,' said Mattie, 'when the house was being used as a convalescent home for hunger strikers. Who remembers the Cat and Mouse Act?'

'Ooh, ooh!' It was Avril, waggling her hand frantically, bouncing up and down with desperation to be asked.

Mattie waited a second or two, on the off-chance that Inez might attempt an answer. Nearly every other hand was raised.

'Ooh, *ooh*!'

'Yes, Avril?'

'They let you out when you were ill, and then made you go back to prison again when you were better.'

'That's right. Hunger strikers were released on licence, and given a date to return to Holloway.'

'But lots of them didn't, and when they were feeling better they went and hid, so the detectives couldn't find them.'

'That was the game what we played last month,' added Elsie. 'Mouse Hunt. Hildegard and Ida were the coppers.'

'And we won,' said Ida.

'Boo!' added Freda.

'You were a good deal more astute and alert than the original detectives,' said Mattie. 'So, my story begins on a wild winter evening. One of the mice was upstairs in her room – it was at the back of the house, facing the Heath, and she was sitting in an armchair. She was a young woman, very brave and daring, and although she'd been greatly weakened by fasting, she was already making plans to leave the house in the guise of a visiting nurse, in order to avoid re-arrest.'

'Miss Simpkin, can I ask something?' said Winnie.

'Of course.'

'Is this story really about you?'

'No. No, I was far from being a young woman when it took place.'

'It's about my mother, I expect,' said Inez, because Miss Simpkin's suffragette anecdotes were *always* about her mother. 'What was she wearing?'

'Wearing?' said Mattie, rather thrown. 'I don't know.'

'Was she in her day clothes, or a dressing gown because she was still ill? What time was it, exactly?'

'I'm not altogether sure. Perhaps ten o'clock.'

'So a nightgown, then. And maybe a wrap.'

'Yes. And as your mother was sitting—'

'And slippers, of course.'

There was an outbreak of giggling from the more distant mattresses. '*What was she wearing?*' repeated someone, wetly. Ida stared at the fire, only half listening as the anecdote progressed (. . . *a scratching at the window, a scream, a white hand behind the glass* . . .), thinking instead about what she'd seen from the bus on the way to the Heath. It had passed the Coronet and she'd spotted Kenneth Billson in the queue for *The Mysterious Lady*, together with that ninny Mary Corrigan. At the time, her only thought had been that Mary was welcome to him, more fool her and her tatty green boa, but now she felt a sudden yearning for a plush seat and a bag of toffees and an arm around her in the dark. The arm would have to belong to someone half decent, mind, who'd treat her properly and wouldn't laugh in her face.

There were one or two gasps beside her, and she realized that she had missed the entire climax of the story, though it had something to do with a detective who'd climbed up a mulberry tree in order to check who was in the house. Involuntarily, she yawned, and Inez turned to look at her, so that their faces were very close together.

'It's terribly bad manners not to cover your mouth when you yawn,' said Inez.

'So*rry*, I'm sure.'

The air between them seemed to scrape and flare, indifference sparking into dislike.

'I think you're actually quite rude,' said Inez.

'I can be a lot ruder than that.' Ida held the stare a moment longer, and then rolled away.

'So it wasn't a real ghost?' said Elsie, disappointed.

Mattie shook her head. 'No, not unless ghosts can fall out of a mulberry tree and break a wrist.'

'But I'd say it's the sort of house that *would* have a ghost, though,' said Freda. 'Did any suffragettes actually die there, Miss Simpkin?'

'No, thank Heaven.'

'I'm glad I live in a *new* house,' said Winnie. 'I wouldn't want to have to worry every time I was opening a door in the dark, or looking in a mirror.'

'Or mopping the floor,' said Inez.

The words were spoken so quietly that it took a moment for Ida to believe what she'd just heard, and then she threw off the blanket and stood up.

'That's it, I'm off.'

She walked swiftly away from the circle, taking the path between the trees to the edge of the copse and then slowing, disorientated in the darkness. Sandy paths formed a pale web across the hillside.

'Ida!'

It was Miss Simpkin, actually running through the trees towards her, and Ida turned to run herself, but knew that she couldn't bolt now and then arrive for work on Monday as if nothing had happened: *Morning, Miss Simpkin.*

179

Yes, thank you very much, I enjoyed the camp out but I suddenly felt bilious. Excuse me, I just need to fetch the soap flakes from the scullery.

She waited.

'Ida, whatever is the matter? Are you unwell?'

How could she not have *noticed*, thought Ida – a person who can point to a dot in the distance and know it's a wren but who can't see what's happening an inch in front of her eye-glasses?

'No, I'm not ill.'

'Then what can be wrong?'

'Inez just said something to me and it made me cross.'

'But what on earth did she say that would make you want to run off?' There was only a shaving of moon, so that Miss Simpkin's face was unreadable, an oblong stitched with shadow, but her tone was one of bafflement at the idea that anyone could scarper because of mere *words*, and Ida didn't know how to explain to someone who'd dodged truncheons what it was like to get sneered at for something that was just your life, something you had to do for money, not something you'd chosen for politics or the Greater Good. Because in spite of the fact that Miss Simpkin wasn't like anyone else – that she threw words around like a circus juggler, that she didn't care two pins for what people said about her, that she strode through life like a painting of a goddess in a helmet – she was still *posh* and, in the end, that made her more like Inez than Ida. Posh people saw things from a different angle, as if they were on stilts; they didn't realize how much easier it was for them to step over obstacles, or catch someone's attention, or keep out of the mud. The best of them might think that they were looking at you eye to eye, but they never were, they were always peering down, watching you mop, as if mopping was the thing that made you what you were, the *identifier*, like spotting a white throat on a crow and knowing that meant it was really a rook.

'Ida?'

'It's not just what she said, it's . . . it's . . .' There was too much to express; the words wedged in her throat like a ball.

'Spit it out!' said Mattie. 'Dare to be a Daniel!' And as she spoke, the moonlight blinked out, doused by cloud, and Ida could see nothing in front of her but a dark shape in darkness, with the campfire a distant flare of orange, and suddenly she could speak, because now it was like those furious conversations she'd sometimes have when she was on her own, arguing with the air as she peeled the spuds, as eloquent as a coster.

'It's not *fair*, Miss Simpkin. Just because Inez's mother was a suffragette, she gets treated as if she's more impor-tant than the rest of us, even though she doesn't answer questions or volunteer or help anyone or have any ideas or even . . . even *pick* anything *up*. It's like in the Bible when that son comes home, the prodigal son, and he's been racketing around and spent all his money and he gets a whole party put on for him, and the other son, who's been trying hard and done everything what he's supposed to do, has to stand and watch while his brother gets a fancy dinner. For doing nothing!' Her voice was a squawk of outrage.

'Excuse me, is everything quite all right?' called a voice from beside the fire.

'Yes, thank you, Freda,' said Mattie. 'Would you like to lead some singing, perhaps?'

There was silence until the first line of 'Bread and Roses' threaded between the trees. *I've gone and done it now*, thought Ida.

'That was really rather an excellent analogy,' said Mattie. Her tone was brooding.

'Was it?' asked Ida, confused.

'Apposite.'

'. . . to what?'

'No, "apposite" means "appropriate", or "befitting".'

'Oh.'

'And you are, in many ways, right,' said Mattie. 'Because of her . . . her *parentage*, I find myself expecting – hoping for – a great deal more from Inez. But as the backbone of our group, Ida, do you have any suggestions as to what it would take to turn her into a true Amazon?'

A boot up the arse.

'I would value your thoughts,' continued Mattie. 'Whatever they are.'

Ida felt her face grow hot and was glad she was invisible. She made an effort to concentrate.

'Maybe if . . . she never tries at anything, does she? So she doesn't know what it's like when you're the person who's done the thing that means your team's won, and everyone's congratulating you and you feel like a . . . a *queen* – and maybe if she could understand what that feels like, for once, it might . . .'

'Buck her up.'

'Yes. Maybe.' Ida had her doubts.

'Thank you. Extremely helpful.'

Something small moved past them in the dark: a soft snuffle, a rustle of grass at ankle height. In the copse, Hildegard was singing a descant, her silvery voice lifting clear of the others.

'And now let's go back, shall we?' said Mattie.

Ida hesitated; somewhere to the west of them, Greta Garbo was gliding across a screen, and there were whispers and promises in the dark, and violet creams . . .

Reluctantly, she plodded after Mattie.

A wreath of white lilies lay on the purple-draped coffin, and there were swags of greenery and more lilies in vases beside the catafalque, whilst across the congregation the same colours were picked out in ribbons and badges, rosettes and sashes, lending an oddly carnival air to the proceedings. Mattie, for the first time, wore her medals: the miniature grille commemorating her incarcerations, the silver disc bearing the dates of hunger strikes, the pin topped with a chip of flint which signified that she had once (several times, as a matter of fact) thrown a stone through a plate-glass window. Similar awards winked from bosoms and lapels in every pew; St John's Smith Square currently contained more convicted criminals than an East End beer-hall.

'Not the best of views,' said Dorothy, for the fourth

time. The Mousehole party had arrived rather late, after meeting Roberta from the Ipswich train, and they were seated near the back of the nave.

'I see Annie Kenney,' whispered The Flea, half rising. 'Annie Taylor, ~~that~~ is. And there's Mrs Despard. And Sylvia and Christabel, of course. No Adela.'

Alice Channing, beside her in the pew, craned her neck. 'Dear, splendid Mrs Despard *still* wearing that extraordinary lace mantilla. Positively Victorian. Though I shouldn't talk, not exactly a fashion plate myself . . .'

Mattie, seated on the aisle, glanced along the row at her old comrades: Alice in black bombazine, her WSPU button badge fastened to her hat band; Dorothy, a whippet in her heyday, now grown rather stout; Roberta, who had proved momentarily unrecognizable on the platform at Liverpool Street, her greying hair newly shingled. And all around, other whispered reunions and half-familiar faces, every pew full, the gallery packed, a mass of sober female respectability – taxpayers, grandmothers, committee members and letter-writers, who had yet, in their time, rolled the world before them like a bowling ball. Lord, what a force they had been! What buoyancy, what momentum in their common aim; she could almost feel it lifting her again, even in these sombre circumstances. And if there had been no Great War, no halting of their forward surge, no splitting of aims, what more might they have achieved? Not painful inroads but a whole new map!

'There's Nellie,' said Dorothy, nudging her, as two women walked up the aisle, bearing flags.

'Nellie Hall?'

'Yes, she was Mrs Pankhurst's goddaughter, you know. A splendid girl, chip off the old block.'

'Who's the other?'

'A Conservative Party member,' hissed The Flea darkly, as a sudden flourish of organ notes heralded both the arrival of the clergy and the widespread creaking of stays occasioned by several hundred middle-aged women standing simultaneously.

It was towards the end of the Reverend Cobb's eulogy that the sudden sharp smell of whisky flooded the rear of the church, accompanied by the words 'Damn it all' and the sound of a glass bouncing twice and then smashing. Mattie's head snapped round like a pointer, and then she was on her feet and moving swiftly towards a stooping figure.

'Hello, Mattie! I only wanted a nip,' said Aileen Gifford, attempting to pick up the shards.

'Let me do that,' hissed Mattie. 'Go into the porch, I'll meet you there.'

'I want to see the service! Darling Mrs Pankhurst!'

The Reverend Cobb had raised his voice, but there were heads turning all over the church and Mattie took Aileen by the elbow and frog-marched her through the door.

They emerged into a gritty wind under a white sky. Two police horses were shifting and stamping at the foot of the steps and a large crowd had assembled on the opposite pavement, its attention immediately riveted by the sight of Aileen trying to ram a bottle back into her Gladstone bag.

'Come along, dear girl,' said Mattie, linking arms.

'Can we not see the service?'

'Perhaps after a little stroll.'

'Oh, I've been so silly,' said Aileen, starting to cry. Mattie guided her into an alcove containing an attenuated marble of the Evangelist, and stood directly in front, blocking the crowd's view. To see Aileen in such proximity was almost painful; like all of them, she had aged – but she was also ruined, her skin rimed with scurf, her eyes the translucent gobstoppers of the alcoholic. 'I missed the train,' she said, Mattie's handkerchief clenched in her hand. 'Forgot to set the alarm, and then it was all helter-skelter, horrible to be so late. Though not as late as Emmeline.' She gave a stifled shriek, a sob muffled in laughter, and looked down at herself, the stain on her blouse, her coat fastened wrongly.

'Let me do that,' said Mattie, starting on the buttons. 'Try and give your nose a good blow.'

'Can I go back in?'

'I think not. I suggest we walk to the cemetery, and if we're brisk about it we should get there before the cortège and then you can pay your respects with a clear head.'

A fire engine passed, bell clanging, the ladder rattling on the roof, and Mattie took advantage of the distraction to guide Aileen down the steps, bypassing a hawker with a tray of memorial cards.

'An angel,' said Aileen, halting suddenly and wafting a hand towards the photographs of Mrs Pankhurst.

'You know very well that she wasn't, Aileen.'

'An angel with a fiery sword!'

'Tuppence apiece,' said the seller, laconically.

'I'll take two hundred and forty.' Mattie stayed Aileen's hand, before it could unroll the note that she'd extracted like a cheroot from her pocket.

'Six,' said Mattie, handing over a shilling.

Aileen fanned the souvenir cards like a hand of rummy. 'Six queens,' she said. 'And you mustn't say a word about her, Mattie.'

'I will say only that she was human. A most magnificent human, but possessed of human failings. And, in the end, she paid no heed to those who had followed her most loyally. Did you have anything to eat this morning?'

'Not a sausage.'

There was a muffin seller at the corner of Smith Square, and Mattie bought three.

'A lady doesn't eat on a public thoroughfare,' said Aileen, who had once unbuckled a policeman's belt, leaving him to choose between arresting a protestor and holding up his trousers. 'Though I must say this smells nice.' She took a tiny bite. 'I was never a big eater.'

'I know.'

'That first day at the Miss Bridges', do you remember? The gravy soup that I poured out of the window?'

'Where are you living now, Aileen?'

'I was staying with my cousin in Woking until last month. Incident with an overflowing bath – very, very little damage to the ceiling, and it was only a *minor* Gainsborough, just a sketch, really.'

'And since then?'

'Lodging with a Mrs Allenthwaite in Winchester, although she mentioned just this morning that she wants me to leave by the end of the week. I'm looking for a country place. I may go in for dog breeding.'

'Come and stay at the Mousehole.'

'No thank you.' She looked at Mattie, and there was a sudden clarity to her blue-green gaze, the lifting of sea-fret to reveal an unexpected calm. 'I would let you down.'

'Nonsense.'

'I would, yes, and I can't bear that. And Florrie shouldn't have to look after me as well as you, silly girl that I am.' And as she spoke, she was snapping open her bag and reaching for the bottle.

'Don't,' said Mattie.

'Just a chaser.'

'Here's a challenge for you: if we reach Brompton before the coffin, I promise to *buy* you a drink.'

'Oh, cunning! I never could resist a challenge.' She closed the bag again, and lengthened her stride, steering an approximate line down the centre of the pavement, Mattie's hand on her arm giving little nudges of correction, as if to a tiller. 'Do you remember the rowing boat we borrowed when we should have been at the Miss Bridges'? Four miles downstream in an hour, four miles back up in – how long was it?'

'Oh Lord,' said Mattie. 'At least half a day. It was dark by the time I reached home; they'd sent the gardener out to look for me.'

'And that was all because you asked me if I could row. And I said I could, though I couldn't, not a stroke.'

'I think I had been reading about galley slaves in Sueto-nius,' said Mattie. Not that Suetonius had been on the curriculum of the small educational establishment opened by Miss Elouise Bridge and her sister in Bedford; Mattie, thirteen at the time, had begged to attend, anticipating rigour and depth, and had received instead a confetti of education, lightly sprinkled over the class and as lightly brushed aside: science confined to the life cycle of the butterfly, geography to the less rugged of the English counties, French restricted to phrases suitable for lady travellers drifting through the emporia of Nice in search of crocheted gloves.

She had complained of the school in her letters to Stephen and in return he had sent her the Suetonius, a Latin grammar and a fair copy of Pliny's account of the eruption of Vesuvius. He had also pointed out that, in two respects at least, her current establishment was an improvement on his own: there was no corporal punishment, and no one expected the pupils to play rugby.

Indeed, they were not expected to play any sports at all, the only form of exercise suggested by the Miss Bridges being a gentle stroll around the school garden, in fine weather only. The fattening of breeding stock for market sprang to mind.

And then, one morning, there had been a new pupil: a girl a little younger than Mattie, with curly hair and cheekbones like a Tartar. Her name was Aileen Latimer and it rapidly became clear that she cared not a fig for any school subject, greeting every new task with dreadful sighs and groans and spending much of the time staring out of the window and whistling under her breath; a brief burst of industry during a Scripture lesson turned out to be not the requested account of the Feeding of the Five Thousand but a full-page drawing of a fish.

Intrigued, Mattie had sought her out – so many of the other girls seemed cut from the same dull pattern, but here was someone as untailored, in her own way, as herself. 'I have never been as bored in my *entire life*,' were Aileen's first words to her.

It transpired that while her parents were abroad she had been sent from her country home to stay with elderly relatives, and these relatives had, after a trying few days of Aileen's company, decided that some daily occupation was needed. She was utterly unteachable, but she was also vastly entertaining – for the two months of her attendance, it was like having a tame bear-cub in the classroom, and, out of it, a wild pony.

'Do you remember the penknife-throwing contest?' asked Mattie. 'We drew a target on a tree. You had seen a stage act, I think.'

'Arcola the Great. I could have done that, I feel.'

'Become a professional knife-thrower?'

'Instead of marrying. Yes, why not?' She stumbled slightly, flinging out an arm to keep her balance, the weighted Gladstone bag describing an arc that could have felled a horse.

'Let me take that,' said Mattie.

'I can think of many things I should have done instead of marry. Crossed the Nubian Desert on a camel. Dived for pearls. You never met Hubert, did you?'

'No.'

'I was never clever, like you and the other comrades . . .

hated reading, brain like an absolute brick, I couldn't paint or . . . or sculpt, only run like a Mohican, and nobody wanted lady athletes, and he was terribly handsome and wealthy and my family had a beast of a house but no money and everyone was fearfully pleased. Of course, he drank, but no one thought . . . you never met him?'

'No,' said Mattie, threading Aileen through the narrow gap between a perambulator and a brace of bull terriers. 'Don't you remember – after you left the Miss Bridges', we didn't meet again until the Albert Hall. More than twenty years.'

'Yes, of course, my banner! And you were tying that scoundrel Winston into *knots*.'

Churchill had been giving a speech about the miners, his staccato delivery a gift to the astute heckler:

'*One great question. Remains to be settled*—'

'And that,' shouted Mattie, leaning forward in the circle, 'is women's suffrage!'

Churchill struggling on amidst shushes and cheers – '*The men have been complaining. Of me*—'

'The women have been complaining of you, too, Mr Churchill!'

'*But in the circumstances. What can we do but*—'

'Give votes to women!'

And from the gods, a great cheer as a banner unspooled, VOTES FOR WOMEN in red paint, dangling twenty feet into the auditorium, and in the meantime, Mattie being dragged from her seat, her jacket torn, her shins bounced on each stair, a ladder of bruises . . .

Afterwards, amidst the dispersing crowds, a woman had rushed up – 'Mattie! It *is* you!' – and it had been Aileen, recognizable as much by that same stamping, restless energy as by her cheekbones. 'Left my husband and found a cause,' she'd said, spanning two decades in a sentence. 'He was rather a terrible man.' And during her marriage, one of those prominent cheekbones had lost its smooth curve, and one of her wrists had set at a slight angle, so that she could throw stones only with her left hand. Spirits, she'd declared, helped with the stiffness. And had gone on helping.

'You know, I'm sure I can walk even faster,' said Aileen.

Mattie checked her wristwatch. 'I think we're doing very well. How are you feeling?'

'Oh, far more sensible. What does this remind you of?' She tapped their linked arms with her free hand.

'The exercise yard.'

'Exactly. Except that we shouldn't be talking.'

'*At six o'clock, Ettie Smyth will be conducting a choir outside the West Wall,*' said Mattie, without moving her lips; Aileen laughed, delightedly.

'You were always very skilled at that. And I remember that you could whistle and hum at the same time.'

'I still can, though there's surprisingly little call for it these days.'

They passed a news stand with the words 'PANK-HURST FUNERAL' chalked above it, and Aileen gave it a shuddering glance, and fell silent. It was another few minutes before Mattie realized that her friend was quietly weeping.

'Perhaps we should have that drink now,' said Mattie, scanning the street ahead for a public house. 'We're not far from the gates.'

'I simply can't think where the time's gone. I simply can't think, I can't *think*.'

'What do you mean, dear?'

'I feel as if Holloway were last week and then there are years and years that have just' – she flapped a hand in disbelief – 'gone. Sand between my fingers. I went into the church and for a moment I wondered whether I were in the wrong place. We're all so *old*, Mattie. It was full of old ladies.'

'You are only fifty-six, Aileen, and in any case, remember Tennyson: "Old age hath yet his honour and his toil." Now, this looks suitable.'

The Lantern was spruce and shining, every wall glittering with mirrors, the smell of polish hanging in the air. It was also empty save for the barman and a single elderly drinker, a white stick propped beside him.

'Two brandies,' said Mattie. The barman shook his head, scarcely pausing as he buffed a glass. 'We don't serve unaccompanied females.'

'Why ever not?'

'Rules.'

'I'm afraid you'll have to be rather more precise than that. Which rule?'

The man jerked his head towards a framed list above the optics.

Mattie leaned across the bar, tilting her eye-glasses to improve her focus.

'The landlord *reserves the right* to . . .' she read out. 'Are you the landlord?'

'No, but I'm in loco, ain't I?'

'You're worried, presumably, that we are prostitutes touting for trade?'

'Now, *now*!' He looked as outraged as if she'd just spat at him. 'It's the look of the thing. Ladies drinking.'

'I need scarcely point out that your only other customer is blind.'

'I'd just like a tiny little brandy,' said Aileen, 'with a splash of soda,' but as she spoke, the door opened, and the barman swung his attention to a group of men and the shrilly yapping Jack Russell that accompanied them; there had been some minor triumph, voices raised, hands clapping the shoulder of one of the crowd, a race won or a bet claimed, and Mattie and Aileen were suddenly no more visible than a couple of tables, obstacles to be avoided on the way to the bar.

'Come along,' said Mattie, taking her friend's arm.

'Even without soda,' said Aileen, plaintively; salt from the tears had formed a fine lacework across her cheeks.

Outside, there was rain in the air, the wind flapping like a damp tea-towel.

'There's bound to be another hostelry nearby,' said Mattie; Aileen's arm was dragging on hers.

'I'm tired.'

'Not far to go now.'

'And my feet hurt. I used to run everywhere.'

'I know.'

'Or even skate – I was a wonderful skater. Do you remember the census? When none of us slept in our own beds because we were protesting . . . what was it, what were we protesting?'

'That we were not recognized as full citizens under the law.'

'Such tremendous fun, the whole of the WSPU shop full of mattresses, and Marian Lawson and I went roller-skating at the Aldwych rink for the entire night, and I could have carried on the next day. I wasn't tired then, I was never tired. I wish – oh, there's a pub!'

The Horse and Dray was neither spruce nor shining, its stucco façade pock-marked, its windows so filthy that it was not until Mattie opened the door that she realized the saloon was crowded.

'It's the Sally Anne,' said a youth just inside the door. 'Where's your tambourines?'

'Just a small brandy,' said Aileen.

There was a crash of skittles from one side of the room, and shouts from the bar, the crowd five-deep, with striped shirtsleeves and the dusty jackets of plasterers, a low roar of conversation, odd faces already turning to look at the incomers, glances of indifference or puzzlement or derision, one fellow nudging another and a burst of laughter from somewhere as Aileen stumbled on the step. Mattie found herself suddenly, unexpectedly, jibbing at the sequence of tiny battles ahead – the ten minutes of vocal sparring, the deft mental footwork and sheer bloody-minded persistence that would be needed simply to cross the bar-room, order a measure and then drink it. She had, for once, no stomach for a fight; the thought was disquieting.

'We should go,' she said. 'It'll take too long.'

'Oh no!' Aileen clutched at the lintel on her way out. 'You promised me.'

'We shall find somewhere private and you can take a little nip from the bottle.'

'Really?' She brightened. 'Where?'

'I have an idea.'

There was something rather suburban about the eastern side of Brompton Cemetery – the headstones of a uniform height, the paths straight, the shrubs clipped. A gardener was edging the lawn, another sweeping the broad path. An elderly couple walked arm in arm, the woman holding a bunch of yellow tulips wrapped in newspaper, their stems dripping a trail across the gravel.

'I can't drink it *here*,' hissed Aileen. 'Not in front of people.'

'Wait just a moment.'

From the direction of the Fulham Road, at the far end of the long lime avenue that bisected the cemetery, came an indefinable noise – a steady murmuring, like bees on blossom.

'What a crowd there must be,' said Mattie. 'Though the cortège can't have arrived yet, if they're still chattering. Now, just over here it all becomes a little more secluded – I once came in search of Fanny Brawne's tomb, and instead stumbled across George Borrow's.'

Crossing the avenue, they entered a region of grieving angels and cracked vaults, elder shoots forcing their way through splits in the masonry, every slab tilting and grouted with moss.

'Did you ever read Borrow's *Wild Wales*?' asked Mattie,

halting beside a weeping Niobe and handing over the Gladstone bag.

'You know quite well that I've never finished a book in my life. And I went to Wales once and they forced me to eat seaweed and since then—' Aileen's fingers nipped ineffectually at the cork. 'I can't, Mattie. You'll have to do it for me. Take some yourself.'

'Afterwards, perhaps.'

She handed back the opened bottle, and Aileen took a small sip.

'There,' she said. 'That's all I wanted. Perhaps *one* more, though.' The second sip was more of a mouthful. 'Can you hear something?' she asked, cocking her head.

The far-off murmur had thickened; as Mattie listened, it rose to a crescendo then abruptly died away. In the silence she could hear the hooting of a tug on the river.

'The cortège must be here,' she said. 'Shall we go?'

She moved to take the bottle, and Aileen swapped it swiftly to her other hand and retreated in the direction of the lime avenue, her expression suddenly shifty and alien, a dragon guarding its hoard.

'Now come along . . .' said Mattie, following. 'Let me cork it, at least. Glenfiddich's far too expensive to hurl around.'

She made another grab for the bottle, and Aileen swung it away and a jet of whisky curved through the air and broke in a pungent wave across the windscreen of a maroon Alvis that had been moving at a stately pace from the Chelsea Lane entrance. The motor-car halted just as

Mattie wrenched the bottle from Aileen's grasp. It was almost empty.

'Oh, *please*,' said Aileen, panting, hands opening and closing in desperation. 'Please, Mattie, please give it back.' The dragon had fled; she was helpless again, and trembling, and Mattie could hardly bear to see her in such a state, on this day, in this place.

'Go on,' she said.

Aileen snatched it back and raised it to her mouth and, in the angle between her profile and the bottle, Mattie saw the door of the motor-car open, and a woman step out on to the drive. It was Jacqueline Fletcher, dressed in black, her mouth an 'O' of amazement. And, possibly, amusement.

'What on earth is going on?' she asked. 'I said to Richard, "Surely that can't be Mattie Simpkin, brawling over a bottle in the middle of the cemetery!"'

'Oh, hello, Jacko,' said Mattie, as if they'd just bumped into each other in the haberdashery department of Dickins & Jones. Embarrassment was not something to which she was prone, but she was conscious of the exceptional awkwardness of the encounter. She eased the bottle from Aileen's fingers and stowed it in the Gladstone bag.

'And is that' – Jacko's expression changed from ersatz shock to the genuine article – 'Aileen?' She was clearly struggling not to stare. 'Oh my word . . . it's been a long time, hasn't it?'

'Hello, Jacko,' said Aileen. 'You look awfully smart and pretty.'

'Thank you.'

Instead of a reciprocal remark, there was a short, painful silence, broken by the squeal of cloth on glass.

'This is my husband, Richard,' said Jacko.

He was tall, with rigidly handsome features, and a complexion scoured by the Antipodean sun; the general impression was that of a classical statue carved out of brisket. He paused in his cleaning of the windscreen, and raised his hat.

Mattie bowed, stiffly.

'I think, in any case, we should walk from here,' said Jacko. 'I'm surprised, though, that you're not at the south entrance, being marshalled by General Drummond.'

'We took a different route,' said Mattie. The phrase seemed to clang with significance.

'Yes, Mattie and I walked the whole way from the church, lickety-spit, I was always a great walker, though I never had a lovely motor-car like yours. I'd call that colour claret, wouldn't you? Do you drive?' asked Aileen, her tone that of a hostess at an amusing dinner, the whisky clearly beginning to take effect.

'I leave the driving to Richard. Shall we go?' said Jacko, taking her husband's arm; alongside her, Aileen rattled on.

'I hadn't known you were married; I was married once, but it was awful. Do you have hordes of children?'

'No,' said Jacko, rather distantly.

'Neither do I. Just as well, I've never had any patience with them, I couldn't have been a teacher, like Mattie was. Did you know that she runs a club for young persons?'

'Yes,' said Jacko. 'As do I. In fact, I rather think that I might have given her the idea in the first place.'

Mattie thought, with instant ire, of Jacko's dismissal of the Amazons in the *Ham & High* article. *Childish games. Classroom debate.*

'Is that true, Mattie?' asked Aileen, gaily, continuing her impression of a one-woman cocktail party.

'It certainly arose out of a discussion about introducing young women to a wider world,' said Mattie.

'Not only young women but also young men, in our case,' said Richard. He had a hoarse edge to his voice, as if he'd been shouting.

Mattie shook her head. 'I'm afraid that I don't consider militarism an introduction to a wider world.'

'It's not militarism but discipline. You'll find that very little can be achieved without it.'

'Discipline need not include drill and uniforms – good God, every woman here today could verify that. Obedience should come from the will, not from the whip.'

'I'm talking about self-discipline.'

'The Amazons have plenty of self-discipline.'

'Yes,' said Jacko. 'We've seen them. Scampering around the Heath.'

'*Rabbits* scamper. My girls are hares and foxes, fit, alert and brimming with initiative.'

Jacko smiled. 'One hardly dares to point out what happens to hares and foxes in real life.'

'In real life they learn to survive,' said Mattie. 'As so many in uniform did not survive, blindly obeying.'

Aileen was looking from one to another, her mouth pinned into a bright smile.

'I'm sure both clubs are simply wonderful. What's yours called, Jacko?'

'The Empire Youth League.'

'How marvellous!'

'*Marvellissimo* would perhaps be more accurate,' said Mattie. 'Given its political tenor. Goose-stepping a speciality.'

'Oh, really, Mattie,' said Jacko. 'Now you're being ridiculous. The League places just as much importance on healthy activities and initiative as your own little club. But we do it with an eye to the future rather than the past.'

'I don't understand,' said Aileen, plaintively. 'Is this politics?'

'One cannot dismiss the past,' said Mattie to Jacko.

'Neither can one live in it, as so many old comrades still seem to. The young should gaze ahead to a brighter future.'

'Illuminated by what, precisely? The Brassoed gleam of their uniform belt-buckles? Zeal without knowledge is fire without light.'

'There's nothing wrong with a little smartness,' said Jacko. 'One doesn't want one's protégés to look like children romping at a party.'

'As opposed to blank-faced recruits, unquestioningly enforcing the leader's wishes. My girls have vim and wit.'

'And also feathers in their hair, so I've heard.'

'Just as long as the feathers don't mean that they're also feather-*brained* . . .' said Jacko's husband, delivering this hammer blow with the expression of someone handing over a pearl.

'Far from it,' said Mattie, crisply. 'In fact, I have no doubt that, in whatever topic or skill you'd care to name, they could knock your bunch for six.'

'Goodness, that's quite a claim.'

'Have you stopped talking politics yet?' asked Aileen. 'Because I never really cared for that side of things. What I loved was being so *busy*, every day filled to bursting and every face a friend. *Dear* old friends.' She missed her step and kicked up a spray of gravel; Mattie steadied her.

In the distance, now, they could see the hearse moving slowly towards them, the two women with flags pacing ahead of it, and behind, a column of women, innumerable and silent. A cluster of undertakers' men marked the site of the grave.

'I want to join all the others,' said Aileen. 'I haven't seen The Flea yet. Or Dorothy. Or Alice. Shall we cut round to them? Are you coming, Jacko?'

'I think we'll pay our respects from here.' Jacko took her husband's arm. 'I've no real wish to dwell on the old days and, in any case, when I was introduced to The Flea after Mattie's lecture, I rather got the impression that she didn't take to me, and it wasn't solely to do with her political views. Dog in a manger, one might say.'

Mattie stared at her. 'What on earth are you talking about?'

'She struck me as' – she took her time choosing her words – 'unnaturally proprietorial. Possibly a little jealous.'

'*Jealous?*'

Jacko's expression was bland.

'Come *on*, Mattie,' said Aileen, pulling on her arm, and

Mattie let herself be steered away, past vaults and memorials, round the raw mounds of recent burials, and towards the great and sombre parade that stretched from the hearse all the way back to the southern gates and beyond.

'We'll never find them!' said Aileen, in despair, but The Flea had been on the look-out, and raised her rolled umbrella and discreetly shook it until they saw her.

'I was wondering where you'd got to,' she said, sotto voce, squeezing Aileen's hand in greeting and turning to Mattie. 'Is everything quite all right?' Her expression sharpened as she scanned Mattie's face. 'Is something wrong? Has something happened?'

'No, no,' said Mattie, turning away as if to look for someone, unable to trust her own expression, which seemed to have come to some concrete conclusion ahead of her nebulous thoughts. 'Nothing at all.'

Ida closed one eye and pressed the other to the microscope. Once you realized that those blurred spokes at the edge were your own eyelashes, you could concentrate on the circle at the centre, on the purple rectangles that shifted into sharpness as you turned the wheel: row after row of narrow, blunted bricks that might have come from an earthworm, or an elephant, or even from Mr Heap, the biology teacher, who had a lisp that they all tried not to laugh at, which was difficult when he was doing a whole lesson on 'thellth'. Behind her, she could hear the heavy breathing of Alan Demetrios, who worked in a cement yard when he wasn't at the continuation school, and whose nose was perpetually blocked from the dust. His eyes were bunged up, too, yellow matter clogging the inner corners. He wanted to be a bank clerk.

'And what about you, Ida?' Mr Heap had asked her, after she'd got nineteen and a half out of twenty in a quiz on digestion (she'd misspelled 'hydrochloric'). She hadn't dared to admit that recently a tiny little impossible thought had begun to roll around inside her head, like a drop of mercury – the idea that she might one day, somehow, become a doctor. Instead, she'd said, 'Biology teacher,' and he'd looked enormously pleased.

'For your homework, read chapter four on the circulatory system and draw a diagram of the cardiac valves.'

'Have a heart, sir,' called out Alan, and everyone laughed. At Ida's old school he'd have got the cane for that, but Mr Heap just smiled, and went round collecting up the slides.

Someone called her name as she left the classroom and she turned to see a heavy-set girl with a great frizz of blonde hair. 'Are you Ida?' she asked.

'Yes.'

'I'm Olive. Someone in my class said you was in that girls' group on the Heath.'

'Oh.' Ida felt the same slight inward droop that might have come from a reminder of a dentist's appointment. 'Yes, I am.'

'Only I'm in the Empire League. You know, we're having that competition with you on Saturday.'

'You're in the League?'

'Yes.'

'But I thought they were all nobs.'

Olive laughed. 'Who said that?'

'There's a girl in the Amazons whose brother's in it, and *she's* a nob.'

'No, me and half the girls from my flats are in it. And two of my cousins are drummers, and so's my boyfriend, Leonard, and he's a window cleaner with his own ladder.' She paused a moment, as if expecting Ida to clap. 'Some of the older boys are posh,' she added. 'You know, like officers.'

'But don't you have to march and salute and all that?'

'So?'

'Well, isn't it all about militarism and following blindly and not thinking for yourself?'

'Who said that?'

'Miss Simpkin.'

'Is she the one with the loud voice? My cousin can take her off to a tee. He says, when she runs, all the streetlamps in Hampstead start to shake. No, it's about, you know, pride in being English and being healthy and better wages for English workers and getting rid of the foreign trouble-makers and looking smart and all that. People are always clapping us and taking photographs. Mrs Cellini said she wanted us girls to look like film stars and we got specially measured for our uniforms and all we had to pay was five shillings and my belt on its own cost six. You'll see it on Saturday. I've just put a poster up – Miss Harris said I could.'

She gestured towards the noticeboard, where the back page of the *Ham & High* had been pinned, with a circle of red crayon highlighting one of the advertisements.

The Empire Youth League
and
The Amazons
Invite spectators, young and old, to
A Display of Youth Skills
And Competitive Games
at
The bandstand field (East of Parliament Hill)
Hampstead Heath
Saturday July 14th, at 2 p.m.
Refreshments will be served!

'I'm in the formation marching team,' said Olive. 'What about you? Your lot don't do marching, do you?'
'No.'
'Nor drumming.'
'No.'
'So what are you going to do for your display?'
'It's a secret.'
Olive looked baffled, as well she might.

'The gauntlet has been thrown down,' Miss Simpkin had announced at an Amazons meeting a fortnight before. 'I have received a letter from the organizers of the League, who wish to pit our two clubs against each other. Do you feel that we could trounce the opposition?'
'At what, Miss Simpkin?'
'Let us weigh up the options.'
There'd been a discussion. The public nature of the competition made slingshots and javelins inadvisable ('I

think, on the whole, we should avoid the accidental impalement of prospective members'), and the fact that there'd been no rain for a month and the grass on the Heath was like straw meant that a demonstration of fire-lighting was out of the question.

'Ju–jitsu?' suggested Avril.

'No, it's not decent,' said Elsie. 'You can't help showing your drawers when you do the kicks.'

Winnie raised a hand. 'Famous statues? And people have to guess what they are? Or three-legged races?'

'Debating?' said Freda. 'Bagsy me.'

Hildegard caught Ida's eye over the heads of the smaller Amazons and grimaced slightly. 'Do we absolutely have to do this, Miss Simpkin?'

'Do what, Hildegard?'

'This challenge. Why can't we just say we'd rather not? What if we end up losing, or what if people laugh at us?'

'I'm quite certain you won't lose,' said Mattie, 'and, frankly, one should treat derision like a light shower of rain. Brush it off and carry on.'

'We could vote,' said Inez, who was sitting on a fallen branch, a yard or two from the rest of them. 'We usually do. On everything.'

Miss Simpkin paused, her features working, as if cross-winds were blowing beneath the skin. 'That, of course, is true,' she said, 'though I think it would be a shame if we passed up this opportunity to show that independence of mind and strength born of friendship is more than a match for the dead hand of authority. But yes, we'll put it to the vote. All those in favour of—'

'Don't we need an argument against?' asked Inez. 'Because all we've heard is you giving one *for*.'

There was a stillness in the group; a quiet sharpening of interest. You could talk to Mattie in a way that you wouldn't ever dare talk to most adults – you could argue and contradict and joke and even cheek, if you did it in the right spirit, but they all knew that, week by week, Inez had been edging towards something more: a sliding insolence, an inch or two further each time, a deliberate prodding at the boundaries. And on each occasion, Mattie seemed to retreat, in the same way that when you touched a snail's horns they humbly withdrew.

'Very well,' said Mattie, a little stiffly. 'Who would like to oppose the motion?'

Ida's hand seemed to go up of its own accord; she started to lower it again, but everyone was looking at her now.

'Ida?'

Ida hesitated, and this time Mattie didn't say, *Spit it out*, or *Dare to be a Daniel*, as she'd done once before on the Heath, but only waited, her expression slightly vexed, so that the argument that had been fluttering in Ida's head – that the best bit about the Amazons was the fact that when you were there, you could say things and do things and try things that you would never do anywhere else, precisely because no one from outside would be watching or judging you – that argument turned to dust, like a clapped moth, and she shrugged awkwardly.

'I just don't fancy it,' she muttered, and flushed at the stupidity of her own reply.

'So shall we vote?' asked Mattie. 'All those in favour?'

There was a thicket of raised arms. 'And against? Very well, carried in favour. Now, let's continue our discussion . . .'

But afterwards, while Ida was sullenly tearing up a newspaper for Fox and Hounds, Mattie came and spoke to her in the old way, using phrases like 'splendid all-rounder' and 'inspiring the small girls', and when she said, 'You won't let the Amazons down, will you, Ida?', Ida agreed that she wouldn't. And here she was now, looking at the newspaper pinned to the board, knowing that, come Saturday, she'd be running around with a red face and her slip showing under a dress she'd had since she was fourteen, in front of someone with a six-shilling belt.

'The commander says, if we win, he'll pay for a bang-up supper and we'll all go on the rowing boats,' said Olive. 'I'll see you then.'

She linked arms with another girl, who'd been waiting for her, and headed for the exit; Ida waited until the door had closed and then took down the sheet of newspaper.

It was dreadfully hot. The Flea had been squeezing lemons since eight in the morning, and by ten was wearing gauntlets of crushed pips. She rinsed her arms under the tap and stepped outside, her head swimming. It was entirely windless, swifts tracing parabolas against a dappled sky; not even the aspen leaves were moving – the garden might have been painted – so that when The Flea saw a patch of air above the Lumbs' wall beginning to shiver and fold she thought for a moment that she must be going to faint. As she stared, more fascinated than frightened, the patch lengthened and became an inverted triangle, trembling and iridescent, and then an insect flew straight into her forehead and she realized that she was looking at a stream of flying ants, boiling out of a crack in the top of the wall, and suddenly the whole garden was full of insects and she retreated into the passage and shut the door.

'Oh, hello!' called a girl's voice from the kitchen. 'The front door was open.'

It was Inez, already seated, her hands folded on her lap as if waiting for a recital to start. 'Am I early?' she asked.

'No, rather late, as a matter of fact. The other girls are already taking the tables and crockery across to the Heath. They'll be back quite soon.'

'Oh. And where's Miss Simpkin?'

'Setting the treasure-hunt clues, I believe.'

The Flea took a cloth and began to wipe the table-top, and Inez sat and watched her. It was the first time that The Flea had ever been alone with the girl, though she had seen her with the other Amazons, participating, though only in the way that you might say a stick participates when borne along by a stream.

'Would you like to help me to make the lemonade?'

'What would I have to do?'

'You can strain the juice, to make sure there's no pips left in it. And after that, you can add the sugar and water. Or would you rather cut up the ginger cake into squares?'

'They're both quite sticky things, aren't they? I don't much like being sticky.'

210

'In that case, could you line these biscuit tins with greaseproof paper? The scissors are in the top drawer.'

Limply, the girl complied. There was nothing *to* her, thought The Flea – she had all the beauty of youth, but none of the essence: its eagerness, its restlessness, even its anger. There was a slyness about her, but no rage, no burning core.

Inez was cutting the oblongs of paper both slowly and carelessly; trapeziums rather than rectangles.

'So, are you looking forward to the afternoon?'

'Not really. It's too hot to run around.'

'But you've still come, which is commendable. In fact, you come every single week, don't you?'

The Flea was not a good actress; she could hear the curiosity in her own voice.

Inez gave her a slanting look. 'Lots of girls come every week.'

'Yes, because they enjoy it. But you don't appear to.'

'No,' agreed Inez. 'I don't.'

For a moment, the only noise was the snip of the scissors, but the straightforwardness of the exchange seemed to have changed something, to have thinned the air between them.

'Do you come to the Amazons to find out more about your mother?' asked The Flea.

'I *did*.'

'She was a brave and spirited young woman.'

'Oh, not you, *too*,' said Inez pettishly, tossing the scissors on to the table, so that they spun across the oilcloth. '*Spirited, spirited, spirited*. I'm so sick of the word; it's all Miss Simpkin ever says, which is why I got so browned off with coming here. It makes me think of an oil-lamp, not

211

a person. And anyway, when people say it, what they really mean is *Why aren't you like her, Inez? What's wrong with you?*' She asked the questions in a voice that viciously approximated Mattie's, looking up at The Flea as if challenging her to contradict, but although there was spite in her face, there was also a glimpse of something else: an awful roaring misery, like that of a toddler standing in a crib, waiting for the nursery door to open.

'Your mother was about your height,' said The Flea. 'And she turned heads.'

'What do you mean?'

'I mean that she was strikingly pretty. And I remember that she had a very direct gaze. And she bounced when she walked.'

'Bounced?'

'Yes, almost as if she were walking on tiptoe. And her hair was the same colour as yours.'

'Was it?' Inez put a hand to her plait, looped with a velvet bow. 'It's only dark brown, after all.'

'Mahogany, I'd say.'

'What else?'

'She had a very nice smile.'

'I don't have any photographs of her smiling.'

'It was the sort of smile that made you want to smile back.'

'I don't have a smile like that.'

'Perhaps you do. I don't think I've ever seen it.'

Inez dropped her gaze and slid the scissors back towards herself, opening and closing them as they lay flat on the table-top.

'So, is there another reason why you keep coming to the Amazons?'

'Father says I have to.'

'Really?' The Flea mentally readjusted her view of Inez's father, whom she had never met but had assumed to be vehemently anti-Amazon. 'Why is that?'

'Because he says I give up on things all the time and I need to apply myself. If I go every week for six months, he'll take me to tea at Harrods. He says I need to learn the habit of persistence.'

'Well . . .' said The Flea. 'I would say he's right. Few worthwhile achievements happen overnight.'

'I suppose you're talking about Votes for Women, *again*.' Her tone was contemptuous.

'Among other things.'

'I'm never going to vote.'

'Why not?'

'Because if you have enough money it doesn't matter who's Prime Minister and because, if it wasn't for the stupid cause, my mother wouldn't be *dead*.'

In the sudden quiet, they could hear the sound of girls' voices outside.

The Flea's mouth seemed full of ash. 'I'm not sure if that's the case, Inez.'

'Of course it is. What on earth would you know about it? It was Father who told me, all the hunger strikes made her so weak that she died of anaemia just after I was born.' Inez stood up, abruptly, the sudden movement sending the greaseproof shapes wafting across the kitchen. 'And she didn't ever get to vote, anyway, so it was all a waste of time, wasn't it?'

She doesn't know that her mother took her own life, thought The Flea. *Of course she doesn't – who would ever tell a child such a thing?* And yet it seemed that the act had left a lacuna in the family, a centre too fragile to approach, so that Venetia was barely spoken of, and Inez gripped by a cramping, bottomless hunger for information, a hunger that pushed aside all other thoughts and feelings. She was like a fledgling waiting solely for the next morsel.

The back door opened and the scullery passage was suddenly full of footsteps and chatter.

'I could drink from a horse trough, I'm that thirsty.'

'Look in the mirror here, Winnie, your face is the colour of an absolute *tomato*.'

'Miss Lee,' said Ida, coming into the kitchen, 'do you have a hammer and nails, one of the table-tops is loose? And could we have some water to drink, please?'

Everyone was pink-faced, blouses limp with sweat, hair damp. Inez stood back, leaning against the Welsh dresser.

'Do remember to keep your hats on, girls. Sunstroke is a horrid thing. And try not to carry too much. Inez, could you take the clubs?'

'Are you coming to watch, Miss Lee?' asked Ida, from behind a tower of biscuit tins.

'Yes, but I'll have a tidy round first. Elsie, I know you're strong, but really, you mustn't try to carry more than one jug of lemonade at a time.'

She followed the girls outside and watched the laden procession heading again for the Heath.

A few ants still hung in the air, but there were hundreds more heaped on the wall, clambering over one another, clumsy and glistening, wings untried.

The heat was stunning. The Flea turned back to the house and the faintness returned with a dip and a swoop; real, this time. She found herself lying on the grass, with a daisy tickling her nose, and no knowledge of how long she might have been there, though the air was full of insects again, and the sun had shifted from its zenith. When she sat up, her heart broke into a stumbling run and she pressed a hand to her breastbone and waited, her fingers cold despite the sun, her mouth dry.

It was just as bad as Ida had imagined; worse, actually, because the members of the Empire League hadn't been hauling tables and tins around for an hour, and so were not only looking smart but as cool as a row of cucumbers – and resembling exactly that, in their dark green uniforms – while the Amazons looked like a bag of bakery seconds, Doris Elphick in a brown gym-slip, Hildegard in a maroon one, Elsie in her older sister's frock, which came halfway down her calves, Avril and Winnie in matching print play-dresses, Freda – for some terrible reason – in a pair of khaki jodhpurs, and on and on, nothing matching or new, only their sashes providing any link between them. As the two teams lined up for photographs, you could see the spectators pointing and grinning as they commented on the difference.

It wasn't a big crowd, thank goodness – it was too hot for that, and mostly it was just small kids, sitting cross-legged with their lemonade and ginger cake, and a cluster of adults standing in the shade of the trees, some of the ladies with parasols. The woman in charge of the Youth League had a lovely pale green duster coat and a white cloche and Miss Simpkin had a straw hat the size of a cartwheel which looked as if someone had recently sat on it. She was talking to a man in a striped blazer, fragments of her speech intermittently audible; Ida heard her declaim the words, 'Say not the needle is the proper pen for women,' and knew she was quoting something – it was astonishing how many quotes were packed into Miss Simpkin's head; it was like a work-box stuffed with coloured wools to match every possible shade and texture. 'We may each have but a single pair of eyes,' she'd said to Ida, 'but if we read, we can borrow the vision of myriad others.' Though only the myriad others who wrote books, of course.

'Who's got the clubs?' asked Doris. 'We're up first, aren't we? Anyone seen the brown canvas bag with the clubs?'

There was a pause; Ida looked at Inez.

'Oh,' said Inez.

'What d'you mean, "Oh"?'

'I think the bag might still be by the back door.'

'What?'

'I had to fasten my buckle and I put it down for a moment.'

'And you didn't pick it up again?'

'I was carrying something else as well.'

'We were *all* carrying something else as well.'

'I'll go back and get it, shall I?' Inez essayed a vague movement in the direction of the house.

'I'll go,' said Doris. 'I'm the fastest runner.'

She was gone in an instant; Inez wrapped her hands around her elbows and gazed over towards the trees, pointedly avoiding the stares of the other Amazons. 'I didn't do it deliberately,' she said.

'I don't suppose you did,' said Freda, 'but you might say sorry, at the very least.'

'Someone's going to have to tell Miss Simpkin,' said Winnie. 'Bagsy not me.'

'Me neither,' said Avril.

'Well, obviously, it should be Inez,' said Freda. 'It's only justice.'

The *Ham & High* had sent along the sports reporter.

'So, hang on,' he said, licking his pencil. 'When you say that it's a political organization . . .'

'Only in the Greek sense.'

'The Greek . . . ?'

'I have no party affiliation, merely the aim of encouraging the girls to take their rightful places in the modern world. Knowledge, confidence, ready laughter and a strong overarm throw will equip them for many arenas.'

She was watching the teams as she spoke: why on earth Jacko had chosen to clothe the League in garments the colour of a municipal drainpipe was quite beyond her. By contrast, the Amazons, aligning themselves for a photograph, were a frieze of splendid non-conformity.

'Glory be to God for dappled things,' she said, 'for skies as couple-coloured as a brinded cow.'

The journalist, frowning, turned a page. 'So there's a religious element, then, to the club?'

'Heaven forbid,' said Mattie.

Jacko, standing close by, gave a chuckle.

'Miss Simpkin is gulling you,' she said to the journalist. 'Verbal sparring is her speciality – beware!'

Mattie managed a stiff smile; Jacko's friendliness had been unexpected and disconcerting. Instead of the preliminary rattle of arms, there had been a ghastly half-hour of Fascist small talk, conversation among the group of League supporters under the trees moving viscously from the Ethiopian Treaty to the Menace of the Trades Unions via the impossibility of hiring a cook.

'Should we start?' asked Mattie, eyeing the scuffles beginning to break out among the smallest of the spectators. 'We are in danger of losing our audience.'

'I think one of your girls is coming over to talk to you,' said Jacko. 'Oh, I recognize her. That's Inez, isn't it? Her brother Ralph's our first officer and a thorough brick.' She swayed nearer to Mattie's ear and lowered her voice. 'You know that their mother was the splendid Venetia Campbell? Though I fear that the splendour may somewhat have bypassed Inez – perhaps she's more her father's child. How do you find her?'

'I find her to be bursting with potential,' said Mattie, tight-lipped.

'Really? Hello, Inez!'

'Hello, Mrs Cellini.'

'I very much like your sash. What are all those gold stars for?'

'One of them is for something to do with initiative, I think. I can't really remember the rest. Miss Simpkin?'

'Yes, Inez?'

'The Indian clubs were accidentally left behind at your house. Doris has gone back for them.'

'Oh. Oh dear.'

'Oh *dear*,' echoed Jacko, sympathetically, in a way that made Mattie want to pick her up like a caber and toss her over the refreshments table. 'Well, it won't really make any difference if we go first, will it? Let me have a word with Richard.'

She left to speak to her husband and Mattie saw him raise an eyebrow; both of them glanced back at her, Jacko's mouth bunched in suppressed amusement.

'They're laughing at us,' said Inez.

'As I've said many times, one should never mind that.' Although, to be frank, she was currently minding it very much indeed.

'My brother Ralph says they call the Amazons "The Raggle-Taggle Gypsies-O".'

'I have been called far worse, Inez, and I can assure you that I've suffered no chronic effects.'

'Ralph's friend Simeon said we're bound to lose the treasure hunt.'

'Why?'

'Because girls talk all the time, so they'll be winning while we're still discussing the clues.'

'How ridiculous. What did you say by way of riposte?'

Inez shrugged. 'I didn't. It doesn't really matter, does it? And if we do win, it won't be anything to do with me, will it? I never know anything.'

'You're part of the team.'

'Not really.'

Her expression was, as always, impassive; Angus, carved from clay. Oh, for something, thought Mattie, that might animate those features; oh, that the afternoon might end in a victory to which Inez had somehow contributed, and in that moment of personal triumph (*and everyone's congratulating you and you feel like a queen,* Ida had said) – in that joyful melee of hats thrown, hands clasped, friendship encircling all like a golden girdle – might the girl not see something beyond herself, a shining city?

'GOOD AFTERNOON.'

The announcement was so loud that one of the lady spectators gave a little shriek. Richard Cellini, dressed in a stalking jacket, had brought a megaphone with him.

'WELCOME TO THE HAMPSTEAD HEATH YOUTH GAMES. THE DISPLAY WILL BEGIN WITH A DEMONSTRATION OF FORMATION MARCHING BY THE EMPIRE YOUTH LEAGUE. FORWARD – THE LEAGUE!!'

The snare drums rattled like a burst of fireworks and the children in the crowd scrambled to their feet.

'Inez,' said Mattie.

'Yes?'

'Later on in the day, remember that ash trees have keys.'

'What?'

'The fruit of the ash tree is called a key. Look, I think I can see Doris on her way back. You'd better join the others.'

Inez drifted away, and Mattie watched the marchers cross and criss-cross in a web of well-drilled pointlessness, the ferocious rhythm of the drums setting up an answering throb in her own head. 'Such discipline,' one of Jacko's friends was saying, 'and how smart they look!' and Jacko herself was taking photographs while her husband stood with his legs apart and his hands behind his back, like an adjutant (though he was nothing of the sort, he'd been head of an insurance firm in Brisbane), and in the distance, behind the rows of swinging arms and blank expressions, Mattie could see Inez slowly approaching the other girls and *Good God*, she thought, *Good God, what was I thinking? What have I done?* And the realization was like a dead weight, impossible for her to carry, and she let it drop and waved encouragingly at Doris, who had trotted the last few yards, apparently still full of puff, swinging the canvas bag. Splendid girls, she thought, they were splendid girls; all of them.

No one could pretend that the club-swinging had gone well. What should have looked effortless felt laboured, and instead of rows of graceful, rhythmic arcs, there were awkward jerks and the intermittent clack of collisions. Worst of all, Elsie's sweaty fingers released a club mid-swing and it flew like a bulbous arrow and hit the journalist from the *Ham & High* on the right shin. One of the League boys shouted, 'LBW!'

After that, there were demonstrations of self-defence, semaphore and Morse code, followed by a brief debate on a subject picked out of a hat ('This House believes that education should be compulsory up to the age of twenty-one' – a motion unpopular with the junior crowd, despite Freda's able defence), and then the Empire League sang 'Marching to the Bright Horizon' and the Amazons sang 'Bread and Roses' and, halfway through the second verse, Winnie was sick on the grass. Ida helped to carry her into the shade.

'I suggest that everyone stays out of the sun for twenty minutes,' said Miss Simpkin, just as Mr Cellini was raising his megaphone.

'THE YOUTH GAMES WILL RECOMMENCE IN TWENTY MINUTES.'

'It's not the sun,' said Avril, charged with applying a cold compress to her sister's forehead. 'It's because she ate five pieces of ginger cake.'

'Four,' said Winnie, feebly.

Ida fanned herself with her hat, relieved that the most public aspect of the display was over. It was odd, she thought, that Miss Lee hadn't come to watch.

'You look awfully hot.'

She turned to see one of the League boys, older than her, all smirk and sparkling buttons.

'Ten out of ten for observation,' she said, tartly, and he grinned, showing teeth like a film star's.

'I've brought you some lemonade.'

'Have you? Why?'

'Don't you want it?'

'All right.' She took the glass and downed it in a couple of gulps. 'Thanks.'

'Have mine as well, if you're that thirsty.'

'No thank you.' She waited for him to go, but he stayed, seemingly perfectly at ease. He looked like John Barrymore, only more handsome. 'Your name's Ida, isn't it?'

'Yes.'

'I was just talking to Inez,' he said. 'Her brother's a great friend of mine.'

'And?'

'And nothing, really. I'm just making conversation.'

'Why?'

'Because despite looking as if you're about to burst into flames, you're very pretty.'

She could hardly get any redder, but she found herself smiling for what was certainly the first time that day.

'I've seen you before,' he said. 'Flag-waving on Parliament Hill. You were quite snappish with me last time as well. I obviously bring out the worst in you.'

'I expect I was concentrating.'

'I expect you were. I'm going to sit down – would you care to join me?'

She hesitated, and then he took out a handkerchief and spread it on the grass for her, so she could hardly refuse, though she twitched it a bit further away from him before she sat.

'My name's Simeon, by the way,' he said. 'Are you enjoying the afternoon?'

'Not much.'

'Nor me. On the whole, I'd rather be swimming. What about you, what would you prefer to be doing?'

'Just . . . sitting in the shade, I think.'

'As you are now?'

'Yes.'

'So I've already made your afternoon perfect!'

She had to laugh a bit. 'Maybe if I had an ice as well.'

He leaned back on his hands, almost inspecting her.

'Are you still at school?' he asked.

'No. Are you?'

'I've just matriculated. So what do you do?'

'If you've been talking to Inez, I bet you know that already. I bet she couldn't wait to tell you where I work.'

'At Big Chief Amazon's?'

'Yes.'

He shrugged. 'I don't mind.'

'What do you mean, you "don't mind"? What's it got to do with you, anyway?'

'You're absolutely right, it's none of my business. I just meant that being Miss Simpkin's daily doesn't make you any less pretty. Or snappish.' He gave her another grin, though this time she was less inclined to smile back.

'I go to classes as well,' she said. 'I want to get on.'

'Do you? Crikey, I don't.'

'Why not?'

'"Getting on" always seems to imply having to work in an office from dawn till dusk. I think I'd like to do something less . . . straitjacketed.'

'Nice to have the choice.'

'Ralph wants to be Prime Minister. He's terribly self-disciplined.'

'Is that Inez's brother?'

'Yes.'

'He doesn't sound much like her.'

'I gather you two don't get on.'

'Is that what she says? We "don't get on"? After I've spent weeks and weeks helping her with everything and trying to be nice, while she looks down her nose at me as if I'm her flipping lady's maid!'

Simeon was looking bemused.

'Don't get cross,' he said. 'Inez is just a silly, rather boring little girl. Nobody takes any notice of her. *I* don't. You're ten times more interesting.'

'How do you know I'm more interesting? We only met about a minute ago.'

'I can sense it.'

'Oh, don't be daft.' She looked away, unsure of whether to feel flattered or angry. It seemed that people like him, people with easy lives, were always assuming things about her: she was stupid because she was a char; she was interesting because she was pretty; she'd be loyal because she was grateful. Nobody except Miss Lee ever asked her what she really thought.

'You're not awfully good at receiving compliments, are you?' said Simeon. 'I was always told that one should simply say thank you.'

'Well, bully for one.' She scrambled to her feet. 'I don't mind saying thank you for the lemonade, though.'

'That's all right.' He looked up at her, squinting at the bright beads of sunlight between the leaves. 'Best of luck for the treasure hunt. Do you have any idea of how it's supposed to proceed?'

'Didn't they tell you?'

'Yes, but I wasn't listening very hard. There was a king-fisher on a post behind RC's head when he was speaking and I couldn't help watching it. Have you ever seen a kingfisher close to?'

'Only flying. Up by the ponds, last month.'

'They're wonderful, aren't they?'

'It was so fast I could hardly see it. Like someone draw-ing a blue line in the air.'

He nodded, slowly. 'I'd say that's a perfect description. And poetic, too. So go on, be charitable, tell me the rules again. There are clues hidden, aren't there?'

'Yes, Miss Simpkin and your leaders made them up. Both teams get given a compass and a clue – the same clue – and they have to work out from it where the next clue's hidden and send out runners to fetch it. And there are five clues altogether. And as well as solving them you have to—' Abruptly, she closed her mouth.

'What?'

She grinned. 'I can't tell you. It's strategy.'

'Aha!' He stood up, and indolently straightened his uni-form. 'Well, as I say, *bonne chance*. If you triumph, may I buy you an ice?'

'All right, then,' she said, emboldened by the sudden ease of the conversation. 'Vanilla wafer, please.'

'And what do I get if my team's the victor?'

'It won't be.'

'You're sounding fearfully confident.'

'Confidence is the staff that supports all our endeavours,' she said, and walked off with her head in the air, knowing that he was watching her. And now, for the first time, she really wanted to win.

'First clue cracked!' said Mattie.

Doris and Avril had broken away from the huddle of Amazons and were sprinting off to the north-east, while the League was still in a cluster, one or two heads turning anxiously to watch the other team. After a few moments, and some worried discussion, a boy and a girl headed off in the same direction as the Amazons.

'I don't think I understand what's happening,' said the journalist.

Richard Cellini cleared his throat, as if about to deliver a lecture. 'The clue will lead to a hiding place containing two further identical clues, one for each team. The new clue must be brought back to be opened and solved, and then the next runners will be sent out.'

'Or *not* solved,' added Mattie. 'I have the feeling – don't you? – that the League has failed with the first puzzle and have simply despatched a pair of hounds to follow my girls in order to find the hiding place. Which, of course, is perfectly acceptable as a tactic. One should always use whatever means are most suited to the occasion – isn't that so, Jacko? Remember how you ambushed Asquith by disguising yourself as a flower-seller?'

'Vaguely,' said Jacko.

'We used to say, "It's hell for leather and it's neck or nothing!"'

'So' – the journalist glanced back at his notepad – 'does that mean that *any* tactic is acceptable?'

Jacko raised an eyebrow. 'Well, I think we're both wedded to fair play, aren't we, Mattie? Youth should remain unsullied by – oh, could you excuse me a moment, a friend has arrived.' She didn't wait for an answer, but walked across to greet a young woman who was bumping a baby-carriage across the grass, and Mattie found herself standing in awful silence beside Cellini. What *did* one say to such a stick?

'When you were in Australia, did you ever see a duck-billed platypus?' she asked.

'No, I didn't.'

'Or an echidna?'

'No.'

'They're the only examples of monotremes in the entire world, I believe.'

The silence stretched.

Doris and Avril were back in ten minutes, Avril with a thread-wrapped piece of paper clutched in a damp fist.

'The League followed us the whole way,' said Doris between gasps, 'but we split up when we got to the pond and that confused them for a couple of minutes. The clue was wedged behind the lifebuoy, like Freda guessed. They'll have found it by now, I think.'

'All right,' said Ida, unwrapping the thread and spreading out the strip of paper. 'Well done. This one says, "HEAD DUE WEST TO ICENI QUEEN'S LAST RESTING PLACE. AT IL DUCE'S COLOURS LOOK FOR BROCK'S FRONT DOOR."'

'Ill what?'

'"Duce", it says. D, U, C, E.'

'Doochay,' said Freda. 'That's what they call Mussolini.'

'Old Baldy Musso?'

'So what's his colours?'

'The Italian flag's white, green and red, isn't it?'

'But I think it's changed now. Yellow, maybe. There might be a ribbon to look out for – or chalks.'

'The rest is easy,' said Ida. 'Boadicea's supposed to be buried in that little wood at the top.'

'The tumulus, you mean?'

'And Brock's a badger!' piped Winnie, from where she was still lying in the shade.

'*Shhhhhhh*,' said everyone, heads swivelling to see if the other group had overheard. The League's two runners were hurtling back across the field towards the group, waving the clue.

'*They'll* know what the Doochay colours are,' said Freda, darkly. 'Why don't we set off and see if we can work it out once we're there. It's me and Evadne next, isn't it?' And she was gone, Evadne just behind her, pigtail flapping beneath her panama.

'It's exciting!' said Elsie, bouncing up and down. 'And after Freda it's you and me, isn't it, Hildegard? And then Winnie and Ida?'

'I don't think Winnie's up to it.'

'I might be,' said Winnie, struggling to sit up.

'Helping to answer the questions is just as useful,' said Ida. She glanced across at the League and saw that Simeon was looking directly at her. He raised a hand, discreetly, and then crooked a finger towards the huddle of League members and shook his head.

'What you laughing at?' asked Elsie.

'Nothing,' said Ida.

Inez quite liked the heat. She never went red in the face like some of the other girls, and she knew that her linen shift from Eaton's suited her well, its colour very nearly matching her eyes. It made everyone else look as if they were dressed in crumpled dishcloths. Not that anybody had commented on her frock – coming to the Amazons was almost like being invisible; the other girls scarcely looked in her direction and, when they did, their gaze skidded straight off again. It was only when she spoke that anyone noticed her. 'Do you think Freda knows that she sticks out one of her feet when she runs?'

'No. But I expect you'll make sure you tell her,' said Ida.

'It looks quite funny, actually. As if she's doing sema-phore with one foot.'

Ida, with a visible effort, turned her back.

'You shouldn't say personal things,' said Avril. 'Not unless you're related to someone. Anyway, you're walking in a funny way yourself today – on tiptoe. You kept bang-ing into people when we were carrying everything across.'

'Did I?'

'You must *know*.'

Inez smiled mysteriously, and moved away. She had, in fact, been trying out her mother's walk, as described by Miss Lee: a sort of gliding bounce, though it was difficult to maintain a straight line while doing so. In photographs, her mother was always sitting; Inez had never imagined her in motion before, with people turning to look as she went past.

There was a shout from the League as two runners tore away, heading for Parliament Hill, their faces set and serious. Inez could see her brother and Simeon watching them, and she tried her gliding walk again, in a direction which took her across Simeon's eyeline.

'Have you hurt your foot, Inez?' called Miss Simpkin, from the shade beside the refreshments.

'No,' said Inez.

Simeon was looking towards her. She attempted the type of smile which made people want to smile back, and for a moment his expression remained blank, and then he absolutely *grinned*, except that she realized, with a jolt, that he was looking not at her but past her, and when she turned her head to see who he was smiling at, it was Ida.

Jacko was holding her friend's infant as if it were an awkwardly shaped vase, rather than with the casual firmness that babies required, and it was emitting thin squeaks as an obvious preliminary to full-scale shrieking.

'There, there,' said Jacko, rather desperately.

'Now hush, little chap,' said Mattie, taking the child's waving fists and blowing a raspberry on each. It stopped squeaking and gazed at her with apparent astonishment, and then spotted its mother approaching, and started wailing in earnest.

'I don't have the knack,' said Jacko, relinquishing the child. 'Clearly.' For a moment she seemed to lose her composure, and Richard's hand was quickly on her shoulder, in a gesture more tender than one might have predicted.

'Nor did I,' said her friend, 'but when the little bundle finally arrives in one's arms . . .' She bent her face towards the child's, lowering her lashes so that she looked like a third-rate copy of a Raphael Virgin.

'Those of us who have never borne a child may yet bear the new world,' said Mattie, rather sharply. 'Now look!' she added, as both pairs of runners reappeared at the same time, pounding down the northern slope of Parliament Hill, Freda and Evadne perceptibly ahead. 'Neck and neck!'

Inez watched Simeon for a while longer, and just once he glanced around and saw her, and gave a little nod, the way you might nod at a coalman, but his gaze kept swivelling back to Ida, who looked as though she had just been scrubbing a floor, her face damp, her stockings wrinkled. Inez, in her pale blue dress, was ignored, the world carrying on around her, Hildegard and Elsie haring off, a peppering of tiny clouds drifting across the sky, children shouting and jumping, a dog sniffing past, the sun pressing on her head like a thumb, and she wished there could be a giant blackboard – here, on the Heath – so she could drag her fingernails down it, very slowly, and everything would come to a halt and everyone would turn and look at her and she'd be right at the centre. They'd all see her then.

The League runners were the first back, followed after nearly a minute of unbearable tension by Elsie, supporting a limping Hildegard.

'We were ahead,' she called breathlessly, almost in tears, 'but I turned my ankle jumping down from a branch. So stupid of me, and Elsie wouldn't go on without me.'

'Good for Elsie, quite right, too,' said Freda, grabbing the clue and unrolling it to reveal a sprinkling of dots and dashes. 'It's in Morse code! Ida, you're wizard at this.'

'And the Empire lot are still puzzling,' called Doris, on the look-out. 'We're still in with a chance.'

Ida stared at the paper. 'Due. East. Near. Green. Shed. Del . . . Delve. Where. Keys. Grow. For. Prize.'

'That's probably the gardener's shed near the bathing pond,' said Freda. 'That's due east, isn't it?'

'But where do keys grow?'

'The League must have cracked it!' said Doris. 'They're off!'

'What does it mean, keys *grow*?'

'In locks, maybe?'

'Just go, Ida,' said Doris. 'Otherwise, there's no chance you'll catch up, and you can try and work it out on the way.'

'But what about Winnie? She's not up to it, is she?'

'I might be,' said Winnie, starting to get up and then immediately sitting down again.

'Go on your own, Ida.'

'Keys grow on ash trees,' said Inez. She was standing a few feet away from the others.

'What?'

'The fruit of the ash is called a key.'

'How do *you* know?' asked Avril, dismissively, already turning away. Inez raised her voice.

233

'I know it because Miss Simpkin secretly told me the answer.'

There was a moment of total silence, like the pause after a firework. And now every eye was on her.

'No she didn't,' said Ida, flatly.

'Yes she did, as a matter of fact. About an hour ago.'

'She'd never do that, that's cheating.'

Inez shrugged. 'Then she cheated.'

'Don't be daft,' said Ida. 'You must think we're all doolally.'

And Inez smiled. 'You'll see,' she said.

Ida's shadow slid before her as she ran; far ahead, she could see two bottle-green dots moving in the same direction, taking a line that led towards the bathing pond, and it seemed impossible that she could catch them, and, moreover, it was hard to buck herself up for the solitary chase. When she'd set off there'd been none of the baying encouragement which had launched the earlier runners, only some half-hearted 'Good luck's and a limp wave from Winnie; instead, the Amazons had drawn together in an uneasy, whispering cluster, shooting glances at Inez, and towards the refreshments table, where Miss Simpkin was tipping crumbs from plates. And now the only sounds were her own breath and the whack of her footsteps and the hiss of long grass around her ankles. She should, she knew, be thinking about the clue, but her thoughts kept bouncing away from the subject.

Ahead, one of the green dots stopped and bobbed down to tie a lace, and Ida plunged onward and had halved the distance between them by the time the pair were off again. When she reached the narrow belt of woodland that separated the hillside from the pond, the shade was like a cold hand on her forehead.

'No key!' said a voice just ahead, and Ida grabbed a branch as a brake. Between the trunks she could see sunlight. She edged forward, until the yellow grass of a clearing was visible, a woodpile stacked in one corner, a roll of chestnut stakes and the remains of a bonfire quite close to her, and on the far side, forty feet away, the green tool-shed. A League boy was rattling the door, and a girl was standing just behind him, hands on hips; it was Olive, the curly-headed one from the continuation school.

'We keep our key under the door-mat,' she said.

'Sheds don't have door-mats.'

'I was just saying. Maybe it's hidden around here.'

'The clue said, "where keys grow".'

'Is it under a plant, then?'

'Which plant? It's all plants, isn't it? Where would we start?'

Ida watched as, rather aimlessly, they began to cast around the shrubby edge of the clearing, and a kind of hopeful window seemed to open in her head, because all the other clues had been quite precise: once the meaning had been pinned down, the hiding place had become suddenly obvious – a lifebuoy or a badger's sett – and the vagueness of Inez's 'ash trees' surely meant that she'd just made the whole thing up and the claim that Miss Simpkin had given her the answer was her usual needling nonsense. This clue, then, like all the others, would lead to a particular spot: the shed roof, maybe, or the woodpile – or the roll of stakes – or the . . .

The hopeful window slammed shut. The bonfire beside her consisted of a few ends of charred wood, and a small pyramid of ash.

Ash.

The League runners were rustling around at the back of the shed. Ida stepped into the clearing and crouched beside the bonfire. A thin gold line was visible in the pale ash, and she nipped it with her nails and drew out a metal disc, twice the diameter of a sovereign. 'TREASURE HUNT WINNERS. HAMPSTEAD HEATH YOUTH GAMES 1928' was engraved on it, with a border of leaves. She sat back on her heels. All the afternoon's tension had gone; she felt as flat as an ironed sheet.

'Hey!' It was Olive, hurtling across the clearing. She stopped when she saw what was in Ida's hand. 'Oh!' she exclaimed. 'You've won. They've won,' she added tragically over her shoulder, towards her team-mate. 'How did you know to look in there?'

'Keys grow on ash trees,' said Ida. 'Ash.'

The boy came across, tall and skinny, with a narrow, lipless face. 'Bugger,' he said. 'No beano for us.'

Olive was looking at Ida curiously. 'What's the matter? Why aren't you going back?'

'Take it,' said Ida, holding out the medal.

'What?'

'We cheated.'

Olive's mouth dropped open.

'You *cheated*?'

'Go on – take it.'

'How did you cheat?'

'One of the girls was given the answer to the last clue.'

'Who by?'

'It doesn't matter. Just take it. You can pretend you found it by yourselves and I'll pretend you got to it before me and no one will know and you'll get your beano.'

The other two exchanged glances. 'All right.' They set off immediately, and Ida stood up stiffly, like an old woman, like her aunt when she'd been lighting the copper. The day had snapped shut. Inside it were the Amazons and Sundays on the Heath and 'all pals together' and shrieks and silliness and feathers in the hair, but she was done with that now. It had never been real, anyway.

The thought of going back to the others was horrible, but if she didn't go, they might start scouring the Heath for her, so she walked very slowly through the trees and across the open hillside, and in the distance she heard applause and cheering, boys' voices as well as girls', and she thought of Elsie and Winnie and Avril, who had been so excited, and she wanted to hit someone, though she wasn't sure whether that 'someone' was Miss Simpkin or Inez – or herself, as a punishment for being hopeful.

The sun was in her eyes now, the view just a golden dazzle, so she kept her gaze on the ground and didn't see the approaching figure until he was just yards away.

'Hello,' said Simeon. 'I volunteered to come and find you. Did you get lost?'

'No.'

'I say, you're not crying, are you?'

'*No*. The sun's in my eyes.'

She turned her head away from him, walking faster.

'I wouldn't hurry back,' he said. 'There's been rather an ugly scene.'

'What are you talking about?'

'Apparently, Inez told your team that Big Chief Amazon gave her the answer to the last question, and word has leaked out. The Cellinis were cock-a-hoop, since they thought the League had won *without* cheating, but Olive was looking very shifty, and has now confessed that you handed them the medal gratis, so the whole thing has slid into farce.' He gave a little huff of laughter. 'The journalist was scribbling away like a good 'un.'

'Is everything a joke to you?' asked Ida.

'Most things, yes. Don't you think life's funny?'

'No.' She wiped her eyes on a sleeve.

'I don't have a clean handkerchief, I'm afraid. But I *do* have a florin, and I'm fully prepared to spend it. Could I buy you an ice?'

'No.'

'Golly, I'd love to hear you say yes to something. Let me have a go – do you like peaches?'

She shook her head.

'Is the sky blue?'

She shrugged.

'Do I reek of sweat?'

'Yes.'

He mimed shock, and she had to bite back a smile.

'That's better,' he said, and then he kissed her, and though she pushed him away, she didn't push very hard.

∽

The Flea heard the back door open, and hurriedly drew herself upright. She was sitting at the kitchen table, topping and tailing a bowl of gooseberries, though her hands were so cold that the scissors felt awkward in her grasp, like rusty pliers.

'Sorry I missed it!' she called. 'I had a dizzy turn, nothing serious, just the heat. Victory, I hope?'

Mattie didn't reply, which was strange; equally odd was the silence that followed – no vigorous footsteps along the scullery passage, no wrenching open of the kitchen door.

'Is that one of the girls?' called The Flea. 'Is that you, Elsie?'

She stood up, taking a moment to steady herself and giving her cheeks a quick pinch to brighten them, and then at last there were footsteps. The door opened and it was Mattie after all, her face shaded by the wide-brimmed hat.

'I've promised some local boys a half-crown to bring the crockery and tables back,' she said, before The Flea could speak. 'They'll be here in a few minutes.' And then she was gone again, through the door into the hall. After a moment, The Flea followed her, and found her in the drawing room, pouring herself a glass of whisky.

'Is something wrong, Mattie? Where are the girls? Has there been an accident?'

'No, no accident, no one has been injured.'

She downed half the glass in one gulp, and closed her eyes at the fiery bloom of the whisky. When she opened them again, she was immediately skewered by The Flea's worried gaze; she swallowed the rest of the measure and poured another. 'Did you say that you'd had a dizzy spell?' she asked, delaying the moment of explanation.

'Oh, it was nothing. I was outside without a hat.'

Mattie put down the glass and withdrew a couple of pins and removed her straw, and the late-afternoon sun seemed to leap into the room.

'I did something rather unfortunate,' she said.

The Flea made a little movement; a silent question.

'During the competition' – it was like trying to swallow a lump of stale bread – 'I behaved in what might be seen as an underhand fashion.'

There was a pause.

'I don't understand,' said The Flea.

'I was talking to Inez and she was . . . not engaged in the proceedings and, in a moment of what I can only call madness, I gave her the solution to one of the clues, thinking it might ignite her spirit – might allow her to participate, to *enjoy* the afternoon. For whatever reason, she informed the Amazons that I had done this, and a great deal – a very great deal – of unhappiness has resulted.'

'Is it true, Miss Simpkin,' Elsie had asked, 'what Inez said you done?' and Mattie had perforce nodded, and that nod – that single nod – had ended everything; the girls had looked at her and left, Winnie and Avril arm in arm for once, Doris holding Elsie's hand, Freda's expression pinched, her gaze studiously avoiding Mattie's, Hildegard

240

holding her head theatrically high; in a straggling line they had walked away along the path towards the bandstand and the bus stop – those marvellous girls, gone; a bunch of roses scattered, a beehive smoked and empty. And all the while, the Cellinis had been watching, and Inez, too, from those faery eyes.

And Mattie – who seldom regretted anything, because life was too large for pettifogging, and brooding over regrets was like swatting midges when one was trying to wrestle a bear – had wanted to stuff her words back into her own foolish, flapping mouth. And as she had walked back across the Heath, the thought that she would be required to actually explain out loud what she had done was almost unbearable, like the prospect of scraping at an already painful graze, and she found herself wishing that the house might be empty for once.

'Is your companion not here?' Jacko had asked earlier, looking round as if she expected to see The Flea hiding behind a bush.

'She's been preparing the refreshments.'

'And very delicious they are, too. How well she looks after you!'

And now The Flea was looking aghast.

'You honestly thought that giving Inez a clue would spring her to life?'

'It was an impulse,' said Mattie, 'not a plan.'

'But good God, I talked to the girl myself today. She doesn't give two hoots about competitions or camaraderie, she doesn't want the answer to a riddle, that's not what she's searching for. How can you not see that? She is not yours to shape – you can't hope to mould a child, when that child doesn't care for you in the slightest. She doesn't want what you are offering, Mattie, she wants her *mother*. Her mother. Only her mother.' The Flea's hands were trembling. 'For all your intellect, you can be an awful fool sometimes. And what on earth did the other girls say? What did Ida say? They must have been so dreadfully upset after all their hard work. You encourage their self-reliance, you praise their initiative and then you . . .' The Flea abruptly sat down. 'I should have said something to you weeks ago. You have been . . . *possessed*, and yet I kept hesitating; I've been cowardly, I was afraid of making you angry. I know your brothers are precious in your memory, but memories are not always exact and Angus may not have been the paragon you seem to recall, and all the while you have been ignoring the treasure in front of you and searching for something that scarcely exists – a . . . a . . . *mirage*.' She shook her head. 'I blame myself,' she said. 'I should have spoken.'

Mattie set down her glass. 'I do not require you to be my conscience, Florrie.'

'But—'

'You have no responsibility for me; my mistakes are my own and I shall deal with them. I do not need you to fret about my every move and decision, I do not need to be *looked after*, nor do I need to be scolded like . . . like an errant spouse.'

Florrie's head jerked back as if she'd been slapped and simultaneously the doorbell jangled and Mattie went to answer it. The whole front garden seemed full of boys and tables and crockery, and she found herself distributing handfuls of change in a distracted manner, barely reacting when a pile of plates hit the sink with a careless smash. A jar of ginger jam was dropped, hitting her squarely on the big toe, a small boy's fingers required attention after being nipped between a table-top and a doorframe, and the ammonite on the windowsill provoked a discussion ('It's a dead snail!') which could only be curtailed by the production of pear drops – and then, at last, limping slightly, she ushered them out and closed the door.

The house was silent, the drawing room empty. Mattie stood at the window for a minute or two, watching swallows loop above the garden, and then she tramped up the stairs and along the corridor to The Flea's room.

'Florrie?'

She could hear movements within. She knocked and waited and then knocked again.

'Would you like a cup of tea? I'll bring one up for you. Florrie?'

There was no reply, only the sound of a drawer being opened. Mattie felt indescribably weary; the day had been absolutely bloody, and if The Flea wished to sulk in her room, then so be it. The memory of her own words, spoken in fury, dipped briefly towards her and then swooped away, unrecoverable.

Back in the drawing room, she took volume one of Fuller's *Worthies* from the bookcase and fell asleep over Thomas de la Lynde, who killed a white hart in Blackmoor Forest and was punished. She didn't hear the front door open, and then softly close again.

PART 3

'I mentioned in my letter that I would need an assistant,' said Mattie to the elderly gentleman who opened the door for her at Ipswich Masonic Hall, an east wind elbowing between them. The cabbie who had driven Mattie from the station helped her to carry in the boxes of glass slides.

The hall itself was almost equally draughty, the canvas screen that hung at the back of the stage bellying like a sail. A lectern stood at the front, and a magic lantern was already in place on a table halfway down the aisle; Mattie arranged the boxes beside it.

'Yes, my great-nephew Roley will be helping you,' said Mr Wilkes, his eyes watery behind pince-nez. 'He's an intelligent boy.'

'It's simply a matter of agreeing on a prearranged signal.' It was the first time she had given a lecture without the aid of The Flea, and she had spent the previous evening whittling down the number of slides so that, instead of the usual six boxes, she need only bring three with her. It had been a complicated and time-consuming exercise, during the course of which, when reaching for a pencil, she had managed to knock two of the glass plates from the desk, and on standing to inspect the damage had

247

inadvertently stepped on another. As ill luck would have it, all had been photographs of the great processions, and it had taken a prolonged search through the cupboards in the lumber room to unearth The Flea's box of 'spares', one of which appeared to show the Coronation March. She had been enraged by her own clumsiness – at one point in the evening, she had stood on the stairs and shouted, 'Damn and blast!' so loudly that her throat was still aching.

No one, obviously, had opened the drawing-room door to enquire tartly what might be the matter.

'Roley, this is Miss Simpkin.'

He was, perhaps, seventeen, shaped like a yardstick – tall but very narrow, his feet the widest part of him – and his expression was that of an Inca sacrifice awaiting slaughter.

'You've operated a magic lantern before?' asked Mattie.

'Yes,' he said, the single syllable covering an octave.

'Very good. Each of these boxes is numbered, as you can see. I shan't be progressing through them in order, so we need to work out a system of signals. I see there's a small bell on the lectern – I can ring it once for Box 1 and twice for Box 2, but to avoid the impression of campanology, I think we should come up with an alternative for Box 3. How would it do if I rapped my knuckles on the lectern instead? And when I give the signal, you must load the next slide from the requisite box and then listen for my verbal cue to actually change it – I shall say, "Slide, please." Does that seem reasonable?'

Roley swallowed, his Adam's apple rising and sinking like a bathysphere.

'Can you say it again, please?'

'Of course. One bell, Box 1; two bells, Box 2; knuckles, Box 3; and then I'll say, "slide, please" – would you like to write it down? I'm certain you'll do a fine job – oh, Mr Wilkes, before I forget, a friend of mine is coming this evening. Could I reserve a seat for her? Her name is Mrs Procter.'

It wasn't until she was waiting in the wings for the lecture to start that Mattie realized that she had forgotten to bring her sash. Absent, too, was her usual sense of eager tension, that feeling of a runner poised for the pistol; she could hear the audience and yet it seemed to stir nothing within her, beyond the thought that on the whole she would rather be spending the evening in front of the fire with a book. She felt unsprung; unleavened.

'. . . fortunate today,' Mr Wilkes was saying, 'in having a very experienced speaker, Miss Simpson, here to tell us about her . . . er . . . experiences. Which I'm sure will be most interesting. Before I forget, after Colonel Duncan's talk on Sarawak last week, a black umbrella was found under a seat, and if anyone . . .'

'I think that was mine,' called a faint, elderly voice.

'Could you see me afterwards, so that I may return it?'

'Does it have a tortoiseshell handle?'

'I believe so.'

'Yes, that's mine. Good. It was my aunt's, you know.'

There was a pause, presumably for Mr Wilkes to ensure that any remaining trace of anticipation had been sluiced from the room, and then Mattie was introduced once more, this time as Miss Timpson, and came on to the stage to a smattering of applause.

'Good evening,' she said. 'My name is Matilda Simpkin.

249

I hope, over the next hour or so, to convey something of the history and methods of the militant suffragette movement . . .'

The lectern lamp was very bright, and she could see little beyond it. Roberta, she knew, was sitting beside the aisle in the fourth row, and Mattie addressed her opening remarks in that direction, flicking the little bell that dangled from the reading light.

'Slide, please,' said Mattie. 'Mary Somerville. Mother of six, self-taught scientist, jointly the first female member of the Royal Astronomical Society. The Oxford college for women is named after her.'

She glanced over her shoulder at the screen, and was reassured to see the expected image: the pleasantly ovine face of a genius. 'I myself studied at that college, although Oxford University did not, and still does not, see fit to award its undergraduettes with a degree, despite exam results which have often exceeded those of the male students.'

'Shame!' called a familiar voice from the fourth row.

'It is indeed a shame,' said Mattie, nodding towards her fellow Somervillian. 'And illustrates a familiar pattern in the struggle of the female for both civil and legal equality, viz: it is not enough for us to match the intellectual and organizational accomplishments of men – it is not even enough for us to outstrip them. Whatever our achievements, we are expected to wait, like patient Griselda, on the whim of those in power.' She tapped the bell. 'Now here is another cloistered member of our sex – one to whom three successive Viceroys of India came for advice. Slide please.'

As Florence Nightingale replaced Mary Somerville, Mattie glanced at the notebook that lay open on the lectern. Usually, she would talk extempore, but on this occasion it was clearly expedient that she stick to an order, and the thought of this marked path, from which she must not stray, made the hour ahead seem like a forced march. She was conscious that her speech was less fluent than normal, its content more pedestrian, the audience no more than politely attentive.

'Any questions?' she asked, after the introduction. 'Before we move on to the birth of the WSPU.'

'Yes, I have one.' It was the quavering voice of the umbrella owner.

'Fire away,' said Mattie, shading her eyes in an attempt to see the questioner.

'Do you think you will be finished by eight o'clock?'

'*Finished?*' Mattie checked her wristwatch. 'I rather doubt it, given that I've only just started and it's already seven forty-five.'

'Oh dear. Only I told Maria that I would be back by ten past eight. I must have got the time wrong. I don't know what to do now.' There was a sigh.

'In 1903—' began Mattie.

'No, I think I should go, or Maria will worry. Excuse me, I'm most awfully sorry, could I just get past?' Inevitably, the speaker was at the centre of a row.

'That rather reminds me,' said Mattie, raising her voice in an attempt to cover the shuffles, apologies and exclamations, 'of the story of the cook Maria, which was sometimes used to illustrate the masculine attitude towards women's talents. "Maria," said her master, "you are a most excellent cook but I can no longer afford to—"'

'Oh, I've forgotten my umbrella – do you have it, Mr Wilkes?'

'Yes, here it is, Miss Carr.'

'"—I can no longer afford to pay your wage. Will you marry me?"'

The joke died quietly, its back broken.

'So where were we?' asked Mattie, slightly rattled, checking her notebook and then flicking the bell twice. 'Yes, 1903, and Mrs Emmeline Pankhurst, together with Mr and Mrs Pethick Lawrence – slide, please – met in Manchester, in order to . . .' There was an odd rustle of laughter. Mattie twisted round to look at the screen and saw three suffragettes dressed as nuns.

'Ah. They met in disguise, obviously,' she said, attempting to salvage the moment. 'No, clearly I've given the wrong signal to our magic-lantern operator.' She rapped her knuckles on the lectern. 'So, as I say, Mrs Pankhurst and the Pethwick Lawrences – slide, please.'

The nuns remained in place.

'Slide, please, Roley.'

'Is it Box 2 when you do that?' His voice was wretched.

'Yes. *No.* I'm so sorry, I'm not being clear. When I give a knock, it's Box 3.' Mattie demonstrated the signal once again.

'Come in!' called a wag.

There were fumbling noises beside the magic lantern, and the squeak of a hinge. Mattie turned back to look at the screen just as the nuns were replaced by a photograph of a poster parade: a long line of suffragettes walking along

252

a road in single file, each wearing a sandwich board that advertised a public meeting. The picture was unfamiliar to her – it was, she realized, the slide she'd found the day before, and which she'd assumed (after briefly raising it to the blueish bulb in the lumber room) showed a march.

'No, that's still not the – oh!' Mattie stopped and stared. A poster parader had merely been an ambulant hoarding, instructed not to engage with the public and to ignore derision or laughter. But the first woman in the line was looking directly at the camera and smiling, her skirts a blur as she strode forward. She was strikingly handsome, dark-eyed, alight with energy; alive with it. Venetia Campbell.

Distantly, a door slammed and a gust of wind swept through the hall, strong enough to set the screen swinging violently. Mattie shot out a hand to steady the lectern, and the bell jingled; there was a panicked movement from behind the magic lantern, followed by a gasp and a monstrously loud crash. Mattie closed her eyes.

'Are you comfortable?' asked Roberta, raising her voice above the engine. The constant vibration made her sound as if she were gargling.

'Not particularly,' said Mattie. 'This seat would seem shaped for someone with a single buttock.'

'Yes, Edward says the same, but I love this little motor-car – Veronica tells me I have four children – her, Crispin, Roger and the Austin – and that I'm fondest of the Austin. And I couldn't manage without it – you know I'm a prison visitor at Norwich? There's no other way to get there apart from a motor-bus that takes *hours*.'

253

'You could thumb a lift in a Black Maria.'

'I'm far too stout these days, they'd never fit me into a cell . . . I've forgotten, did you ever drive?'

'In Serbia. Ambulances. Though one didn't so much drive as wrestle; it took two hands to change gear while one steered with one's knees.' She looked over her shoulder at the boxes, wedged in the gap between the seats.

'I'll go very slowly,' said Roberta. 'We don't want to break anything else. Oh, that poor boy, though, I thought he would die of mortification – you were very restrained, I must say.'

'*Tout passe, tout lasse, tout casse*,' said Mattie. '*Casse* being the operative word in this case.' Twelve slides had been broken. 'Frankly, short of felling him with an upper cut and then setting fire to the hall, I really could think of no adequate response. And in any case, I must shoulder my share of the blame. I confused the boy.'

'But what on earth will Florrie say?'

The Austin turned a corner and the headlights caught a fox in the lane ahead, its eyes like silver buttons.

'Shoo!' shouted Roberta.

It fled into the verge.

'I may as well tell you,' said Mattie, 'that I haven't spoken to Florrie since July.'

'What?' Roberta actually turned to look at her, mouth open, before snapping her gaze back to the road. 'What do you mean? You've not talked to each other in *four months*?'

'She is no longer living at the Mousehole.'

'But – no, hang on, we're nearly back home, I can't

drive and think about this at the same time. This lane is all pot-holes.'

Frowning, she fixed her gaze on the untarred track, and Mattie looked out of her window at the overgrown hedge-row, though the darkness had stripped it of all texture; they might have been passing a cement wall topped with spikes. A visit to Roberta had always been a treat – a house full of pets and jolly children, a river where one could fish, long walks and rooks roosting in the stubble, and gentle, kindly Edward, a classicist who handled books as if they were made of gold leaf, and played chess like a devil. But now there was a conversation to be had. A headache dropped behind her eyes, like someone lowering a heavy crate.

Roberta turned off the road and eased the car to a halt. Lights were on in the windows of the large, square house, and a lamp in the porch threw a pale semicircle across the gravel. Above the ticking of the engine, Mattie could hear the river.

'Tell me in here,' said Roberta. 'Otherwise we'll have to fight to find a quiet space. Tell me why The Flea has gone, and where she's gone and why you're not speaking.' Roberta, for all her artistic bent, had a lawyer's brain.

'We had a disagreement.'

'So Florrie isn't unwell?'

'Not as far as I know.'

'But you said in your letter that she wasn't coming to the lecture because she was ill. Mattie, you *never* lie.' Roberta was looking aghast, her round face hatched by shadow, the effect almost cubist in the half-light. 'So what was the disagreement? Surely you've had a thousand disagreements before – neither of you has ever fought shy of having an opinion.'

There was a long silence.

'Do tell me, Mattie.'

'Should I pretend that I'm a prisoner you're visiting?'

'If you like. There's very little I haven't heard.'

'To be frank, I've made a hash of things.'

The dark booth of the motor-car was somewhat reminiscent of a confessional, with its lure of absolution. Best out with it, thought Mattie; best admit the whole, ghastly chain of events. Roberta listened carefully, with the odd painful interjection.

'So she's Angus's child?'

'Yes.'

'Well, he was always something of a lecher – yes, he *was*, Mattie, there's no need to flinch. He stroked my bottom once, in Hyde Park, when I was already engaged to Edward, and I wasn't the only one, far from it. Anyway, go on.'

A lecher. The word seemed to stay in the air, reverberating thinly beneath the narrative. The car grew chilly. There was an odd dislocation to seeing one's breath whilst talking about a day of exceptional heat.

'And what did the journalist write?'

'A rather bald description. "Day of Sports marred by accusations of Unsporting Behaviour". I received five letters of complaint from parents.' And on the following Sunday, and the three after that, she had waited on Parliament Hill at the usual time, but no girls had arrived. Each week, the summer had retreated a little further, the leaves dulling, the baked grass regaining its colour in the rain. Once, she had seen Freda and her white dog in the distance, but neither had come any nearer, though Mattie had waved.

'So did Florrie leave a note?' asked Roberta.

'Merely one stating that she would send a carrier for her trunk. He came a day or two later.'

'But no address?'

'No.'

'But presumably her employer will know her whereabouts.'

'Presumably.'

'You haven't asked?'

'Florrie wrote to Alice Channing to say that she would rather not see any of her old friends for a while, and charged her to tell me.'

'Oh dear. And what about the girl?'

'Inez?'

'The one you hit with a bottle.'

'Ida. I must assume she has found alternative employment.'

'You haven't seen her, either?'

'No. Not since the Sports Day.'

'Good God, Mattie, you're like Rapunzel in the tower. What on earth have you been doing with yourself?'

It was difficult to give a precise answer, to define the hiatus that had begun with the serial removal of every normal activity. First had come the cancellation of her weekly column in the *Ham & High* ('the Editor regrets that, following the recent events . . .') and then – after three weeks of dropped-jam-jar-induced limping, her big toe resembling an illustration of a bletted plum – came the diagnosis of a fracture, with the injunction from the doctor that if she didn't rest with her bandaged foot on a stool, like some gouty dowager, she would be forever impaired.

As autumn splashed and loured outside, she had sat in the drawing room in a state of ghastly impotence, unable, in her usual manner, to stride away from introspection; stewing in it, in fact, like a dumpling in mutton soup. She had let the Amazons down, she had hitched her wagon to an ersatz star, she had ignored the obvious, she had embraced the unlikely, she had chosen speculation and ignored truth, she had gilded the past and pawned the present. She had rewarded loyalty with blows; she had accepted ammunition from the enemy; she had chosen a missile which might wound, and had flung it, deliberately, into the face of a friend. She had embraced pride and made a sad fool of herself, at the expense of others.

And then, since one could only self-flagellate so many times before numbness set in, she had sat and read: all her favourites, Sterne and Fuller, Boswell and Eliot, the crystal labyrinth of Browne and Dickens' foggy alleyways, Montaigne and Surtees, and Somerville and Ross. She had finished one book and picked up another. The house had grown dusty and she had eaten bread and cheese for nearly every meal, and apples from the back garden, before the first hard frost had blackened them. And when she could once more manage without a stick, she had begun to walk a little further each day, and walking, as ever, had uncoiled her thoughts, so that she could follow them again – each a guideline rather than a noose.

'I have, I suppose, been listening to the metaphorical voice of the magistrate.'

Roberta gave a cluck of amusement. 'Well, that would make a change – you were certainly splendid at ignoring the real ones. Do you remember King's Thursday? – fourteen of us in the dock, one after another, brought in and then removed for misbehaviour? Genevieve tried to climb over the rails and I think Aileen threw a boot at the constable and I kept shouting, "Shame! Shame!" until they dragged me out again, but you managed the entire catechism, I think – "I believe in Votes for Women on the same terms as men, I believe in . . . in . . ."'

'". . . in the policy of the Women's Social and Political Union. I believe in the equality of the sexes, Representation for Taxation, the necessity for militant tactics and Freedom Everlasting!"' How clean, how simple, the aims had been – an arrow, straight and true; one fight, one victory. How muddy, by comparison, the present.

'So what's to be done?' asked Roberta. 'I presume that part of the reason Florrie was upset was because you implied that her friendship was unnatural, though why on earth you would listen to the insinuations of Jacqueline Fletcher I have no idea, when Florrie's worth fifty of her. And in any case, aren't Sapphists allowed friendships, too? Just think of Ethel Smyth and Mrs Pankhurst. Besides – oh!' she added, startled, as a tall shape loomed at the side window of the Austin.

'Good evening, ladies,' said Edward, bowing like a butler. 'I gather that a conference is in progress, so I have brought refreshments.' Two glasses of punch steamed briskly on a tray.

'Oh, you are thoughtful,' said Roberta, opening the window. 'Are the children in bed?'

'No. They never listen to me and, besides, they want to stay up in order to see Mattie.'

'Tell them we shan't be long,' said Roberta.

'Chess later, Mattie?'

'Of course. I shall be storming your Sicilian Defence.'

They watched him walk back to the porch, his shadow impossibly long.

'He's a dear man,' said Mattie. There was a liberal measure of brandy in the punch.

'He is,' said Roberta, rather sombrely. 'I know that I've been fearfully lucky to have Edward and the children – and of course I have brothers that I love, just as you did, but I still think that there was never a family as close to me and as true as the one I had with my sisters in the cause.' With her free hand, she reached out and squeezed Mattie's arm. 'And all families have their disagreements.'

'And some are forever estranged.'

'Oh, Mattie!'

'I am under no illusion as to the amount of damage that I have wrought. I must try to make amends.' But she felt ready, now – as if visiting Roberta were a stirrup-cup, rallying her for the journey. 'Do you remember the lyrics of "March of the Women"?' she asked. ' "Life, strife. These two are one." '

'"Nought can ye win but by faith and daring,"' capped Roberta, smartly. 'Shall we go in?'

∽

Miss F. Lee
c/o Public Health Department
Pancras Road, NW1
November 20th, 1928

Dear Florrie,
After living like an anchorite for much of the last few months, I have now exited my cell, free, I think, of the peculiar obsession that gripped me over the summer. During our last exchange I spoke to you in anger, after a day – after an entire season – ruined by my own folly. I am profoundly sorry. You have been the most loyal and perceptive of friends, and I was a clod not to recognize the wisdom of your words. The past, I have realized, should not be revisited; one is but a spectator there, stamping one's feet in impotent anguish. Better, always and ever, to raise one's eyes to the road ahead. I hope you will forgive me, Florrie. As you correctly pointed out, I can be an awful fool.

By way of a handshake, I would like to offer you a parcel of domestic news, though little of it is cheering, and most of it reflects badly on myself.

Having neglected the garden to the extent that I feared that one day soon I would open the back door only to be felled by a poison dart from a tribe of pygmy head-hunters, I have now set to with pruning-hook and hoe, and last

*week built a splendid bonfire; so splendid, in fact, that
Major Lumb threatened to telephone the London Fire
Brigade. It occurred to me that learning to transmit smoke
signals would have been an excellent activity for the
Amazons – we could have had two fires separated by the
brow of a hill, and a vaporific conversation; however, this
cannot be; a flourishing meadow has been scythed and
ploughed, and in its place grow rows of turnips – by which
I mean that, due entirely to my actions, the Amazons is no
more, while the League appears to have doubled in size,
so that one can hear their profoundly dissonant rendition of
'Salute We the Flag' from as far away as Parliament Hill.
More of this, later.*

*Besides the garden, you may be astonished to hear that I
have – at last – cleared the attic, discovering several items
dating back to suffragette days, and even earlier, judging by
the patent bustle that I found in a trunk. One might wish
that there was a Museum of Obsolescence to which it could
be donated, so that future schoolgirls could marvel at the idea
of attempting to run and jump with what appears to be a
giant tea-strainer buckled to one's rear end. The saleable
items I donated to a bazaar to raise money for the Six Point
League and, having been recruited (by Alice Channing) to
run a bric-a-brac stall, I am delighted to inform you that I
sold every item thereon, including three bundles of stair rods
and a Tyrolean walking stick of unsurpassed ugliness.*

*To further prove that I have not been entirely inert,
I have visited an exhibition of Brancusi sculptures
(covetable), attended a lecture given by Maud Hepplewhite
of the National Spinsters' Pension Association (overlong)*

and attempted to make apple jelly using your own recipe.
Should you need a strong and pungent adhesive, I have
fourteen jars of the stuff.

To return to news of the Empire Youth League: I'm
afraid, Florrie, that I have twice glimpsed Ida marching
among their ranks; were a vengeful God to choose my
punishment, He could scarcely have come up with an
improvement. Like yourself, Ida has left the Mousehole,
sending me her notice in a letter (incidentally, she writes
clearly and well). I'm sure she has no wish to see me, but,
equally, I feel that I should apologize to her in person, not
to mention handing across the week's wage that she is still,
after all this time, owed. I don't suppose, Florrie, that you
could drop me a line with Ida's address? I remember you
mentioning that she lived with an aunt.
    If I don't hear from you I shall visit the continuation
school on the Euston Road and try to find her there.
I shall send her your best wishes; your kindness to her
has been unfaltering.
    In friendship,
    Mattie

♾

'Ida Pearse,' repeated Mattie. In the room next door to the
secretary's office, a class was chanting French verbs, and
the secretary herself had a head cold, her strained wisp of
a voice scarcely audible beneath the bellowed declension
of *être*.

'Oh, you mean the red-headed—'

'ILL AY ELL AY.'

'Yes.'

'She stopped coming. I don't think we've seen her this term.'

'But why?'

'Often when our—'

'JER SWEE TOO AY.'

'I'm sorry, I couldn't hear you.'

'If our pupils change jobs, their new employers often refuse to give them leave to take time off, and we really have no—'

An electric bell shrilled and the secretary sat back with a sigh, indicating with a wave of her handkerchief that, for the time being, further speech would be impossible.

Mattie turned to watch the stream of young people passing the open door, and then stepped to one side as three girls entered.

'Miss Hopkins, Monsewer Bernard isn't feeling well,' said one of them. 'He says he's sorry but he's not going to be able to take the three o'clock class.'

'He's sweating like a horse,' added one of her companions, with relish.

'Oh dear, what's wrong?'

'He says it's the grip.'

'The grip?'

'Influenza,' said Mattie. '*La grippe*.'

'Goodness, I hope not,' said Miss Hopkins. 'Perhaps

he's just caught my cold. Oh, Olive,' she added, as the girls turned to leave. 'Don't you know Ida Pearse?'

Olive had a great bush of hair, anchored with a grid of pins. 'Yes,' she said, cautiously.

'This lady is looking for her.'

Olive shifted her gaze, and her eyes widened. 'Oh!' she said, and her mouth contracted into a smirk.

'Miss Simpkin,' said Mattie, extending a hand. 'I gather that you recognize me.'

Olive nodded, her hand limp in Mattie's. 'I saw you on . . .'

'The Heath. The Sports Day. When I admitted to having cheated.'

Olive reddened. 'Yes.'

'Then I surmise that you're in the Empire Youth League, with Ida. I would very much like to speak to her.'

'I haven't seen her for a fortnight – or three weeks, maybe. She got ill when we were on parade.'

'Dropping like flies,' said Miss Hopkins, blowing her nose.

'Mrs Cellini had to take her home. In a motor-car, the lucky thing.'

'In that case, could you tell me where she lives?'

'Top floor of Alma Buildings in Wilson Road. My cousin lives just downstairs and he says Ida's aunt's a right old . . . not very nice,' she amended.

'You mean she's *une vraie vipère*?' asked Mattie. 'It's the French equivalent for "a right old cow" – literally, "a true snake". Though I suspect Monsieur Bernard hasn't taught you that.'

Mutely, Olive shook her head.

'Are you fluent, Miss Simpkin?' asked Miss Hopkins. 'Only we're always on the look-out for fresh blood . . .'

∞

Ida's aunt had given her a bundle of plain lawn squares, which, when hemmed and embroidered, could be re-sold as handkerchiefs for a shilling each. Ida was working on a moss-stitch rose, concentrating every speck of her attention on the task because that way she could avoid having to think about anything else. She kept forgetting to blink, so that her eyes felt roasted.

'Drink your tea,' said Aunt Lilias. 'And you needn't make it so perfect, it's not worth your time for what people will pay for them. If you cross-stitch a double border, that's enough.'

Ida took an obedient mouthful and pulled a face. 'Too much sugar.'

'It's good for you. There's a nice pear if you're hungry.'

'I'll have it later.'

The knock made both of them jump.

'It'll be the tally-man . . .' said her aunt, rising, but it wasn't. The sound of Miss Simpkin's voice rose above the blare of a passing train, and Ida started up, the handkerchief dropping to the floor.

'You can just turn right round and go away again,' said her aunt. The view to the door was blocked by a drying rack, and Ida edged forward until she could see between the pillow cases. She could tell from the angle of her aunt's back that Miss Simpkin would be coming no nearer than the outside landing, and from the tone of her aunt's voice that there would be no interrupting her, no wedging of justifications between the hammered sentences – every word had been waiting, primed for use.

'No, she doesn't want to see you, and for two pins I'd chase you down the road. Miss Lee said you'd stick with Ida. She said, "Mrs Beck, I can promise you that Miss Simpkin's a sticker," but you didn't stick, did you? You didn't stick and you let Ida down, you got her hopes up and then turned your back on her and gave a leg-up to someone that didn't need it, someone who has it all on a plate, and then afterwards nothing – you didn't come here then, did you, not a word of apology, you might as well have slapped her down, and I hold you, Miss Simpkin, I hold you *responsible* – you should be ashamed of yourself, with all your talk of everyone together and all's fair, and telling the girls that the Empire lot were bad when Mrs Cellini's been ten times the help you have, *ten* times. If it wasn't for Mrs Cellini . . .'

There was a fractional pause. Ida held her breath.

'. . . So don't go thinking you'll get round her now,' said her aunt, violently changing tack, her tone relentless. 'It'll take a hayload more than "sorry". No,' she continued, over a comment from Mattie, 'she's not ill, who told you she was ill? There's nothing wrong with her. No, she's helping me, she doesn't have time for running about, she's got to make her own way, just like I had to make my own way, the world's not moved on an inch, all those *new women* in the magazines, it's all lies, it's all nonsense, it's – what's in that? Is that her wages? About time. Yes, I'll give it to her, and you can go now.'

The door clapped shut.

Ida's aunt stood, breathing heavily, an envelope balled in her hand. 'Don't, Ida,' she said, not looking round. 'Don't cry. You won't get anywhere by crying.'

'I'm not.' Though she was. She wiped her eyes on her sleeve, and then her aunt was back by her side, taking one of the handkerchiefs that Ida had embroidered – a tumble of pastel flowers on one corner – and pressing it into her hand.

'Blow your nose.'

'I've just finished making it.'

'And it's a pretty thing. Almost good enough for you.' Her aunt gave Ida's hand a swift pat – half admonition, half affection – and went back to her ironing.

Dear Florrie,

I have spent the day with Mr Arnold, who came this morning to clean out the gutters. Since he arrived with the same ladder as last year (do you remember? It has a distinct starboard slant) and no boy accompanying him (Reginald has had enough of working outside in all weathers, and is now on the glove counter at Debenhams, much to his father's disgust), I felt obliged to act as anchor, and was therefore unable to escape a two-hour monologue on the history of the British Monarchy, of which Arnold senior appears to be chief archivist. In case you didn't

*know, Florrie, the Regency Act of 1830 made provision
for a change in the line of succession had a child been born
to William IV after his death, a fact that I shall doubtless
mull over during the long winter evenings.*

*All of which lengthy preamble is merely a way of
delaying having to tell you that I did not manage to speak
to Ida. Her aunt, a tigress of rare stripe, sent me on my
way with a clawed ear, and I barely glimpsed her niece
amongst the washing.*

*After giving some thought as to what course I should
take, on Tuesday I visited Pomeroy at his office. I have
settled money on Ida, to enable her to continue her
education, should she wish; Pomeroy will deal with all
correspondence, since I think it would be expedient to keep
myself at a remove. I have also given him a letter for Ida,
which I hope she will be generous enough to read.*

*An unexpected and tangential result of the above events
has meant that I can now introduce myself to you as
Mademoiselle Simpkin, as I am styled for my weekly
French lesson at the Euston Road Continuation School.
I am also teaching English, and have chosen to begin with*
Macbeth, *given the ample opportunity it provides for
re-enacting scenes of gore and violence – I have never
before taught boys, but this has always proved a fruitful
approach with the gentler sex.*

*You would like my pupils, Florrie; they are raw and loud
and eager. The answers they gave to my question 'Describe
Lady Macbeth in a single sentence' might not be acceptable
in an examination – or, indeed, in polite society – but
nevertheless strike truly at the heart of the matter.*

269

*I am writing to you from the drawing room, and among
the cards and invitations on the mantelpiece is one from
Roberta, asking you to The Beeches for Christmas. I hope
you will accept it. Or, if not, I hope that your current
lodgings will provide you with congenial company. I have an
errand or two to run, and shall therefore remain at the
Mousehole for the festive season, should anyone wish to
drop by. I have been making sloe gin, as evidenced by the
indelible stains on my fingers. Out, damned spot . . .*
   In friendship,
   Mattie

Fifty-three, Ailsbury Gardens had a pokerwork sign on
the gatepost which read 'Beware of the Children', and an
obviously home-made holly wreath drooping asymmet-
rically from the door knocker; the pleasantly informal
impression was deepened by a distant woofing that became
rapidly louder and nearer the second Mattie lifted her
finger from the doorbell.

'Get in there,' said a female voice. '*Get in!*' There was the
scuffle of toenails on tile, and then an inner door slammed,
muffling the barking. Shortly afterwards, the front door
opened to reveal a parlour maid, apron askew, her breath
somewhat short.

'Good afternoon, Madam. Can I help you?'

'Yes, I have something for Inez.'

'For Miss Inez?'

'Yes.' Mattie took the square, well-padded parcel out of

her bag. 'Could you please tell her that it's fragile, and to unwrap it very carefully?'

'May I say who called, Madam?'

'Yes, my name is Miss Simpkin, but there is a card attached.'

The maid took the package with requisite care, and Mattie had just turned to go when there was an exclamation from within the house and a Jack Russell shot up the passage and halted at her feet, yipping insistently, teeth bared, eyes boggling with hatred.

'Sorry, terribly sorry,' said a man's voice.

'What *are* you doing, little chap?' asked Mattie, bending to scratch the dog's head. It instantly stopped barking and writhed on the door-mat, belly uppermost. The maid stooped for its collar and dragged it back up the hall.

'Sorry,' said the man again. 'Paddy thinks everyone's a burglar. You're not hurt, are you?'

'Not at all.'

'Campbell. Leo.' He held out a hand.

'Matilda Simpkin,' said Mattie, shaking it.

'Oh.' He looked at her, apparently startled. 'You're Miss Simpkin.'

'Yes.'

'Oh,' he said again, shoving his hands into his pockets like a schoolboy, and then straight away removing them, as if he'd just been reminded of his manners; he was in his late forties, with sandy hair in a tonsure and a mild, anxious face. 'Do come in,' he added.

'I was not, in fact, visiting – merely leaving a gift for Inez.'

'But if you have the time. I'd actually been intending to . . . now you're here . . .' He didn't finish the sentence, but opened the door more widely, and Mattie managed a nod. It was not an interview she would have sought, but it was one that it would be cowardice to avoid.

'Thank you,' she said.

In the study, Campbell cleared a flotilla of paper boats from a chair, and gestured for Mattie to sit.

'My wife's taken the children to see a pantomime – the three youngest, that is; the other two are in the house somewhere . . . too old for *Mother Goose*. Should I ring for some tea?'

'Not on my account, thank you.' Glancing at the books on the nearest shelf, she adjusted her eye-glasses and peered more closely. There were seven copies of the same volume.

'*Xylem Transport* by Dr L. Campbell. Is that you?'

'Yes.'

'You're a botanist?'

'A dendrologist, specifically. Though my youngest thinks I'm a woodcutter, like Hansel and Gretel's father.'

'I had no idea. I thought . . .' What had she thought? That Venetia's husband, who had insisted that she left the WSPU, who had kept her in seclusion, must be a thought-less brute, a blank-faced gaoler? Campbell shifted in his chair, and removed something from beneath one buttock.

'French militia,' he said, inspecting the lead soldier, before placing it on the desk and looking at Mattie. 'I . . . um . . . wanted to thank you,' he said.

'*Thank* me?'

'For your efforts with Inez. Who doesn't usually take kindly to outdoor activities. Or any activities at all, it has to be said, beyond visiting Regent Street. But you managed to get her camping and lighting fires. And throwing a javelin.'

'She has quite a good arm. As had her mother.'

His smile faded. 'You knew Venetia well, of course.'

'Yes.'

'It's hard to see her in Inez, isn't it?'

'Quite hard.'

'Ralph, too, for that matter. He's a tremendous stickler. Martinet. Chief whip in the making, Jenny says.'

There was a pause. 'That's my wife. My second wife,' he added. 'Jenny.'

He stopped speaking again, and rubbed his forehead, as if wiping the smears from a window; in the silence, Paddy could be heard, sniffing at the door.

'Of course, neither of them really knew their mother and we've never told them the whole truth; it seemed too brutal. When Venetia was in the asylum for the first time—'

Mattie wasn't aware that she'd spoken or moved, but Campbell glanced at her. 'You didn't know?'

'No.'

'She had, um . . . it was quite a specific condition. Postpartum psychosis. It began just a day or two after Ralph was born. Venetia kept trying to hide from us, she was terrified, she told the nurse she'd been kidnapped, she couldn't remember having had a child – it all happened within hours – the speed of it was . . .' He shook his head, lips pinched at the memory. 'She was in the asylum for weeks and weeks and then she started to come back to her old self again. I suppose you would have first met her a year or so after that – my own mother was a keen suffragist. She took Venetia to a meeting and there was a speaker there from the WSPU. It was like lighting a match, she said. Like setting off a firework.'

He picked up the lead soldier again, and idly, perhaps unconsciously, scraped its tiny bayonet along the desk top.

'She had splendour,' said Mattie. 'I recently came across a magic-lantern slide that I hadn't seen before – it shows Venetia striding along like a Valkyrie. I brought it with me, as a gift for Inez.'

'I'm sure she'll be pleased,' said Campbell, but he sounded distracted. 'There's actually another reason why I wanted to see you—' He stood up, abruptly, and went over to the window. There was no view; merely the side-wall of the next house, the bricks purplish in the early twilight, but he stood looking out at it, the back of his head towards Mattie, hands once again plunged into his pockets.

'We were . . . um . . . we were told that Venetia should never have another child, which, of course, we accepted. So when she . . . it was . . . we both knew that Inez wasn't mine. And then, just a day after the birth, the same thing happened, exactly the same thing, the terror and the confusion – only my mother was unwell by then and couldn't help with the children, and it was the war and there were factory jobs, no one wanted to be a nursemaid. And then one day in the asylum someone left Venetia's room unlocked and she found her way to a medicines cupboard. It was . . . well, you can imagine. Much later on, months later, I found a letter hidden in one of her shoes, in this house. From . . .'

'From my brother, Angus.'

'Yes.' He swung back to look at her, relief flooding his face. 'Jenny was right – she was certain you knew. So when did you find out that you had a niece?'

'I had no idea that Inez existed until she came to see me. And then I guessed.'

'Because of a . . . a strong physical resemblance?'

'Yes. You know – you do know that my brother was mortally wounded very early in the war?'

Campbell nodded, soberly. 'I can't pretend that I wasn't thrown when I found out who was running Inez's club. But Jenny said, "Let's just see what happens," and you showed such . . . patience. And perseverance. And I gather from Ralph that it was your efforts to encourage Inez that led to the, er . . .'

'Downfall of the Amazons,' said Mattie. 'Yes.'

'So now you no longer have the chance to see her' – he took a short breath, a nip of air to brace himself – 'we've discussed this, Jenny and I, and we agree that if you wanted to visit us occasionally – as an acquaintance – a family friend . . . ?'

It took Mattie a moment to absorb the astonishing generosity of the offer, and in that disorientating second she had the sense of staring at a weather house, at one figure swinging back into the shadows while another came into the light, and it was Angus, her dear Angus, who was disappearing from view, and Campbell, shining with decency, who emerged.

'Thank you,' she said. 'I would like that. Although perhaps Inez would not.'

'To be honest, we find it terribly hard to know what would please Inez. Harrods. She's very keen on Harrods. But she's still young, and we love her dearly and we hold out hope that, with time, there may be a change . . .'

'It is never too late to be who you might have been,' said Mattie.

Campbell smiled and looked suddenly ten years younger.

'My mother used to quote that,' he said. 'A sentiment true of all of us, I'd like to think.'

It was windless outside, the air hazed with chimney smoke and Venus like a rusty pin above the rooftops. Mattie paused beside the streetlight and pulled on her gloves. She could still hear Paddy barking behind the closed door of number 53, and she glanced back at the house. On the first floor, in the uncurtained bay window, stood Inez. She was holding something up to the glass – a snowflake, cut from tissue paper, delicate and lacy – and she was speaking to someone over her shoulder; her hair had been bobbed since the summer, and she looked painfully young. After a moment or two Leo Campbell appeared, holding a glue pot and brush. Carefully, he anointed the snow-flake and then feinted a dab at Inez's nose; her shriek was audible even through the glass.

Mattie, smiling, continued down the road, and turned on to Highgate Hill, taking her torch from her bag as she reached the shuttered tea-stall at the entrance to the Heath.

The Mousehole was due west, no more than a mile and a half as the owl flew, and it was dry underfoot, so that she was able to leave the gravelled path and take the slowly climbing track towards Parliament Hill. The Heath lay like a vast blanket dropped over the lit streets. Just visible to her left was the pale sombrero of the bandstand roof; beyond that lay the stretch of grass where the Sports Day displays had taken place, and the copse where Jacko had said of The Flea, 'How well she looks after you.'

She knew now how she should have answered. Instead of bridling at the implication, instead of feeling obscurely patronized, she should have replied, 'Yes, and how lucky I am.'

The dense shadow ahead of her separated into the trunks of a grove of beeches. I shan't visit Inez, thought Mattie, with sudden certainty – or I shall visit only once, in thanks, and then never again. She is loved and cherished and I am not needed there – nor, in all honesty, wanted. And besides, she thought, as her torch beam slid through fallen leaves, besides, I have a close, true family of my own.

1929

Bending to fasten her shoes had left The Flea a little short of breath. She sat at the dressing table and rubbed cold cream into her hands and watched the morning light slide round the curtains; a bird was singing in the ivy, though she'd never been able to tell one birdsong from another – 'A goldfinch,' Mattie would announce, cocking an ear to an indistinguishable twittering. 'Surely you can hear the *sweesweesweeswee*?'

This song, though, seemed particularly distinctive, reminiscent of a street-corner fiddler tuning up, each line repeated with an identical flourish. Or perhaps it was simply that she had never properly listened before; there had always been reports to write and to read, buses to catch, appointments to meet, lists to be compiled, tasks completed and tasks begun. And now that she could no longer work, there was both plenty of time, and not enough.

'I've brought you a cup of tea,' called Mattie, knocking.

'Yes, do come in. What's this bird?'

Mattie listened for perhaps half a second. 'That's the wise thrush,' she said. 'He sings each song twice over, lest you think he could never recapture that first, fine, careless rapture. Now, I'm boiling you an egg. Would you like your breakfast brought up here?'

'No, thank you.'

'Are you sure? The taxi will be here in forty-five minutes.'

'Don't fuss, Mattie, I'll be down very shortly.'

'You have a letter, incidentally.'

The Flea took the envelope and angled it in order to read the postmark.

'Norwich,' said Mattie, pre-empting her. 'I imagine it's from Roberta. Oh, and there was a note from Aileen as well, addressed to both of us, though I'm surprised the postman could read it without recourse to a cryptographer. I'm afraid she can't come after all.'

'Oh dear.'

'Something to do with a dog. Or a log, possibly. Or even a leg.'

The doorbell rang for the second time that morning.

'I imagine that's either the butcher or the baker,' said Mattie. 'The order from the candlestick-maker isn't due for a couple of days. You don't have to laugh,' she added over her shoulder, heading for the stairs.

'Then I shan't.'

The Flea opened the envelope and withdrew a card that flashed as it caught the morning sun, the broad, gold 'X' on the front surrounded by hand-painted garlands in purple, green and white.

TO MISS FLORENCE LEE
X
THE LONG OVERDUE GIFT OF
A VOTE!

Inside, Roberta had written, 'Happy Polling Day,' and signed it from the whole family, adding, 'Sorry I can't come for the party, but do come and see us – I will drive down and collect you!'

As if on cue, a motor-car hooted outside, and there was the sound of raised voices. The Flea stood up, her heart hopping a beat or two before pattering back into its usual rhythm. 'You have some medical knowledge, of course,' the physician had said, 'so I shan't need to use the usual lay analogies of water pipes and village pumps. Your mitral valve has been damaged by rheumatic fever and you have resulting atrial dilatation,' – but all the same, she couldn't help but think of her heart as a faulty clockwork bird, the sort that pecked on the spot when wound up but which faltered if tipped or turned. And slowly, inevitably, ran down.

'Was it the fever you caught from that baby?' Mattie had asked. 'The one you carried halfway across London.'

'Far more likely to be one I encountered ten years ago.'

'But it can be treated, presumably?' It was odd how firmly Mattie, never ill herself, trusted in the efficacy of medicine.

'Treated to a certain extent, but not cured.' She rattled with pills, but every month an ordinary walk seemed a little more effortful, as if the streets of London were slowly tilting upwards.

'Give me a chance! What's your bloody hurry?' someone was shouting. The Flea parted the curtains and saw a large vehicle with a loudspeaker bolted to its roof, and a brace of Unionist posters in the window; it was being driven by a young woman, while another was gesturing from the passenger seat at the butcher's boy as he slowly wheeled his bicycle through the ruts towards the Wimbournes' house.

'I think they've taken a wrong turn,' shouted Mattie from the front hall. 'Unless there's been a sudden surge in the squirrel vote.'

Every newspaper article was calling it 'The Flapper Election', and certainly almost every canvasser who had called at the Mousehole had been young and female. 'We know that politics can seem awfully dull and complicated for us ladies, but we've come to talk to you about the Liberal Party,' one innocent had chirruped. The Flea, seated in the drawing room, had caught only the odd word of the subsequent conversation, but afterwards Mattie looked as if she had just won a hundred-yard dash against all-comers, and they had received no further visits from the Liberals.

The Flea herself had answered the door to George Balfour, the sitting Conservative and Unionist MP, and had heard herself say, 'Not today, thank you,' as if he were the milkman, before closing the door on his astonished, walrus face. When she'd heard about it, Mattie had laughed until she cried. Almost every other house on the lane was sporting Balfour's card in their front window, and the Allard-Browns had a poster showing a respectable lady and gentleman being throttled in the coils of a giant snake labelled 'SOCIALISM' while a Jew, a woman in a tie and a girlish-looking man stood by and laughed. 'As usual,' said The Flea, 'the enemy consists of those who do not fit the mould.'

'Though there's nothing very pythonish about the Labour candidate,' said Mattie, who had been to the hustings. 'He looks like a stockbroker.'

'Nevertheless, I shall be voting for him,' said The Flea. 'Imagine if we had a Socialist Government!' She saw parity spreading across the land, like sun after the passing of a cloud; healthy children in school, hot running water and a WC in every dwelling, the sick and the elderly no longer terrified of penury, every baby welcome and warm.

'You'll never guess who else I saw at the hustings,' Mattie said. 'Jacko and her husband, distributing leaflets.'

'Did you speak?'

'No. Jacko was preoccupied with the contents of a baby-carriage and Richard made me the sort of stiff little bow that rival beaux give each other in the novels of Austen; I'm sure if we'd been near enough he'd have slapped me with a glove.'

Outside in the lane, the motor-car disappeared towards the dead end of the Vale of Health, and The Flea sat down again at her dressing table. Her normally pale face was marked these days by a flare of red along the cheekbones – her heart's attempt to perfuse the peripheries. At a casual glance she might be thought to be looking well. She brushed her hair and then opened her jewellery case, actually an old watercolours box that Mattie had found in the attic; The Flea kept her brooches and necklaces in the brushes tray, and items of paperwork in the space beneath: her certificate from the Sanitary Institute, her will, a birthday card from her mother, Mattie's letters tied with a ribbon, the invitation to her friend Etta's wedding, a photograph of herself as a solemn child, another of her at her desk at the WSPU offices in Kingsway, with Alice Channing as a passing blur in the background. Alice would be coming to the Mousehole in the afternoon, together with Ethel-wynne and Dorothy and half a dozen others – old comrades all. Mattie had been practising the piano in anticipation, crashing out 'March of the Women' with variable accuracy. 'I have noticed,' she'd shouted yesterday, above the climbing chords of the bass, 'that the newspapers seem to regard this election as the line drawn under female ambition. "Thus far and no further. You have gained an equal vote and must now be forever content." No hint that it is merely a springboard.' Though Mattie had not yet settled on the particular pool into which she would be diving next. 'Perhaps a return to studies,' she'd said. 'Macbeth, amongst others, hath murdered sleep, and I've been doing a great deal of midnight reading. Slaking an old thirst. And if I decide to drink more deeply, Bedford College is apparently accepting doctoral students.'

It seemed, to The Flea, a good plan; suitably ambitious, yet lacking the inevitable scrapes and collisions of Mattie's usual grand schemes – a plan that could safely be carried out solo, without the necessity for someone to precede her with a red flag.

From the lane came a sudden crackling roar, a brutal brick of sound which shattered into words as it came nearer.

'BALFOUR. VOTE FOR BALFOUR. SAFETY FIRST. PLACE YOUR TRUST IN BALFOUR. YOU'LL NEED FIRST GEAR FOR THIS STRETCH, VERONICA.'

The motor-car ground past again, heading this time towards the metalled road to Hampstead.

'*Safety first!*' called Mattie derisively up the stairs. 'What a stunningly retrogressive slogan! With that as his motto, Early Man would have rejected the wheel. Your egg is nearly ready.'

The Flea picked out the brooch of enamelled violets that had been her mother's, and held it against her leaf-green dress to check the effect, before pinning it on. She stood carefully, and smoothed down her skirts. Breakfast of an over-boiled egg awaited. She was, for the first time in her adult life, being looked after – with strong tea and nips of crème de menthe, with fires built and windows closed in case of draughts, with interesting items read out of the newspaper and dreadful puns to make her laugh. If she hadn't absolutely insisted that she was still capable of cooking the dinner, then she would also have been the recipient of meals consisting mainly of inadequately peeled potatoes and chicken roasted to the consistency of a bale of wool.

'It only takes a second or two longer to take the eyes out of the potatoes, you know,' she'd said to Mattie. 'It's not difficult.'

'It is, however, dull.'

'Most people spend a large portion of their lives doing dull things.'

'Then I have clearly been lucky.'

As have I, thought The Flea. She missed work far less than she would have imagined; the entertainments that had previously been fitted into odd moments had expanded to fill the whole. She had become, as Mattie put it, 'mad for the wireless', with a particular fondness for the Morning Play. Her erstwhile colleague Etta, married now, but not yet pregnant, and monumentally bored, had decided to write a novel about her experiences as a health visitor, and was regularly consulting The Flea about its contents. There were visits from friends, there were letters to write and there were outings; at the recent Hampstead Oil-painting Association exhibition that she'd attended with Mattie ('Clearly the art of perspective has yet to percolate these regions') they had encountered Winnie and Avril, trailing round after their parents. Avril had darted away, but Winnie had lingered.

'I miss the Amazons,' she'd said.

'So do I,' said Mattie. 'Its demise is entirely my fault, and I'm sorry.'

Winnie had turned pink. 'Grown-ups never apologize.'

'Whereas I would counter that learning to apologize is part of growing up. Do you ever see any of the other girls?'

'I meet Elsie in Chalk Farm Library on Saturday afternoons. I'm helping her with her arithmetic.'

'That's very kind.'

'Yes, that's what she says,' said Winnie, complacently. 'But I don't mind. And she's doing quite well.' Patronage suited her; she seemed somehow less squashed.

They had not seen Ida. Pomeroy had written recently to say that he'd heard from her aunt that she was attending classes again, at an afternoon school in Silverdale.

'I've sent her a note,' said The Flea. 'Just to say that we're thinking of her, and that we're pleased she's studying.' She had not yet received a reply.

'Your egg is *ready*!' called Mattie.

The Flea closed the jewellery box. She herself had never replied to the three letters she'd received from Mattie. They had arrived at the Public Health Department after she had already been forced to take sick leave, and for some reason had not been forwarded to her lodgings. So when Mattie had knocked on the door of 19, Greenwood Road, Finchley, it had come as a complete shock. 'A friend of yours is here, Miss Lee,' the landlady had said, and in had come Mattie, like a storm blast.

'But this place is *frightful*,' she'd announced, after Mrs Crewe was out of earshot.

'The landlady's very kind.'

'Nevertheless, it smells of boiled cod. And' – she'd looked around, aghast – 'what are all these?'

'Her daughter makes pictures out of shells.'

Mattie gazed at the nearest, and then peered at it more closely, frowning.

'It's the Last Supper,' said The Flea, slightly defensively. Mattie let out a shout of laughter.

'Shall we go, then?' she asked.

'*Go?* What are you talking about? Marching in here and demanding that—'

'I said in my last letter that I would come and fetch you, unless instructed to the contrary. Alice coughed up your address.'

'I didn't receive a letter.'

'Really? But I sent three.'

'None arrived.'

'I sent them to your place of work.'

'Ah.' The Flea, who had stood when Mattie arrived, saw the room begin slowly to rotate. 'I haven't been into work for a while,' she said, sitting. 'I've been unwell.'

'An infection?'

'No. So what were these letters?'

'I—' For the first time, Mattie seemed discomposed. 'They contained home news. And my profound apologies. After the events of the summer, I did a great deal of thinking, much of it rather chastening.'

'I see.'

'I may have quoted Fuller.'

'You usually do.'

'Ha! *Touché.*'

'Which quote?'

'I'm not sure if it's one you know, but it is both true and apposite.' She paused before speaking, her grey eyes on Florrie's. 'He said, *A good friend is my nearest relation.*' Her expression was wholly serious, even humble; a supplicant's.

In the sudden blurring of her vision, The Flea felt, rather than saw, Mattie's hand clasp her own.

'Please come home,' said Mattie. 'We do very well together, don't we?'

The Flea could only nod and then untuck her handkerchief from her sleeve, and watch as Mattie cast around the room for something.

'What are you looking for?' she asked, blowing her nose.

'Do you have a carpet bag, or a suitcase? Ah!' She stooped and pulled The Flea's valise from beneath the bed.

'You mean, go *now*? But I've paid next month's rent.'

'Really? Well, I suppose I could ask the taxi to wait till February . . .'

The thrush had started singing again. The Flea paused to hear it repeat itself and then closed the bedroom door and followed the smell of burned toast along the landing. She could hear music coming from the wireless – 'The Blue Danube', an orchestral version that seemed to sway the air with gaiety and colour, so that, although she was walking down the stairs with careful slowness, she might almost be descending to a ballroom, like one of the twelve dancing princesses. Oh *really,* Florrie, she thought, how fanciful! But as she walked along the passage towards the kitchen, she could still feel herself being swung through a waltz, the world a bright blur, the music playing.

1933

'Stay there,' said Ida. 'Don't move. I won't be long – maybe five minutes. You can eat this,' she added, fishing an apple out of her bag. 'It's a nice one.'

The Mousehole looked no different. The front door had been repainted, but in the same maroon colour as before, and the boot-scraper was still bent from when Doris Elphick had stood on it during a game of off-ground tig. Ida removed some of the yellow mud from her shoes; the lane was thick with it. It had rained every single day for the last month, which was yet another thing she wouldn't miss, and judging by the sky there was more on the way. She straightened her coat and adjusted her hat, for no reason other than nervousness.

She'd forgotten how quiet it was here. Just birdsong.

The door opened as she was reaching for the bell, and a short woman, with a tonged fringe and a green wool coat that had belonged to Miss Lee, started violently and then fanned herself with one hand. 'Gave me a fright. You call-ing?' she asked.

'Yes.'

'Miss Simpkin's in the study – here, I'll . . .' The woman gave a tug on the bell, and the familiar jangle sounded. The movement dislodged the napkin that covered the top of her basket, revealing it to be completely full of damsons. Avoiding Ida's eye, she drew the cloth over them again. 'You've got a visitor, Miss Simpkin!' she called over her shoulder into the house. 'Toodle-oo. See you on Wednesday! Can you make certain to order some scouring powder for next time?' And then she was away, lugging her basket up the path and leaving the door half open. Ida could see from the light slanting into the hall that whoever had just mopped the floor had left pools of water among the flagstones. Slattern.

'Hello?' she called. 'Miss Simpkin?' She edged into the hall, feeling suddenly sick at the import of what she was about to do, at the speed with which she needed to do it. The place was freezing, as usual; she closed the front door. 'Miss Simpkin?'

'Yes, in here. Who is it?'

'It's Ida Pearse.'

There was a pause, and then the thud of a dropped book and the rattle and crash of a door being wrenched open.

'Great Heavens!' said Mattie, bursting into view. 'Ida! You're taller than I am! You've shot up like a telescope – did you find a cake labelled "Eat Me"? Come through to the drawing – no, let's go to the kitchen and I can make some tea. What a splendid surprise – Pomeroy informed me in the summer that you passed your nursing exams with flying colours. Is that correct?'

'Yes,' said Ida, feeling dazed. Mattie seen from above looked all wrong, as if she'd been compressed. 'I came second in my year.'

'The silver medal – what a tremendous feat!' And there

was, thought Mattie, something burnished about Ida now: not only taller, but honed, primed – a drawn sword, the scabbard thrown aside. 'I, too, have been studying, as a matter of fact. A doctorate on Thomas Fuller; you must have heard me quote him an infuriating number of times: "All things are difficult before they are easy. Abused patience—"'

'"—turns to fury."'

'Well remembered. And by God, it does. It does.' She tilted her chin up and looked Ida in the eye. 'Thank you so much for coming to see me – and do sit down.'

She turned to fill the kettle. Ida remained standing, fingers knitted to stop them from trembling. There was a scattering of books and newspapers on the kitchen table, and the heel of a loaf next to the butter-dish, but no smell of cooking and no plates on the rack. It was more like a common-room than a kitchen, in a college with just one student.

'I was so sorry to hear about Miss Lee,' she said.

'Dear Florrie.' Mattie paused beside the range. 'Our dear Florrie. She would have been prouder than anyone to hear of your success. She was your unswerving champion from the moment she met you; she knew your worth from the first.' She smiled. 'Of course, if she were here now, you would be subject to some *very* precise questions about your nursing curriculum, whereas I simply expect you to tell me everything you've been doing for the last four years.'

'Miss Simpkin—'

'Let me just see if I can—'

'*Miss Simpkin—*'

She had meant to sound urgent, but the words came out as a panicky yelp. Mattie looked round enquiringly from the cupboard in which she'd been searching.

'What's the matter, Ida?'

'I've got to . . .' She realized that she was actually wringing her hands. 'I don't know how to start,' she said. She looked at the kitchen clock and it had been far more than five minutes – what was she *thinking*? – and she said, 'Just a moment,' and went into the passage and back outside again, and round the corner of the house to where a bench was tucked beneath the drawing-room window, facing west to catch the evening sun. He stood up when he saw her.

'Come along, then,' she said, taking his hand.

'Who's this?' asked Mattie. Ida was accompanied by a small boy in a mackintosh too large for him, and with a peculiar gait, his right leg hitched up at every stride.

'He's called Noel,' said Ida. Her heart was beating so fast that she could feel the pulse in the palms of her hands. 'But I can't talk in front of him,' she said. 'Can I put him in the drawing room?'

'Of course,' said Mattie. 'Would you believe, though, that I haven't a single toy in the house? You might give him that ammonite on the windowsill.'

She made the tea, trying not to advance along the path of speculation, and heard the mismatched footsteps retreating and then Ida's smartly returning. The kitchen door closed.

'He's four and a half,' said Ida, standing beside the table, looking down at her short, square-cut fingernails digging into the grain. 'Today's the first time I've seen him since the day after he was born. He caught poliomyelitis – infantile paralysis – when he was one, and he's been in a home in Barnet ever since, but I didn't know that till yesterday. I've just stolen him.'

She had worn her uniform to the Barnet Hospital for Incurables, found an orderly pushing a basketful of sheets, and had lied, with all the authority she could muster: she was a visiting nurse with especial credentials and she was here to see a particular child.

'He's the one at the back, with the ears,' the orderly had said, pointing through the window towards a crocodile of children progressing through the damp garden, all lurch and hop and shuffle, leg-irons and splints, crutches and straps, limbs like asparagus stalks. Ida had met them at the door. 'I'm collecting Noel Cellini – his parents have arranged for him to move to another hospital,' she'd said to the man in pince-nez who was leading the little parade, his arms full of schoolbooks, and she'd walked straight past him towards the child. No one had turned to watch her go as she'd led him away. He limped, but no worse than children she'd seen playing in the street outside the flats, no worse than the night sister on Male Surgical.

Once outside the hospital gates, she'd picked him up and walked fast, stopping in an alley between two shops in order to remove her cloak and starched hat, and taking her coat out of her bag and buttoning it over her uniform.

'We're going on a lovely outing,' she said to the child.

'Where?'

'You'll see.'

He said nothing on the bus, but placed his hands on the window and stared between them, his nose dabbing the glass whenever they went round a corner.

He looked completely unfamiliar.

'He's mine,' she said to Mattie. 'I fell pregnant that summer, after the Sports Day, and then I fainted on parade at the League and Mrs Cellini took me home, and she guessed what was the matter, and she offered to adopt the baby because she thought she couldn't have any of her own. She *thought*.'

'The child's father . . . ?'

Ida shook her head. 'It wasn't . . . It wasn't like that. He didn't ever know.'

'So that day when I called at Wilson Road . . .'

'I was four or five months gone. I stayed indoors. No one round there knew anything about it.'

She had spent the last few weeks in a nursing home in the countryside – a motor-car had called to take her, she'd worn a big old coat and carried a bag in front of her, and she had ridden like a lady out of London, through lanes of cherry blossom, past fields of horses, cottages like the ones in fairy tales – thatched roofs, gardens nodding with roses – so that none of it seemed real, not even the pain, not even the slippery skinned rabbit that had flexed and screamed. Afterwards she'd been able to pretend that it had happened to someone else, only a faint few silvery streaks on her stomach remaining as evidence, like a letter in invisible ink.

'You can start again now,' her auntie had said. They'd had the letter from Mr Pomeroy by then. Nothing from

Simeon, ever; he'd gone off to Cambridge, though it might as well have been Timbuctoo.

'So let me see if I have this correctly,' said Miss Simpkin, her expression not shocked, but that of someone working her way through a tricky examination question. 'You wish to take him back, although, legally, he's the Cellinis' child?'

'No, *no*, you don't understand. It's not about that, I didn't ever want a baby' – she thought of her mother's house, small hands always snagging you, everywhere sticky, crowded, roaring, everything broken, surrendered, shared ten ways – 'I thought everything was solved, I thought he was being looked after properly, in a family, I would never have tried to see him, and then yesterday—'

Only yesterday! She felt as if a year had passed. She'd been in the Italian haberdasher on the Euston Road, buying webbing for her cabin-trunk. A large young woman holding an infant had said, 'Ida! Long time no see!' and it had taken her a moment to recognize Olive Hickman, from the Empire League, and then she'd had to stand for a polite ten minutes while Olive described, in detail, the christening gown for which she was buying two yards of crewel-work, the baby in question champing quietly on a bone teething-ring, its cheeks aflame.

'And what about you?' Olive had asked, at last.

Ida had allowed herself a tiny, pleasurable pause. 'I'm going to Gibraltar.'

'You never! When?'

'The day after tomorrow. I'm going to be working on the Queen Mary surgical ward at the Colonial Hospital.'

The head of the nursing school had recommended her; she'd had to take an extra examination, and had been interviewed by a woman so grand it might as well have been Queen Mary herself, and then the letter had come, on thick cream paper. 'Oh, Ida . . .' her auntie had said, running a finger across the embossed coat of arms.

'You know who else I heard had gone to Australia this year?' asked Olive.

'Gibraltar's not in—'

'The Cellinis! Because Mr Cellini is going to stand for Parliament there. My husband – do you remember, he's got his own cleaning business, three people under him now – he used to do their windows. He said they were always good payers. You all right, Ida? You look a bit . . .'

'Gone back to Australia?' said Ida, her voice sounding falsely bright; she felt as if someone had smashed a hole in the wall next to her and stuck their head through it. 'The whole family? They've got a . . . a son, is it?'

'And two little girls, twins – Mrs Cellini had a terrible time having them, they had to be cut out of her – but they're not taking the boy, because he's had polio and he's in a home – seems a shame, doesn't it, but they say the heat's bad for cripples.'

Ida couldn't remember what she'd said during the rest of the conversation, but when she arrived back at the flat, she realized that she still had a rigid smile pinned to her face, like a forgotten mask.

'*Infamous*,' said Mattie.

'The twins were Mrs Cellini's. I mean, by birth. They're

only a year younger than him. I suppose once she'd got babies of her own . . .'

'It's just as Florrie always said: all those deemed weak or imperfect, all those who cannot or will not march in step, are pushed aside. As ever, your instincts do you credit, Ida. How did you find out where the boy was?'

'I went to the library at St Thomas's, they've a directory of homes, and telephone numbers, but what it is – why I'm here – I can't keep him, Miss Simpkin, I'm not keeping him, I didn't ever want to keep him, and we're going on Friday, we're all packed, it's been planned for months, I paid for the tickets weeks ago, we can't change everything—'

'We?' asked Mattie, grasping at a single word, amidst the torrent.

'Me and my auntie, of course. She's coming with me, she's earned it. She can put her feet up now and sit in the sun, and she still can't believe it, she keeps checking the tickets, and I'm not – I'm not smashing all that to bits.'

'But does your aunt know you've taken the child?'

'She doesn't know anything – I didn't even tell her about meeting Olive. What good would that have done? I didn't even know I'd take him before I took him. It wasn't a – a *plan*.'

'And yet you brought him straight here?'

'Yes.'

There was a muddy footprint near the hem of Ida's coat – she must have carried the child up the lane, thought Mattie.

'But what do you want me to do with him?' she asked.

Ida made an impatient gesture; how many times did you have to explain to people who had everything that they *had everything*? 'I don't know,' she said, 'but you know who to talk to, it's easier for you, people listen to you, you can find a way for him to be looked after the way he ought to be looked after.'

'But—'

'You have *money*!' Her voice was close to a shout, and for a moment she couldn't believe that she was speaking to Miss Simpkin in that way, but the words seemed borne on a hot breeze, as if coming back here had opened a door on to that scorching day five years ago and on the far side of the door stood another Ida. *That* Ida might have gone even further. That Ida might one day, just possibly, have written 'Dr' in front of her own name.

'After you came to my aunt's flat, you sent me a letter,' she said, looking past Mattie and towards the wide view beyond the garden wall. 'You said in it you were sorry. You said you wouldn't ever let me down again. You said that this time you'd stick by me through thick and thin. Do you remember?'

'Yes.'

'Well, now I don't need help – not any more – but he does, Miss Simpkin. I need you to stick by *him*.'

Outside, the sky was darkening.

'Please,' said Ida.

She left through the back door, so she wouldn't have to pass by the drawing room. Zygotes, she told herself, picking her way between the ruts, rain beginning to fall;

zygotes and cell division, nuclei and cilia, an embryo like a comma, bone marrow blooming, erythrocytes and lymphocytes, smooth and striated muscle, keratin for hair and cartilage for ears, and he is just another human being, no more miraculous than any life is miraculous, no more her own than any child on the ward. She felt the tarmacadam of East Heath Road beneath her feet, and scraped her shoes on the kerb edge until barely a trace of the lane remained. There; gone; forgotten. Clumsily tucking a few stray hairs into her hat, she walked towards the Tube station.

Mattie stood in the kitchen. The house felt peculiar, as if it had changed shape, had been expanded or else tunnelled into, an unfamiliar wind blowing through the passages. And yet there was only silence from the drawing room.

He was sitting in the chair by the window, the ammonite on his lap, one finger tracing the curve. The movement halted when she entered.

'Good afternoon,' she said, sitting down on the sofa a few feet away. 'My name is Mattie.'

'Good afternoon,' he said, formally, and resumed drawing a finger along the spiral.

'What you're holding is a fossil called an ammonite,' she said. 'Millions upon millions of years ago, it was a living creature, rather like a snail. It lived in the same world as the dinosaurs.'

He looked at her impassively. His hair was unprepossessingly short, his ears large, and his face had the flour-and-water plainness of a child in a Bruegel painting.

'When am I going home?' he asked.

'By "home" . . .' She paused, wondering how to phrase it. 'You mean, where you were this morning? With all the other children?'

'Yes.'

'Do you like it there?'

His eyes shifted, examining her face. Possibly, she thought, the question had no meaning for him; the word 'like' implied comparison, and how could there be a comparison if he remembered nothing else?

'Have you ever had a holiday?' she asked.

'Tiger Tim did.'

'I beg your pardon?'

'Tiger Tim went on holiday.'

His accent was odd – a burr of Scottish, a sawn-off edge of London. Absorbed, perhaps, from the nurses who looked after him.

'Is Tiger Tim in a storybook?'

He nodded.

'And where did he go to on holiday?'

'Under the sea.'

There was a pause. His gaze slid past her and began to poke around the room: the cushions on the window seat, the bookshelves, the vase of dried teazels, the log-pile, the Klee print, the jade horse, the framed photograph of The Flea at her desk, the carillon that played the '1812 Overture' on a row of tinkling bells when you lifted the lid, the giant clam shell sent back from South Africa by Stephen.

'Would you like to explore? I don't mind at all if you touch things.'

Was there doubt in his expression? He looked at the table beside him, where the chess set was laid out for a Hungarian opening. 'Do you know what that game is?' she asked.

A head shake. He reached out a hand and carefully pressed a fingertip on to the crenellations of the white castle.

'That piece is called a castle, or rook.'

His hand moved towards the large edition of *Roget's Thesaurus*, next to the board, and rested on the front cover.

'That's not a storybook and it has no pictures, but it is, in its own way, full of wonders.'

He sat back and looked at her; a sober, watchful presence, lacking the restless speed of childhood, the inconsequent chatter. Mattie glanced around the room herself and caught The Flea's sharp gaze: *What on earth are you waiting for, Mattie? It's perfectly obvious what you should do.*

'Would you like to stay and have a holiday here? It'll probably be drier than the one Tiger Tim went on, but if we go to the ponds, we might find some sticklebacks to catch.'

He shifted slightly in the chair, but his eyes remained fixed on her.

'Would I have things to eat?'

'Are you hungry now?'

He nodded.

'Come along, then. Let's see what we can find.'

He creaked as he moved; a corset of some kind, she supposed, supporting his back. Halfway down the passage, he stopped and looked in the mirror. The bottom of the frame was at the same level as the bridge of his nose, and he looked first at himself – eyeball to eyeball for a good five seconds – and then upwards at Mattie's reflection.

'Are you a nurse?' he asked.

'No.'

'Are you a doctor?'

'No.' She paused. 'Well, I shall be soon, but a doctor of words rather than medicine. Did anyone ever read you *Alice through the Looking-Glass*?'

He shook his head.

'If you stay, we could make a start on it tonight. Now, what would you like to eat? Bread and butter and jam? A glass of milk?'

'Yes, please.'

She made herself a pot of tea, and sat opposite him as he ate. 'Do you remember ever living in a house?' she asked. He appeared to think about the question, before shaking his head.

'Do people come to visit you at the home?'

This time, the shake of the head was immediate. He finished his bread and jam, picked up all the crumbs on the plate with a damp finger and then folded his hands, waiting for what might happen next.

'So what would you like to do now?'

He said nothing, but his pupils widened. Perhaps, she thought, he was unused to the idea of choice.

'On an ordinary weekday, what might you do in the afternoon?'

'We go for a nap.'

'Would you like a nap now?'

Cautiously, eyes on hers, he mouthed the word 'no'.

'Good decision; neither would I. Napping in the afternoon is for infants and those in their dotage. What else might you do?'

'We walk in the garden.'

'That sounds like an excellent idea. It's stopped raining for the time being.'

And if there happened to be a neighbour nosing over the fence, she could always claim the child as a young relative, or perhaps a godson come to stay.

There was a snapping wind. Only odd leaves were left on the fruit trees, and the grass was lumpy with windfalls.

'I like to leave a few for the birds,' said Mattie. 'Do you have a favourite fruit? Pears? Plums? Goosegogs?'

'Pineapple.'

'Ah, one that I have so far singularly failed to grow. Look, here's someone come for his dinner. A rook.'

It tilted on the wall, waiting for them to leave. The boy said something inaudible.

'What was that?' asked Mattie.

'Or castle,' he said, more loudly.

It took Mattie a second to grasp his meaning. 'I say, well *done*!' she said. 'What a memory!' She broke into applause and the rook – or castle – flapped off again.

They walked slowly around the beds. 'Nothing's in bloom,' said Mattie, 'but if you shake one of these for me' – she snapped off a poppy head on a long stem – 'you can spread some seeds for next year.'

He waved the stem slowly, watching the breeze catch

the fine black specks, pulling them like a thread of smoke across the garden.

'There's a little house,' he said.

'Yes, it's called a summer house, and it harbours a surprise – one can use it to follow the sun. Here, come and stand on it.'

She waited until he'd stepped up on to the strip of porch and then she leaned against the rail on one side, and pushed. The summer house rotated very slowly through a quarter of a turn and then stopped with a jerk. The boy sat down, hard.

'I am *so* sorry,' said Mattie. 'I think the mechanism must have rusted.' She helped him up; there was a faint colour in his cheeks. 'Are you all right? Not hurt at all?'

He shook his head. 'Can we do it again?' he asked.

Acknowledgments

Thank you to my husband, James Connell, and my friend Kate Anthony for endless listening and invaluable suggestions; to Mervyn Heard, for his expertise on magic-lantern lectures; to Susannah Stapleton and Doug Castle, for their generous help with specific gaps in my knowledge, and to Jennifer R. Haynes, whose PhD thesis 'Sanitary Ladies and Friendly Visitors' was wonderfully useful when writing about The Flea's job. Once again, the London Library served me both as a lovely place to write and as a rich source of research material. Among the many books I used, Elizabeth Crawford's *The Women's Suffrage Movement – A Reference Guide* was invaluable, while Emmeline Pankhurst's *My Own Story* was the direct source of Mattie's heckles in the Albert Hall, since I thought the originals were unimprovable. I hasten to add that any historical inaccuracies in the text are mine, all mine.

And thank you, as ever, to Bill Scott-Kerr for his superhuman patience and never-failing enthusiasm, and to Georgia Garrett for practically everything.

About the Author

A former radio and television producer, Lissa Evans is the author of three previous novels, including *Crooked Heart* and *Their Finest*, which were both longlisted for the Orange Prize (now called the Baileys Women's Prize for Fiction). She lives in London with her family.

ALSO BY LISSA EVANS

THEIR FINEST
A Novel
Available in Paperback, eBook, and Digital Audio
"A beautifully written, minutely observed and researched, evocative and very funny tale."
—*The Guardian* (London)
From the author of the acclaimed *Crooked Heart* comes another "smart, funny, ingenious, revealing tale of London life during the Second World War" (*The Independent*)—longlisted for the Orange Prize upon its original publication in England.

CROOKED HEART
A Novel
Available in Hardcover, Paperback, eBook, and Digital Audio
"Glorious. I loved every line of this book."
—Paula Hawkins, author of
The Girl on the Train
Paper Moon meets the Blitz in this original black comedy, set in World War II England, chronicling an unlikely alliance between a small time con artist and a young orphan evacuee.

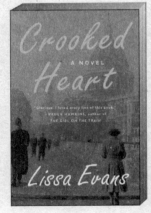